A CLASH OF HONOR

(BOOK #4 IN THE SORCERER'S RING)

MORGAN RICE

Copyright © 2013 by Morgan Rice

All rights reserved. Except as permitted under the U.S. Copyright Act of 1976, no part of this publication may be reproduced, distributed or transmitted in any form or by any means, or stored in a database or retrieval system, without the prior permission of the author.

This book is licensed for your personal enjoyment only. This book may not be re-sold or given away to other people. If you would like to share this book with another person, please purchase an additional copy for each recipient. If you're reading this book and did not purchase it, or it was not purchased for your use only, then please return it and purchase your own copy. Thank you for respecting the hard work of this author.

This is a work of fiction. Names, characters, businesses, organizations, places, events, and incidents either are the product of the author's imagination or are used fictionally. Any resemblance to actual persons, living or dead, is entirely coincidental.

ISBN: 978-1-939416-26-1

Books by Morgan Rice

THE SORCERER'S RING
A QUEST OF HEROES (BOOK #1)
A MARCH OF KINGS (BOOK #2)
A FEAST OF DRAGONS (BOOK #3)
A CLASH OF HONOR (BOOK #4)
A VOW OF GLORY (BOOK #5)
A CHARGE OF VALOR (BOOK #6)
A RITE OF SWORDS (BOOK #7)
A GRANT OF ARMS (BOOK #8)
A SKY OF SPELLS (BOOK #9)
A SEA OF SHIELDS (BOOK #10)
A REIGN OF STEEL (BOOK #11)

THE SURVIVAL TRILOGY
ARENA ONE (Book #1)
ARENA TWO (Book #2)

the Vampire Journals
turned (book #1)
loved (book #2)
betrayed (book #3)
destined (book #4)
desired (book #5)
betrothed (book #6)
vowed (book #7)
found (book #8)
resurrected (book #9)
craved (book #10)

"Be not afraid of greatness:
some are born great,
some achieve greatness,
and some have greatness thrust upon them."

—William Shakespeare
Twelfth Night

CHAPTER ONE

Luanda charged across the battlefield, narrowly avoiding a galloping horse as she weaved her way towards the small dwelling that held King McCloud. She clutched the cold, iron spike in her hand, trembling, as she crossed the dusty grounds of this city she once knew, this city of her people. She had been forced all these months to witness their being butchered—and she'd had enough. Something inside her snapped. She no longer cared if she went up against the entire McCloud army—she would do whatever she could to stop it.

Luanda knew that what she was about to do was crazy, that she was taking her life into her hands, and that McCloud would likely kill her. But she pushed these thoughts from her mind as she ran. The time had come to do what was right—at any cost.

Across the crowded battlefield, amidst the soldiers, she spotted McCloud in the distance, carrying that poor, screaming girl into an abandoned dwelling, a small clay house. He slammed the door behind them, raising a cloud of dust.

"Luanda!" came a shout.

She turned and saw Bronson, perhaps a hundred yards behind, chasing after her. His progress was interrupted by the endless stream of horses and soldiers, forcing him to stop several times.

Now was her chance. If Bronson caught up to her, he would prevent her from going through with it.

Luanda doubled her speed, clutching the spike, and tried not to think how crazy this all was, how slim her chances were. If entire armies could not bring down McCloud, if his own generals, his own son, trembled before him, what chance did she, alone, possibly have?

Moreover, Luanda had never killed a man before, much less a man of McCloud's stature. Would she freeze up when the time came? Could she really sneak up on him? Was he impervious, as Bronson had warned?

Luanda felt implicit in this army's bloodshed, in the ruin of her own land. Looking back, she regretted that she had ever agreed to marry a McCloud, despite her love for Bronson. The McClouds, she had learned, were a savage people, beyond correction. The MacGils had been lucky that the Highlands divided them, she realized that now, and that they had stayed on their side of the Ring. She had been naïve, had been stupid to assume that the McClouds were not as bad as she had been raised to think. She thought that she could change them, that having a chance to be a McCloud princess—and one day queen—was somehow worth it, whatever the risk.

But now she knew that she was wrong. She would give up everything—give up her title, her riches, her fame, all of it—to have never met the McClouds, to be back in safety, with her family, on her side of the Ring. She was mad at her father now for having arranged this marriage; she was young and naïve, but he should have known better. Was politics so important to him, to sacrifice his own daughter? She was mad at him, too, for dying, for leaving her alone with all of this.

Luanda had learned the hard way, these last few months, to depend on herself, and now was her chance to make things right.

She trembled as she reached the small clay house, with its dark, oak door, slammed shut. She turned and looked both ways, expecting McCloud's men to bear down on her; but to her relief, they were all too preoccupied with the havoc they were wreaking to notice.

She reached up, the stake in one hand, and grabbed the knob, turning it as delicately as she could, praying she did not alert McCloud.

She stepped inside. It was dark in here, and her eyes adjusted slowly from the harsh sunlight of the white city; it was cooler in here, too, and as she stepped across the threshold of the small house, the first thing she heard was the moans and cries of the girl. As her eyes adjusted she looked over in the small house and saw McCloud, undressed from the waist down, on the floor, the girl undressed, struggling beneath him. The girl cried and screamed, her eyes bunched up, as McCloud reached up and clamped her mouth shut with his beefy palm.

Luanda could hardly believe this was real, could hardly believe she was really going through with this. She took a tentative step forward, her hands shaking, her knees weak, and prayed that she would have the strength to carry through. She clutched the iron spike as if it were her lifeline.

Please, god, let me kill this man.

She heard McCloud grunting and groaning, like a wild animal, having his fill. He was relentless. The girl's screams seemed to amplify with his every move.

Luanda took another step, then another, and was just feet away. She looked down at McCloud, studied his body, trying to decide the best place to strike. Luckily he had removed his chainmail and wore only a thin, cloth shirt, now drenched in sweat. She could smell it from hear, and she recoiled. Removing his armor was a careless move on his part, and it would be, Luanda decided, his last mistake. She would raise the spike high, with both hands, and plunge it into his exposed back.

As McCloud's groans reached their peak, Luanda raised the spike high. She thought of how her life would change after this moment, how, in just seconds, nothing would ever be the same. The McCloud kingdom would be free of their tyrant king; her people would be spared from further destruction. Her new husband would rise and take his place, and finally, all would be well.

Luanda stood there, frozen with fear. She trembled. She knew that if she did not act now, she never would.

She held her breath, took one final step forward, raised the spike high overhead with both hands, and suddenly dropped to her knees, plunging the iron down with all she had, preparing to drive it through the man's back.

But something happened which she did not expect, and it all happened in a blur, too fast for her to react: at the last second McCloud rolled out of the way. For a man with his bulk, he was much faster than she could imagine. He rolled to one side, leaving the girl beneath him exposed, and it was too late for Luanda to stop the plunge.

The iron spike continued, to Luanda's horror, plunging all the way down—and into the girl's chest.

The girl sat straight up, shrieking, and Luanda was mortified to feel the spike piercing her flesh, inches deep, all the way to her heart. Blood gurgled from her mouth and she looked at Luanda, terrified, betrayed.

Finally, she lay back down, dead.

Luanda knelt there, numb, traumatized, hardly grasping what had just happened. Before she could process it all, before she could realize that McCloud was safe, she felt a stinging blow on the side of her face, and felt herself go down to the ground.

As she flew through the air, she was dimly aware that McCloud had just punched her, a tremendous blow, to the face, had sent her flying, had indeed anticipated her every move since she had walked into the room. He had feigned ignorance. He had waited for his moment, waited for the perfect chance to not only dodge her blow, but to trick her into killing this poor girl at the same time, to put the guilt of it on her head.

Before her world dimmed, Luanda caught a glimpse of McCloud's face. He was grinning down, mouth open, breathing hard, like a wild beast. The last thing she heard, before his giant boot rose up and came down for her face, was his guttural voice, spilling out like an animal:

"You did me a favor," he said. "I was through with her anyway."

CHAPTER TWO

Gwendolyn ran down the twisting side streets of the worst part of King's Court, tears streaming down her cheeks as she ran from the castle, trying to get as far away from Gareth as she could. Her heart still raced since their confrontation, since seeing Firth hanging, since hearing Gareth's threats. She desperately tried to extricate the truth from his lies. But in Gareth's sick mind, the truth and lies were all twisted together, and it was so hard to know what was real. Had he been trying to scare her? Or was everything he'd said true?

Gwendolyn had seen Firth's dangling body with her own eyes, and that told her that perhaps, this time, all of it was true. Perhaps Godfrey had indeed been poisoned; perhaps she had indeed been sold off into marriage, and to the savage Nevaruns no less; and perhaps Thor was right now riding into an ambush. The thought of it made her shudder.

She felt helpless as she ran. She had to make it right. She could not run all the way to Thor, but she could run to Godfrey and could see if he was indeed poisoned—and if he still lived.

Gwendolyn sprinted deeper into the seedy part of town, amazed to find herself back here again, twice in as many days, in this disgusting part of King's Court to which she had vowed to never return. If Godfrey had truly been poisoned, she knew it would happen at the ale house. Where else? She was mad at him for returning, for lowering his guard, for being so careless. But most of all, she feared for him. She realized how much she had come to care for her brother these last few days, and the thought of losing him, too, especially after losing her father, left a hole in her heart. She also felt somehow responsible.

Gwen felt real fear as she ran through these streets, and not because of the drunks and scoundrels all around her; rather, she feared her brother, Gareth. He had seemed demonic in their last meeting, and she could not get the image of his face, of his eyes, from her mind—so black, so soulless. He looked possessed. His sitting on their father's throne had made the image even more surreal. She feared his retribution. Perhaps he was, indeed, plotting to marry her off, something she would never allow; or perhaps he just wanted to throw her off guard, and he was really planning to assassinate her. Gwen looked around, and as she ran, every face seemed hostile, foreign. Everyone seemed like a potential threat, sent by Gareth to finish her off. She was becoming paranoid.

Gwen turned the corner and bumped shoulders with a drunken old man, knocking her off balance, and she jumped and screamed involuntarily. She was on-edge. It took her a moment to realize it was just a careless passerby, not one of Gareth's henchmen; she turned and saw him stumble, not even turning back to apologize. The indignity of this part of town was more than she could stomach. If it were not for Godfrey she would never come near it, and she hated him for making her stoop to this. Why couldn't he just stay away from the alehouses?

Gwen turned another corner and there it was: Godfrey's tavern of choice, an excuse of an establishment, sitting there crooked, door ajar, drunks spilling out of it, as they perpetually did. She wasted no time, and hurried through its open door.

It took her eyes a moment to adjust in the dim bar, which reeked of stale ale and body odor; as she entered, the place fell silent. The two dozen or so men stuffed inside all turned and looked at her, surprised. Here she was, a member of the royal family, dressed in finery, charging into this room that probably hadn't been cleaned in years.

She marched up to a tall man with a large belly whom she recognized as Akorth, one of Godfrey's drinking companions.

"Where's my brother?" she demanded.

Akorth, usually in high spirits, usually ready to unleash a tawdry joke that he himself was too satisfied with, surprised her: he merely shook his head.

"It does not fare well, my lady," he said, grim.

"What do you mean?" she insisted, her heart thumping.

"He took some bad ale," said a tall, lean man whom she recognized as Fulton, Gareth's other companion. "He went down late last night. Hasn't gotten up."

"Is he alive?" she asked, frantic, grabbing Akorth's wrist.

"Barely," he answered, looking down. "He's had a rough go. He stopped speaking about an hour ago."

"Where is he?" she insisted.

"In the back, missus," said the barkeep, leaning across the bar as he wiped a mug, looking grim himself. "And you best have a plan to deal with him. I'm not going to have a corpse lingering in my establishment."

Gwen, overwhelmed, surprised herself and drew a small dagger, leaning forward and holding the tip to the barkeep's throat.

He gulped, looking back in shock, as the place fell deadly silent.

"First of all," she said, "this place is not an *establishment*—it is an excuse of a watering hole, and one that I will have razed to the ground by the royal guard if you address me that way again. You may begin by addressing me as *my lady*."

Gwen felt outside of herself, and was surprised by the strength overcoming her; she had no idea where it was coming from.

The barkeep gulped.

"My lady," he echoed.

Gwen held the dagger steady.

"Secondly, my brother shall not die—and certainly not in this place. His corpse would do your establishment far more honor than any living soul who has passed through here. And if he does die, you can be sure the blame will fall on you."

"But I did nothing wrong, my lady!" he pleaded. "It was the same ale I served to everybody else!"

"Someone must have poisoned it," Akorth added.

"It could have been anyone," Fulton said.

Gwen slowly lowered her dagger.

"Bring me to him. Now!" she ordered.

The barkeep lowered his head in humility this time, and turned and hurried through a side door behind the bar. Gwen followed on his heels, Akorth and Fulton joining her.

Gwen entered the small back room of the tavern and heard herself gasp as she saw her brother, Godfrey, laid out on the floor, supine. He looked more pale than she had ever seen him. He looked a step away from death. It was all true.

Gwen rushed to his side, grasped his hand and felt how cold and clammy it was. He did not respond, his head lying on the floor, unshaven, greasy hair clinging to his forehead. But she felt his pulse, and while weak, it was still beating; she also saw his chest rise with each breath. He was alive.

She felt a sudden rage well up within her.

"How you could leave him here like this?" she screamed, wheeling to the barkeep. "My brother, a member of the royal family, left alone to lie like a dog on the floor while he's dying?"

8

The barkeep gulped, looking nervous.

"And what else was I supposed to do, my lady?" he asked, sounding unsure. "This is not a hospital. Everyone said he was basically dead and—"

"He is *not* dead!" she screamed. "And you two," she said, turning to Akorth and Fulton, "what kind of friends are you? Would he have left you like this?"

Akorth and Fulton exchanged a meekish glance.

"Forgive me," Akorth said. "The doctor came last night and looked at him and said he was dying—and that all that was left was for time to take him. I didn't think anything could be done."

"We stayed with him most the night, my lady," Fulton added, "at his side. We just took a quick break, had a drink to pass our sorrows, and then you came in and—"

Gwen reached up and in a rage swatted both of their mugs from their hands, sending their cups of ale flying to the floor, the liquid spilling everywhere. They looked up at her, shocked.

"Each of you, grab one end of him," she ordered coldly, standing, feeling a new strength rise within her. "You will carry him from this place. You will follow me across all of King's Court until we reach the Royal Healer. My brother will be given a chance for real recovery, and will not be left to die based on the proclamation of some dim-witted doctor.

"And you," she added, turning to the barkeep. "If my brother should live, and if he should ever return to this place and you agree to serve him a drink, I shall see to it firsthand that you are thrown in the dungeon never to come out."

The barkeep shifted in place and lowered his head.

"Now move!" she screamed.

Akorth and Fulton flinched, and jumped into action. Gwen hurried from the room, the two of them right behind her, carrying her brother, following her out the bar and into daylight.

They began to hurry down the crowded back streets of King's Court, towards the healer, and Gwen only prayed that it was not too late.

CHAPTER THREE

Thor galloped across the dusty terrain of the outer reaches of King's Court, Reece, O'Connor, Elden and the twins by his side, Krohn racing beside him, Kendrick, Kolk, Brom and scores of Legion and Silver riding with them, a great army heading west to meet the McClouds. They rode as one, heading east to liberate the city, and the sound of hooves was deafening, rumbling like thunder. They had been riding all day, and already the second sun was long in the sky. Thor could hardly believe he was riding with these great warriors, on his first real military mission. He felt that they had accepted him as one of theirs. Indeed, the entire Legion had been called up as reserves, and his brothers in arms rode all around him. The Legion members were dwarfed by the thousands of members of the king's army, and Thor, for the first time in his life, felt a part of something greater than himself.

Thor also felt a driving sense of purpose. He felt needed. His fellow citizens were under siege by the McClouds, and it was left to them to liberate them, to save his people from a horrible fate. The importance of what they were doing weighed on him like a living thing—and it made him feel alive.

Thor felt security in the presence of all these men, but he also felt a sense of worry, too: this was an army of real men, but that also meant that they were about to face an army of real men. Real, hardened warriors. It was life and death this time, and there was far more at stake here than he had ever encountered. As he rode, he reached down instinctively and felt reassured by the presence of his trusted sling, by the presence of his new sword. He wondered if by the day's end it would be stained with blood. Or if he himself would be wounded.

Their army suddenly let out a great shout, louder even than the horses' hooves, as they rounded a bend and on the horizon spotted for the first time the besieged city. Black smoke rose up in great clouds from it, and the MacGil army kicked their horses, gaining speed. Thor, too, kicked his horse harder, trying to keep up with the others as they all drew their swords, raised their weapons, and headed for the city with deadly intent.

10

The massive army was broken down into smaller groups, and in Thor's group their rode ten soldiers, legion members, his friends and a few others he did not know. At their head rode one of the king's army's senior commanders, a soldier the others called Forg, a tall, thin man with a wiry build, pockmarked skin, cropped, gray hair and dark, hollow eyes. The army was breaking down into smaller groups and forking in every direction.

"This group, follow me!" he commanded, gesturing with his staff for Thor and the others to fork off and follow his lead.

Thor's group followed orders and fell in behind him; as they went, he found they were forking farther away from the main army. Thor looked back and noticed that his group forked farther than most, the army becoming more distant, and just as Thor was wondering where they were being lead, Forg shouted:

"We will take up a position on the McCloud flank!"

Thor and the others exchanged a nervous and excited look as they all charged, forking until the main army was out of sight.

Soon they were in a new terrain, and the city fell out of sight completely. Thor was on guard, but there was no sign of the McCloud army anywhere.

Finally, Forg pulled his horse to a stop before a small hill, in a grove of trees. The others came to a stop behind him.

Thor and the others looked at Forg, wondering why he had stopped.

"That keep there, that is our mission," Forg explained. "You are young warriors still, so we want to spare you from the heat of battle. You will hold this position as our main army sweeps through the city and confronts the army. It is unlikely any McCloud soldiers will come this way, and you will be mostly safe here. Take positions around it, and stay here until we say otherwise. Now move!"

Forg kicked his horse and charged up the hill, and Thor and the others did the same, following him. The small group rode across the dusty plains, kicking up a cloud, with no one in site as far as Thor could see. He felt disappointed to be removed from the main action; why were they all being so sheltered?

The more they rode, the more something felt off to Thor. He couldn't place it, but his sixth sense was telling him that something was wrong.

As they neared the hilltop, atop which sat a small, ancient keep, a tall, skinny tower that looked abandoned, something within Thor told him to look behind him. As he did, he saw Forg. Thor was surprised to see that Forg had gradually dropped behind the group, gaining more and more distance, and as Thor watched, Forg turned around, kicked his horse and without warning, galloped the other way.

Thor could not understand what was happening. Why had Forg left them so suddenly? Beside him, Krohn whined.

Just as Thor was beginning to process what was happening, they reached the hilltop, reached the ancient keep, expecting to see nothing but wasteland before them.

But the small group of legion members pulled their horses to an abrupt stop. They sat there, all of them, frozen at the site before them.

There, facing them, waiting, was the entire McCloud army.

They had need led right into a trap.

CHAPTER FOUR

Gwendolyn hurried through the winding streets of King's Court, Akorth and Fulton carrying Godfrey behind her, pushing her way as she cut a path through the common folk. She was determined to reach the healer as soon as possible. Godfrey could not die, not after all they had been through, and not like this. She could almost see Gareth's self-satisfied smile as he received news of Godfrey's death—and she was intent on changing the outcome. She only wished she had found him sooner.

As Gwen turned a corner and marched into the city square, the crowds became particularly thick, and she looked up and saw Firth, still swinging from a beam, the noose tight around his neck, dangling for all to gawk at. She instinctively turned away. It was an awful site, a reminder of her brother's villainy. She felt she could not escape his reach, wherever she turned. It was odd to think that just the day before she had been talking to Firth—and now he hung here. She couldn't help but feel that death was closing in all around her, and was coming for her, too.

As much as Gwen wanted to turn away, to choose another route, she knew that heading through the square was the most direct way, and she would not shirk from her fears; she forced herself to march right past the beam, right past the hanging body in her way. As she did, she was surprised to see the royal executioner, dressed in black robes, blocking her way.

At first she thought he was going to kill her, too—until he bowed.

"My lady," he said humbly, lowering his head in deference. "Royal orders have not yet been given as to what to do with the body. I have not been instructed whether to give him a proper burial or throw him in a mass pauper's grave."

Gwen stopped, annoyed that this should fall on her shoulders; Akorth and Fulton stopped right beside her. She looked up, squinted in the sun, looking at the body dangling just feet from her, and she was about to move on and ignore the man, when something occurred to her. She wanted justice for her father.

"Throw him in a mass grave," she said. "Unmarked. Give him no special rites of burial. I want his name forgotten from the annals of history."

He bowed his head in acknowledgment, and she felt a small sense of vindication. After all, this man had been the one who had actually killed her father. While she hated displays of violence, she shed no tears for Firth. She could feel her father's spirit with her now, stronger than ever, and felt a sense of peace from him.

"And one more thing," she added, stopping the executioner. "Take down the body now."

"Now, my lady?" the executioner asked. "But the king gave orders for it to hang indefinitely."

Gwen shook her head.

"Now," she repeated. "Those are his new orders," she lied.

The executioner bowed and hurried off to cut down the corpse.

Gwen felt another small sense of vindication. She had no doubt that Gareth was checking on Firth's body out his window throughout the day—its removal would vex him, would serve as a reminder that things would not always go as he planned.

Gwen was about to go when she heard a distinctive screech; she stopped and turned, and up high, perched on the beam, she saw Estopheles. She raised her hand to her eye to shield the sun, trying to make sure her eyes weren't playing tricks on her. Estopheles screeched again and opened her wings, then closed them.

Gwen could feel the bird bore the spirit of her father. His soul, so restless, was one step closer to peace.

Gwen suddenly had an idea; she whistled and held out one arm, and Estopheles swooped down off her perch and landed on Gwen's wrist. The weight of the bird was heavy, and her claws dug into Gwen's skin.

"Go to Thor," she whispered to the bird. "Find him on the battlefield. Protect him. GO!" she screamed, lifting her arm.

She watched as Estopheles flapped her wings and soared, higher and higher into the sky. She prayed it would work. There was something mysterious about that bird, especially its connection to Thor, and Gwen knew that anything was possible.

Gwen continued on, hurrying through the winding streets towards the healer's cottage. They passed through one of several arched gates heading out of the city, and she moved as fast as she could, praying that Godfrey hung in there long enough for them to get help.

The second sun dipped lower in the sky by the time they climbed a small hill on the outskirts of King's Court and the healer's cottage came into view. It was a simple, one-room cottage, its white walls made of clay, with one small window on each side and a small, arched oak door in front. Hanging from its roof were plants of every color and variety, framing the cottage—which was also surrounded by a sprawling herb garden, flowers of every color and size making the cottage look as if it were dropped into the midst of a greenhouse.

Gwen ran to the door, slammed the knocker several times. The door opened, and before her appeared the startled face of the healer.

Illepra. She had been healer to the royal family her entire life, and had been a presence in Gwen's life ever since she could walk. Yet still, Illepra managed to look young—in fact, she barely looked older than Gwen. Her skin positively glowed, radiant, framing her kind, green eyes and making her seem to be hardly more than 18 years. Gwen knew she was a good deal older than that, knew that her appearance was deceiving, and she also knew that Illepra was one of the smartest and most talented people she had ever met.

Illepra's eyes shifted to Godfrey as she took in the scene at once. She did away with pleasantries as her eyes opened wide with concern, realizing the urgency. She brushed past Gwen and hurried to Godfrey's side, laying a palm of his forehead. She frowned.

"Bring him in," she ordered the two men, hastily, "and be quick about it."

Illepra went back inside, opening the door further, and they followed on her heels as they rushed into the cottage. Gwen followed them in, ducking at the low entrance, and closed the door behind them.

It was dim in here, and it took her eyes a moment to adjust; when they did, she saw the cottage exactly as she had remembered it as a young girl: small, light, clean, and overflowing with plants, herbs and potions of every variety.

"Set him down there," Illepra ordered the men, as serious as Gwen had ever heard her. "On that bed, in the corner. Remove his shirt and shoes. Then leave us."

Akorth and Fulton did as they were told. As they were hurrying out the door, Gwen grabbed Akorth's arm.

15

"Stand guard outside the door," she ordered. "Whoever came after Godfrey might want a chance at him still. Or at me."

Akorth nodded and he and Fulton exited, closing the door behind them.

"How long has he been like this?" Illepra asked urgently, not looking at Gwen as she knelt at Godfrey's side and began to feel his wrist, his stomach, his throat.

"Since last night," Gwen answered.

"Last night!" Illepra echoed, shaking her head in concern. She examined him for a long time in silence, her expression darkening.

"It's not good," she said finally.

She placed a palm on his forehead again and this time closed her eyes, breathing for a very long time. A thick silence pervaded the room, and Gwen was beginning to lose her sense of time.

"Poison," Illepra finally whispered, her eyes still closed, as if reading his condition through osmosis.

Gwen always marveled at her skill; she had never been wrong once, not in her lifetime. And she had saved more lives than the army had taken. She wondered if it was a learned skill or if it was inherited; she knew that Illepra's mother had been a healer, and her mother before her. Yet at the same time, Illepra had spent every waking minute of her life studying potions and the healing arts.

"A very powerful poison," Illepra added, more confident. "One I encounter rarely. A very expensive one. Whoever was trying to kill him knew what he was doing. It is incredible he did not die. This one must be stronger than we think."

"He gets it from my father," Gwen said. "He had the constitution of a bull. All the MacGil kings did."

Illepra crossed the room and mixed several herbs on a wooden block, chopping and grinding them and adding a liquid as she did. The finished product was a thick, green salve, and she filled her palm, hurried back to Godfrey's side, and applied it up and down his throat, under his arms, on his forehead. When she finished, she crossed the room again, took a glass and poured several liquids, one red, one brown and one purple. As they blended, the potion hissed and bubbled. She stirred it with a long, wooden spoon, then hurried back to Godfrey and applied it to his lips.

Godfrey did not budge; Illepra reached behind his head and lifted it with her palm, and forced the liquid into his mouth. Most of it spilled down the side of his cheeks, but some of it went down his throat.

Illepra dabbed the liquid from his mouth and jaw, then finally leaned back and sighed.

"Will he live?" Gwen asked, frantic.

"He might," she said, somber. "I have given him everything I have, but it won't be enough. His life is in the hand of the fates. Only the gods can say now."

"What can I do?" Gwen asked.

She turned and stared at Gwen.

"Pray for him. It will be a long night indeed."

CHAPTER FIVE

Kendrick had never appreciated what freedom was like—true freedom—until this day. The time he had spent locked away in the dungeon had shifted his view on life. Now he appreciated every little thing—the feel of the sun, the wind in his hair, just being outside. Charging on a horse, feeling the earth speeding by beneath him, being back in armor, having his weaponry back, and riding alongside his brothers in arms made him feel as if he had been shot out of a cannon, made him feel a recklessness which he had never experienced before.

Kendrick galloped, leaning low into the wind, his close friend Atme at his side, so grateful for the chance to fight with his brothers, to not miss this battle, and eager to liberate his home city from the McClouds—and to make them pay for invading. He rode with an urge for bloodshed, though even as he rode he knew that the real target of his wrath was not the McClouds but his brother, Gareth. He would never forgive him for imprisoning him, for accusing him of his father's murder, for taking him away in front of his men—and for attempting to execute him. Kendrick wanted vengeance on Gareth—but since he could not have it, at least not today, he would take it out on the McClouds.

When Kendrick returned to King's Court, though, he would settle things. He would do whatever he could to oust his brother, and to instill his sister Gwendolyn as the new ruler.

As they neared the sacked city, huge, billowing black clouds rolling towards them and filling Kendrick's nostrils with acrid smoke, it pained him to see a MacGil city like this. If his father had still been alive, this would have never happened; if Gareth had not succeeded him, this would have never have happened either. It was a disgrace, a stain on the honor of the MacGils and The Silver. Kendrick prayed they were not too late to rescue these people, that the McClouds had not been here too long, and that too many people had not been injured or killed.

He kicked his horse harder, riding out in front of the others, as they all charged, like a swarm of bees, towards the open-gate entrance to the city. They stormed through, Kendrick drawing his sword, preparing to encounter a host of the McCloud enemy as they charged into the city. He let out a great shout, as did all the men around him, steeling himself for impact.

But as he passed through the gate, as he entered the dusty square of the city, he was stumped by what he saw: nothing. All around him were the telltale signs of an invasion—destruction, fires, looted homes, corpses piled, women crawling. There were animals killed, blood on the walls. It had been a massacre. The McClouds had ravaged these innocent folk. The thought of it made Kendrick sick. They were cowards.

But what stumped Kendrick as he rode was that the McClouds were nowhere in sight. He could not understand it. It was as if the entire army had evacuated deliberately, as if they had known they were coming. Fires were still alight, and it was clear that they had been lit with a purpose.

It was beginning to dawn on Kendrick that this was all a decoy. That the McClouds had wanted to lure the MacGil army to this place.

But why?

Kendrick suddenly spun, looked around, desperate to see if any of his men were missing, if any contingent had been lured away, to another spot. His mind was flooding with a new sense, a sense that this had all been arranged to cordon off a group of his men, to ambush them. He looked everywhere, wondering who was missing.

And then it hit him. One person was missing. His squire.

Thor.

CHAPTER SIX

Thor sat on his horse, atop the hill, the group of Legion members and Krohn beside him, and looked out at the startling site before him: as far as the eye could see were McCloud troops, sitting on horseback, a vast and sprawling Army, clearly awaiting them. They had been set up. Forg must have led them here on purpose, must have betrayed them. But why?

Thor swallowed, looking out at what appeared to be their sure death.

A great battle cry rose up, as the McCloud army suddenly charged them. They were but a few hundred yards away, and closing in fast. Thor glanced back over his shoulder, but there were no reinforcements as far as he could see. They were completely alone.

Thor knew they had no other choice but to make a last stand here, on this small hill, beside this deserted keep. It was impossible odds, and there was no way they could win. If he was going to go down, he would go down bravely, and face them all like a man. The Legion had taught him that much. Running was not an option, and Thor prepared himself to face his death.

Thor turned and looked at his friends' faces, and he could see they, too, were pale with fear; he saw death in their eyes. But to all of their credit, they remained brave. Not one of them flinched, even though their horses pranced, or made a move to turn and run. The Legion was one unit now. They were more than friends: the Hundred had forged them into one team of brothers. Not one of them would leave the other. They had all taken a vow, and their honor was at stake. And to the Legion, honor was more sacred than blood.

"Gentlemen, I do believe we have a fight before us," Reece announced slowly, as he reached over and drew his sword.

Thor reached down and drew his sling, wanting to take out as many as he could before they reached them. O'Connor drew his short spear, while Elden hoisted his javelin; Conval raised a throwing hammer, and Conven a throwing pick. The other boys with them from the Legion, the ones Thor did not know, drew their swords and raised their shields. Thor could feel the fear in the air, and he felt it too, as the thunder of the horses grew, as the sound of the McClouds' cry reached the heavens, sounding like a rolling clap of thunder about to hit them. Thor knew that they needed a strategy—but he did not know what.

Beside Thor, Krohn snarled. Thor drew inspiration from Krohn's fearlessness: he never whimpered or looked back once. In fact, the hairs rose on his back, and he slowly walked forward, as if to meet the army alone. Thor knew that in Krohn he had found a true battle companion.

"Do you think the others will reinforce us?" O'Connor asked.

"Not in time," Elden answered. "We've been set up by Forg."

"But why?" Reece asked.

"I don't know," Thor answered, stepping forward on his horse, "but I have a sinking feeling it has something to do with me. I think someone wants me dead."

Thor felt the others turn and look at him.

"Why?" Reece asked.

Thor shrugged. He did not know, but he had some inkling it had to do with all the machinations at King's court, something to do with the assassination of MacGil. Most likely, it was Gareth. Perhaps he viewed Thor as a threat.

Thor felt terrible for having endangered his brothers in arms, but there was nothing he could do about it now. All he could do now was do his best to defend them.

Thor had enough. He shouted and kicked his horse, and he burst forward at a gallop, charging out before the others. He would not wait here to be met by this army, by his death. He would take the first blows, maybe even divert the blows from his brothers in arms, and give them a chance to run if they decided to. If he was going to meet his death, he would meet it fearlessly, with honor.

Shaking inside but refusing to show it, Thor kicked his horse and burst forward, farther and farther from the others, charging down the hill towards the advancing army. Beside him, Krohn sprinted, not missing a beat.

Thor heard a shout, and behind him, his fellow Legion members raced to catch up. They were hardly twenty yards away, and they galloped after him, raising a battle cry. Thor remained way out in front, yet still, it felt good to have their support behind him.

Before Thor a contingent of warriors broke out from the McCloud army, charging ahead to meet Thor, perhaps fifty men. They were a hundred yards ahead and closing in fast, and Thor pulled back his sling, took aim and hurled. He aimed for the lead warrior, a large man with a silver breastplate, and his aim was perfect. He hit the man at the base of the throat, between the plates of armor, and the man fell from his horse, landing on the ground before the others.

As he fell, his horse fell with him, and the dozen horses behind him piled up, sending their soldiers hurling to the ground, face first.

Before they could react, Thor placed another stone, reached back and hurled it. Again, his aim was true, and he hit one of the lead warriors in the temple, at the spot exposed from his raised faceplate, and knocked him sideways off his horse, into several other warriors, taking them down like dominoes.

As Thor galloped, a javelin flew by his head, then a spear, then a throwing hammer and a throwing pick, and he knew his Legion brothers were supporting him. Their aim was true, too, and their weapons took down the McCloud soldiers with deadly precision, several of them falling from the horses and crashing into others who fell with them.

Thor was elated to see that they had already managed to take down dozens of McCloud soldiers, some of them with direct hits but most being tripped up by falling horses. The advance contingent of fifty men was now down on the ground, lying in great heaps of dust.

But the McCloud army was strong, and now it was their turn to fight back. As Thor came within thirty yards of them, several threw weapons his way, too. A throwing hammer came right at his face, and Thor ducked at the last moment, the iron whizzing by his ear, missing by an inch. A spear came flying at him just as quickly and he ducked the other way, as the tip grazed the outside of his armor, luckily just missing him. A throwing pick came right for his face, and Thor raised his shield and blocked it. It stuck to his shield, and Thor reached over, pulled it off, and threw it back at his attacker. Thor's aim was true, and it lodged in the man's chest, piercing his chainmail; with a scream the man cried out and slumped over his horse, dead.

Thor kept charging. He charged right into the thick of the army, into a sea of soldiers, prepared to meet his death. He shouted and raised his sword as he did, letting out a great battle cry; behind him, his brothers in arms did, too.

With a great clash of arms, there came impact. A huge, full-grown warrior charged for him, raised a double-handed ax, and brought it down for Thor's head. Thor ducked, the blade swinging by his head and slashed the soldier's stomach as he rode past; the man screamed out, and slumped over on his horse. As he fell he dropped his battle ax, and it went flying end over end, into another McCloud horse, who shrieked and pranced, throwing off his rider into several others.

Thor kept charging, right into the thick of the McCloud warriors, hundreds of them, cutting a path right through them, as one after the other swung at him with their swords, axes, maces, and he blocked with his shield or dodged them, slashing back, ducking and weaving, galloping right through. He was too quick, too nimble, for them, and they had not expected it. As a huge army, they could not maneuver fast enough to stop him.

There rose up a great clash of metal all around him, as blows hailed down on him from every direction. He blocked one after the other with his shield and sword. But he could not stop them all. A sword slash grazed his shoulder, and he cried out in pain as it drew blood. Luckily the wound was shallow, and it did not prevent him from fighting. He continued to fight back.

Thor, fighting with both hands, was surrounded by McCloud warriors, and soon the blows began to lighten, as other Legion members joined the pack. The clang of grew greater as the McCloud men fought against the Legion boys, swords striking shields, spears hitting horses, javelins being thrust into armor, men fighting in every way. Screams rang out on both sides.

The Legion had an advantage in that they were a small and nimble fighting force, the ten of them in the midst of a huge and slow-moving army. There was a bottleneck, and not all the McCloud warriors could reach them at once; Thor found himself fighting two or three men at a time, but no more. And with his brothers now at his back, it prevented him from being attacked from behind.

As a warrior caught Thor off guard and swung his flail right for Thor's head, Krohn snarled and pounced. Krohn leapt high into the air and clamped down on his wrist; he tore it off, blood flying everywhere, forcing the soldier to change direction right before the flail impacted Thor's skull.

It was like a blur as Thor fought and slashed and parried in all directions, using every ounce of his skill to defend, to attack, to watch out for his brothers, and to watch out for himself. He instinctively summoned his endless days of training, of being attacked from all sides, in all situations. In some ways, it felt natural to him. They had trained him well, and he felt able to handle this. His fear was always there, but he felt able to control it.

As Thor fought and fought, his arms growing heavy, his shoulders tired, Kolk's words rang in his ears:

Your enemy will never fight on your terms. He will fight on his. War for you means war for someone else.

Thor spotted a short, broad warrior raise a spiked chain, with both hands, and swing for the back of Reece's head. Reece did not see it coming, and Thor knew that in a moment, Reece would be dead.

Thor leapt off his horse, jumping in mid-air and tackling the warrior right before he released the chain. The two of them went flying off the horses and landed hard on the ground, in a cloud of dust, Thor rolling and rolling, the wind knocked out of him, as horses trampled all around him. He wrestled with the warrior on the ground, and as the man raised his thumbs to gouge out Thor's eyes, Thor suddenly heard a screech—and saw Estopheles swoop down and claw the man's eyes right before he could hurt Thor. The man screamed, clutching his eyes, and Thor elbowed him hard and knocked him off of him.

Before Thor had a chance to revel in his victory, he felt himself kicked hard in the gut, knocked onto his back. He looked up to see a warrior raise a two-handed war hammer, and bring it down for his chest.

Thor rolled, and the hammer whizzed by him, sinking into the earth all the way up to the hilt. He realized it would have crushed him to death.

Krohn pounced on the man, leaping forward and sinking his fangs into the man's elbow; the soldier reached over and punched Krohn, again and again. But Krohn would not let go, snarling, until finally he tore the man's arm off. The soldier shrieked and fell to the ground.

A soldier stepped forward and slashed his sword down at Krohn; but Thor rolled over with his shield and blocked the blow, his entire body shaking with the clang, saving Krohn's life. But as Thor knelt there he was exposed, and another warrior charged over him with his horse, trampling him, knocking him down face first, the horse hooves feeling like they were crushing every bone in his body.

Several McCloud soldiers jumped down and surrounded Thor, closing in on him.

Thor realized he was in a bad place; he would give anything to be back up on his horse now. As he lay there on the ground, his head ringing with pain, out of the corner of his eye he saw his other Legion members fighting, and losing ground. One of the Legion boys he did not recognize let out a high-pitched scream, and Thor watched as a sword punctured his chest, and he slumped over, dead.

Another one of the Legion Thor did not know came to his aid, killing his attacker with a thrust of his spear—but at the same time, a McCloud attacked him from behind, thrusting a dagger into his neck. The boy screamed and fell off his horse, dead.

Thor turned and looked up to see a half dozen soldiers bearing down on him. One raised a sword and brought it down for his face, and Thor reached up and blocked it with his shield, the clang resonating in his ears. But another raised his boot and kicked Thor's shield from his hand.

A third attacker stepped on Thor's wrist, pinning it to the ground.

A fourth attacker stepped forward and raised a spear, preparing to drive it through Thor's chest.

Thor heard a great snarl, and Krohn leapt on the soldier, driving him back and pinning him down. But a soldier stepped forward with a club and swiped Krohn, hitting him so hard that Krohn went tumbling over with a yelp, and landed on his back, limp.

Another soldier stepped forward, standing over Thor, and raised a trident. He scowled down, and this time there was no one to stop him. He prepared to bring it down, right for Thor's face, and as Thor lay there, pinned, helpless, he could not help but feel that, finally, his end had come.

CHAPTER SEVEN

Gwen knelt by Godfrey's side in the claustrophobic cottage, Illepra beside her, and could stand it no longer. She had been listening to her brother's moans for hours, watching Illepra's face grow increasingly grim, and it seemed certain that he would die. She felt so helpless, just sitting here. She felt that she needed to do something. Anything.

Not only was she racked with guilt and worry for Godfrey—but even more so, for Thor. She could not shake from her mind the image of him charging into battle, set up for a trap by Gareth, about to die. She felt she had to do something. She was going crazy sitting here.

Gwen suddenly rose to her feet, and hurried across the cottage.

"Where are you going?" Illepra asked, her voice hoarse from chanting prayers.

Gwen turned to her.

"I will be back," she said. "There is something I must try."

She opened the door and hurried outside, into the sunset air, and blinked at the site before her: the sky was streaked with reds and purples, the second sun sitting as a green ball on the horizon. Akorth and Fulton, to their credit, still stood there, on guard, and they jumped up and looked at her, concern on their faces.

"Will he live?" Akorth asked.

"I don't know," Gwen said. "Stay here. Stand guard."

"And where are you going?" Fulton asked.

An idea had occurred to her as she looked into the blood red sky, felt the mystical feeling in the air, she knew that there was one man who might be able to help her.

Argon.

If there was one person Gwen could trust, one person who loved Thor and who had remained loyal to her father, one person who had the power to help her in some way, it was he.

"I need to seek out someone special," she said.

She turned and hurried off, across the plains, breaking into a jog, running, retracing the steps to Argon's cottage.

She hadn't been here in years, ever since she was a child, but she knew he lived high on the desolate, craggy planes. She ran and ran, barely catching her breath, as the terrain became more desolate, more windy, grass giving way to pebbles, then to rocks. The wind howled, and as she went, the landscape became eerie; she felt as if she were walking on the surface of a star.

She finally reached his cottage, out of breath, and pounded on the door. There was no knob anywhere she could grab onto, but she knew this was his place.

"Argon!" she shrieked. "It is me! MacGil's daughter! Let me in! I command you!"

She pounded and pounded, but all that came back in return was the howling of the wind.

Finally, she broke into tears, exhausted, feeling more helpless than she ever had. She felt hollowed out, as if she had nowhere left to turn.

As the sun sank deeper into the sky, its blood-red giving way to twilight, Gwen turned and began to walk back down the hill. She wiped tears from her face as she went, desperate to figure out where to go next.

"Please father," she said aloud, closing her eyes. "Give me a sign. Show me where to go. Show me what to do. Please don't let your son die on this day. And please don't let Thor die. If you love me, answer me."

Gwen walked in silence, listening to the wind, when suddenly, a flash of inspiration struck her.

The lake. The Lake of Sorrows.

Of course. The lake was where everyone went to pray for someone who was deathly ill. It was a pristine, small lake, in the middle of the Red Wood, surrounded by towering trees that reached into the sky. It was considered a holy place.

Thank you father, for answering me, Gwen thought.

She felt him with her now, more than ever, and she burst into a sprint, racing towards Red Wood, towards the lake that would hear her sorrows.

*

Gwen knelt on the shore of the Lake of Sorrows, her knees resting on the soft, red pine that encased the water like a ring, and looked out at the still water, the stillest water she had ever seen, which mirrored the rising moon. It was a brilliant, full moon, more full than she had ever seen, and while the second sun was still setting, the moon was rising, casting both sunset and moonlight over the Ring. The sun and the moon reflected together, opposite each other in the lake, and she felt the sacredness of this time of day. It was the window between the close of one day and the start of another, and at this sacred time, and in this sacred place, anything was possible.

Gwen knelt there, crying, praying for all she was worth. The events of the last few days had been too much for her, and now she let it all out. She prayed for her brother, but even more so for Thor. She could not stand the thought of losing them both on this night, of having no one left around her but Gareth. She could not stand the thought of she, herself, being shipped off to be wed to some barbarian. She felt her life collapsing around her, and she needed answers. Even more, she needed hope.

There were many people in her kingdom who prayed to the God of the Lakes, or the God of the Woods, or the God of the Mountains, or the God of the Wind—but Gwen never believed in any of these. She, like Thor, was one of the few who went against the grain of belief in her kingdom, and followed the radical path of believing in just one God, just one being who controlled the entire universe. It was to this God that she prayed.

Please God, she prayed. *Return Thor to me. Let him be safe in battle. Let him escape his ambush. Please let Godfrey live. And please protect me—don't let me be taken away from here, wed to that savage. I will do anything. Just give me a sign. Show me what you want from me.*

Gwen knelt there for a long time, hearing nothing but the howling of the wind, racing through the endlessly tall pine trees of Red Wood; she listened to the gentle cracking of the branches as they swayed above her head, their needles dropping in the water.

"Be careful what you pray for," came a voice.

She spun, flinching, and was shocked to see someone standing there, not far from her. She would have been scared, but she recognized the voice immediately—an ancient voice, older than the trees, older than the earth itself, and her heart swelled as she knew who it was.

She turned and saw him standing over her, wearing his white cloak and hood, eyes translucent, burning through her as if he were peering into her very soul. He held his staff, lit up in the sunset and the moonlight.

Argon.

She stood and faced him.

"I sought you out," she said. "I went to your cottage. Did you hear me knock?"

"I hear everything," he answered cryptically.

She paused, wondering. He was expressionless.

"Tell me what I have to do," she said. "I will do anything. Please, don't let Thor die. You can't let him die!"

Gwen stepped forward and grasped his wrist, pleading. But as she touched him she was scorched by a burning heat, traveling through his wrist and onto her hands, and she pulled back, overwhelmed by the energy.

Argon sighed, turned from her, and took several steps towards the lake. He stood there, looking out at the water, his eyes reflected in the light.

She walked up beside him and stood there silently, for she did not know how long, waiting until he was ready to speak.

"It is not impossible to change fate," he said. "But it exacts a heavy price on the petitioner. You want to save a life. That is a noble endeavor. But you cannot save two lives. You will have to choose."

He turned and faced her.

"Would you have Thor live on this night, or your brother? One of them must die. It is written."

Gwen was horrified by the question.

"What kind of choice is that?" she asked. "By saving one, I condemn the other."

"You do not," he responded. "They are both meant to die on this night. I am sorry. But that is their fate."

Gwen felt as if a dagger had been plunged into her stomach. Both of them meant to die? It was too awful to imagine. Could fate really be that cruel?

"I cannot choose one over the other," she said, finally, her voice weak. "My love for Thor is stronger, of course. But Godfrey is my flesh and blood. I cannot stomach the idea of one dying at the expense of the other. And I don't think either of them would want that."

"Then they both shall die," Argon replied.

Gwen felt flooded with panic.

"Wait!" she called out, as he began to turn away.

He turned and looked at her.

"What about me?" she asked. "What if I should die in their stead? Is it possible? Can they both live, and I will die?"

29

Argon stared at her for a very long time, as if taking in her very essence.

"Your heart is pure," he said. "You are the most pure-hearted of all the MacGils. Your father chose wisely. Yes, he did…"

Argon's voice trailed off as he continued to look into her eyes. Gwen felt uncomfortable, but did not dare look away.

"Because of your choice, because of your sacrifice on this night," Argon said, "the fates have heard you. Thor will be saved on this night. And so will your brother. You will live, too. But a small piece of your life must be taken. Remember, there is always a price. You will die a partial death in return for both of their lives."

"What does that mean?" she asked, terror-stricken.

"Everything comes with a price," he answered. "You have a choice. Would you rather not pay it?"

Gwen steeled herself.

"I will do anything for Thor," she said. "And for my family."

Argon stared right through her.

"Thor has a very great destiny," Argon said. "But destiny can change. Our fate is in our stars. But it is also controlled by God. God can change fate. Thor was meant to die on this night. He will live only because of you. You will pay that price. And the cost will be high."

Gwen wanted to know more, and she reached out to Argon, but as she did, suddenly, a bright light flashed before her, and Argon disappeared.

Gwen spun, looking for him in every direction, but he was nowhere to be found.

She finally turned and looked out at the lake, so serene, as if nothing had happened here on this night. She saw her reflection, and she looked so far away. She was filled with gratitude, and finally, with a sense of peace. But she couldn't help but also feel a sense of dread for her own future. As much as she tried to put it out of her mind, she couldn't help but wonder: what price would she pay for Thor's life?

CHAPTER EIGHT

Thor lay on the ground in the midst of the battlefield, pinned down by McCloud soldiers, helpless, hearing the clash of battle, the screams of horses, of men dying all around him. The setting sun and the rising moon—a full moon, fuller than any he had ever seen—was suddenly blocked by a huge soldier, who stepped forward, raised his trident and prepared to bring it down. Thor knew that his time had come.

Thor closed his eyes, preparing for death. He did not feel fear. Only remorse. He wanted more time to be alive; he wanted to discover who he was, what his destiny was, and most of all, he wanted more time with Gwen.

Thor felt that it wasn't fair for him to die like this. Not here. Not this way. Not on this day. It wasn't his time yet. He could feel it. He was not ready yet.

Thor suddenly felt something rising up within him: it was a fierceness, a strength unlike any he had ever known. His entire body grow hot and tingly, as he felt a new sensation shoot through him, from the soles of his feet, through his legs, up his torso, through his arms, until his fingertips were positively burning, sparking with an energy he could barely understand. Thor shocked himself by letting out a fierce roar, like a dragon rising from the depths of the earth.

Thor felt the strength of ten men course through him as he broke off the soldiers' grips and leapt to his feet. Before the soldier could bring the trident down, Thor stepped forward, grabbed him by his helmet and head butted him, cracking his nose in two; he then kicked him so hard he went flying backwards like a cannonball, knocking down ten men with him.

Thor shrieked with a newfound rage as he grabbed a soldier, raised him high overhead and threw him into the crowd, taking down a dozen soldiers like bowling pins. Thor then reached out and snatched a flail with a ten foot chain from a soldier's hands, and swung it overhead, again and again, until screams rose up all around him, taking down all the soldiers within a ten foot radius, dozens of them.

31

Thor felt his power continue to surge, and he let it take over. As several more men charged him, he reached up and held out a palm and was surprised to feel a tingling and then watch a cool mist fly from it. His attackers suddenly stopped, blanketed in a sheet of ice. They stood frozen in place, blocks of ice.

Thor turned his palms in each direction, and everywhere men became frozen; it looked like blocks of ice had dropped down all over the battlefield.

Thor turned to his brothers in arms, and saw several soldiers about to land fatal blows on Reece, O'Connor, Elden and the twins. He raised a palm in each direction and froze the attackers, saving his brothers from instant death. They turned and looked at him, relief and gratitude welling in their eyes.

The McCloud army began to notice, and became wary of approaching Thor. They started to create a safe perimeter around him, all of these warriors afraid to get too close, as they saw dozens of their comrades frozen in place on the battlefield.

But then there came a roar, and a man stepped forward, five times the size of the others. He must have been fourteen feet tall, a giant, and he carried a sword bigger than Thor had ever seen. Thor raised a palm to freeze him—but it didn't work against this man. He merely swatted the energy away as if it were an annoying insect, and continued to charge for Thor. Thor was beginning to realize that his power was imperfect; he was surprised, and did not understand why he was not strong enough to stop this man.

The giant reached Thor in three long steps, surprising Thor with his speed, and then backhanded him, sending Thor flying.

Thor hit the ground hard, and before he could turn, the giant was on him, picking him up over his head with two hands. He threw him, and the McCloud army screamed in triumph as Thor went flying through the air, a good twenty feet, landing on the ground and tumbling hard, until he rolled to a stop. Thor felt as if all of his ribs had been cracked.

Thor looked up to see the giant bearing down on him, and this time, there was nothing left he could do. Whatever power he had had been exhausted.

He closed his eyes.

Please God, help me.

As the giant bore down on him, Thor began to hear a muted buzzing in his mind; it grew and grew, and soon, it became a buzzing outside of his mind, in the universe. He felt a strange sensation he never had before; he began to feel in unison with the very material and fabric of the air, the swinging of the trees, the movement of the blades of grass. He felt a great buzzing amidst all of them, and as he reached a hand up, he felt as if he were gathering this buzzing, from all corners of universe, summoning it to his will.

Thor opened his eyes to hear a tremendous buzzing overhead, and watched in surprise as a massive swarm of bees materialized from the sky. They poured in from all corners, and as he raised his hands, he felt that he was directing them. He did not know how he was doing it, but he knew that he was.

Thor moved his hands in the direction of the giant, and as he did, he watched as a swarm of bees darkened the sky, dove down and completely covered the giant. The giant raised his hands and flailed, then shrieked, as they all devoured him, stinging him a thousand times until he collapsed to his knees, then to his face, dead. The ground shook with the impact of his body.

Thor then directed his hand towards the McCloud army, who sat on their horses, staring back at him, watching the scene, in shock. They began to turn to flee—but there was no time to react. Thor swung his palm in their direction, and the swarm of bees left the giant and began to attack the soldiers.

The McCloud army let out a shout of fear, and as one they turned and rode, stung countless times by the swarm. Soon the battlefield was emptying of them, as they disappeared as fast as they could. Some of them could not manage to ride away in time, and soldier after soldier fell, filling the field with corpses.

As the survivors kept galloping, the swarm chased them all the way across the field, into the horizon, the great sound of buzzing blending with the thunder of horses' hooves and of men's shouts of fear.

Thor was astounded: within minutes, the battlefield was vacant, still. All that remained was the moaning of the McCloud wounded, lying in heaps. Thor looked around and saw his friends, exhausted, breathing hard; they seemed to be badly bruised, covered in light wounds, but okay. Aside, of course, from the three legion members he did not know, who lay there, dead.

There came a great rumbling on the horizon, and Thor turned in the other direction and saw the King's army charging over the hill, racing towards them, Kendrick leading the way. They galloped for them, and within moments they came to a stop before Thor and his friends, the lone survivors on this bloody field.

Thor stood there, in shock, staring back, as Kendrick, Kolk, Brom and the others dismounted and walked slowly towards Thor. They were accompanied by dozens of Silver, all the great warriors of the King's Army. They saw that Thor and the others stood there alone, victorious, in the bloody battlefield, riddled with the corpses of hundreds of McClouds. He could see their looks of wonder, of respect, of awe. He could see it in their eyes. It was what he had wanted his entire life long.

He was a hero.

CHAPTER NINE

Erec galloped on his horse, racing down the Southern Lane, charging faster than he ever had, doing his best to avoid the holes on the road in the black of night. He had not stopped riding since he had received news of Alistair's kidnapping, of her being sold into slavery and taken to Baluster. He could not stop reprimanding himself. He'd been stupid and naïve to trust that innkeeper, to assume that he would be good to his word, would keep up his end of the deal and release Alistair to him after he had won the tournament. Erec's word was his honor, and he assumed that others' word was sacred, too. It was a foolish mistake. And Alistair had paid the price for it.

Erec's heart broke at the thought of her, and he kicked his horse harder. Such a beautiful and refined lady, first having to suffer the indignity of working for that innkeeper—and now, being sold into slavery, and to the sex trade no less. The thought of it infuriated him, and he could not help but feel that he was somehow responsible: if he had never showed up in her life, had never offered to take her away, perhaps the innkeeper never would have considered this.

Erec charged through the night, the sound of his horse's hooves ever-present, filling his ears, along with the sounds of his horse's breathing. The horse was beyond exhausted, and Erec feared he might ride him to the ground. Erec had gone right to the innkeeper after the tournament, had not stopped to take a break, and he was so weary with exhaustion, he felt as if he might just slump and fall off his horse. But he forced his eyes to stay open, forced himself to stay awake, as he rode beneath the last vestiges of the full moon, heading ever south for Baluster.

Erec had heard stories of Baluster throughout his life, though it was a place he had never been; from the rumors, it was known to be a place of gambling, of opium, of sex, of every imaginable vice in the kingdom. It was where the disgruntled poured in, from all four corners of the Ring, to exploit every sort of dark festivity known to man. The place was the opposite of who he was. He never gambled, and rarely drank, and preferred to spend his free time alone, training, sharpening his skills. He could not understand the types of people who embraced sloth and revelry, the way the frequenters of Baluster did. It did not bode well, his being brought there. Nothing good could come of it. The very thought of her in such a place made his heart sink. He knew he had to rescue her quickly, and get her far from here, before any damage was done.

As the moon fell in the sky, as the road grew wider, more well-traveled, Erec caught his first glimpse of the city: the endless number of torches lighting its walls made the city appear like a bonfire in the night. Erec was not surprised: its inhabitants were rumored to stay up all hours of the night.

Erec rode harder and the city neared, and finally he rode over a small wooden bridge, torches on either side, a sleepy sentry nodding off at its base, who jumped up as Erec stormed past. The guard called out after him: "HEY!"

But Erec didn't even slow. If the man mustered up the confidence to chase after Erec—which Erec doubted very much—then Erec would make sure it was the last thing he did.

Erec charged through the large, open entranceway to this city which was laid out in a square, surrounded by low, ancient stone walls. As he entered, he charged down the narrow streets, so bright, all lined with torches. The buildings were built close together, giving the city a narrow, claustrophobic feeling. The streets were absolutely mobbed with people, and nearly all of them seemed drunk, stumbling to and fro, screaming loudly, jostling each other. It was like a huge party. And every other establishment was a tavern or gambling den.

Erec knew this was the right place. He could sense Alistair here, somewhere. He swallowed hard, hoping it was not too late.

He rode up to what appeared to be a particularly large tavern in the center of the city, throngs of people milling outside, and figured it would be a good place to start.

Erec dismounted and hurried inside, elbowing his way past the people rowdy with drink, and making his way up to the innkeeper, who stood in the back, in the center of the room, writing down people's names as he took their coins and directed them to rooms. He was a slimy looking fellow, wearing a fake smile, sweating, and he rubbed his hands together as he counted their coins. He looked up at Erec, a plastic smile on his face.

"A room, sir?" he asked. "Or is it women you want?"

Erec shook his head and came in close to the man, wanting to be heard above the din.

"I'm looking for a trader," Erec said. "A slave trader. He rode this way from Savaria, but a day or so ago. He brought precious cargo. Human cargo."

The man licked his lips.

"What you seek is valuable information," the man said. "I can provide that, just as easily as I can provide a room."

The man reached forward and rubbed his fingers together, and held out a palm. He looked up at Erec and smiled, sweat forming on his upper lip.

Erec was disgusted by this man, but he wanted information, and didn't want to waste time, so he reached into his pouch and put a large gold coin in the man's hand.

The man's eyes opened wide as he examined it.

"King's gold," he observed, impressed.

He looked Erec up and down with a look of respect, and of wonder.

"Have you ridden all the way from King's Court, then?" he asked.

"Enough," Erec said. "I'm the one asking questions. I have paid you. Now tell me: where is the trader?"

The man licked his lips several times, then leaned in close.

"The man you seek is Erbot. He comes through once a week with a new batch of whores. He auctions them off to the highest bidder. You'll likely find him in his den. Follow this street to the end, and his establishment lies there. But if the girl you seek is of any worth, she's probably gone already. His whores don't last long."

Erec turned to go, when he felt a warm, clammy hand grab his wrist. He turned, surprised to see the innkeeper grabbing him.

"If it is whores you seek, why not try one of mine? They are just as good as his, and half the price."

Erec sneered at the man, revolted. If he had more time, he would probably kill him, just to rid the world of a man such as he. But he summed him up, and decided he wasn't worth the effort.

Erec shook his hand off, then leaned in close.

"Lay your hands on me again," Erec warned, "and you will wish that you hadn't. Now take two steps back from me before I find a nice spot for this rapier in my hand."

The innkeeper looked down, eyes opened wide in fear, and took several steps back.

Erec turned and stormed from the room, elbowing and shoving patrons out of his way as he burst back outside and through the double doors. He had never been so disgusted by humanity.

Erec mounted his horse, which was prancing and snorting at some drunk passersby who were eyeing it—no doubt, Erec figured, to try to steal it. He wondered if they would have actually attempted it if he had not returned until a few minutes more, and he made a note to himself to tie his horse more securely at the next place. He marveled at the vice of this town. Still, his horse, Warkfin, was a hardened warhorse, and he knew that if anyone tried to steal him, he would trample them to death.

Erec kicked Warkfin, and they went charging down the narrow street, Erec doing the best he could to avoid the throngs of people. It was late in the night, yet the streets seemed to become more and more dense with humanity, people of all races mingling with each other. Several drunk patrons screamed out at him as he charged past them too quickly, but he didn't care. He could feel Alistair within reach, and he would stop at nothing until he had her back.

The street ended in a stone wall, and the last building on the right was a leaning tavern, with white clay walls and a thatched roof, which looked as if it had seen better days. From the looks of the people going in and out, Erec sensed this was the right place.

Erec dismounted, tied his horse securely to a post, and burst through the doors. As he did, he stopped in his tracks, surprised.

The place was dimly lit, one big room, a few flickering torches on the walls, a dying fire in the fireplace in the far corner, and strewn with rugs everywhere, on which lied scores of women, scantily dressed, chained to each other and chained to the walls. They all appeared to be on drugs, and Erec could smell the opium in the air, and saw a pipe being passed around. A few well-dressed men walked through the room, kicking and nudging the feet of the women here and there, as if testing out the merchandise and deciding what to buy.

In the far corner of the room there sat a single man on a small, red velvet chair, wearing a silk robe, women chained to either side of him. Standing behind him were huge, muscular men, their faces covered in scars, taller and broader even than Erec, looking as if they would be thrilled to kill somebody.

Erec took in the scene and realized exactly what was going on: this was a sex den, these women were for hire, and that man in the corner was the kingpin, the man who had snatched Alistair, and probably snatched all of these women, too. Even now Alistair might be in this room, Erec realized.

He burst into action, frantically hurrying through the aisles of women and scanning all the faces for hers. There were several dozen women in this room, some passed out, and the room was so dim, it was hard to tell right away. He looked from face to face, walking through the rows, when suddenly a large palm smacked him in the chest.

"You pay yet?" came a gruff voice.

Erec looked up and saw a huge man standing over him, scowling down.

"You want to look at the women, you gotta pay," the man boomed in his low voice. "Those are the rules."

Erec sneered back at the man, feeling a hatred rising up within him, and then faster than the man could blink, he reached up and struck him with the heel of his palm, right in his esophagus.

The man gasped, eyes opened wide, then dropped to his knees, clutching his throat. Erec reached up and elbowed him in the temple, and the man fell flat on his face.

Erec walked quickly through the rows, scanning the faces desperately for Alistair, but she was nowhere in sight. She was not here.

Erec's heart was pounding as he hurried to the far corner of the room, to the older man sitting in the corner, watching over everything.

"Have you found something you like?" asked the man. "Something you want to bid on?"

"I'm looking for a woman," Erec began, his voice steel, trying to keep calm, "and I'm only going to say this once. She's tall, with long blond hair and green-blue eyes. Her name is Alistair. She was taken from Savaria but a day or two ago. I'm told she was taken here. Is that true?"

The man slowly shook his head, grinning.

"The property you seek has already been sold, I'm afraid," the man said. "A fine specimen, though. You do have good taste. Choose another, and I will give you a discount."

Erec glowered, feeling a rage within him unlike any he'd ever felt.

"Who took her?" Erec growled.

The man smiled.

"My, you do seem fixed on this one particular slave."

"She is not a slave," Erec growled. "She is my *wife*."

39

The man looked back, shocked—then suddenly threw his head back and roared with laughter.

"Your *wife*! That's a good one. Not anymore, my friend. Now she is someone else's play thing." Then the innkeeper's face darkened, into an evil scowl, as he gestured to his henchmen, and added, "Now get rid of this piece of trash."

The two muscle-bound men came forward, and with a speed that surprised Erec, they both lunged him at once, reaching out to grab his chest.

But they did not realize who they were attacking. Erec was faster than them both, sidestepping them, grabbing the wrist of one of them and bending it back until the man fell flat on his back, and then elbowing the other in the throat at the same time. Erec stepped forward and crushed the windpipe of the man on the floor, knocking him out, then leaned forward and head-butted the other one, who was grasping his throat, knocking him out, too.

The two men lay there, unconscious, and Erec stepped over their bodies and towards the innkeeper, who was now shaking his chair, eyes opened wide in fear.

Erec reached forward, grabbed the man by the hair, yanked back his head, and held a dagger to the man's throat.

"Tell me where she is, and I might just let you live," Erec growled.

The man stammered.

"I will tell you, but you are wasting your time," he answered. "I sold her to a lord. He has his own force of knights and lives in his own castle. He is a very powerful man. His castle has never been breached. And beyond that, he has an entire army on reserve. He's a very rich man—he has an army of mercenaries willing to do his bidding at any moment. Any girl he buys, he keeps. There is no way you will ever get her free. So go back to wherever it is you came from. She is gone."

Erec held the blade tighter to the man's throat until he began to draw blood, and the man cried out.

"Where is this lord?" Erec snarled, losing patience.

"His castle is west of town. Take the Western gate of the city, and go until the road goes no further. You will see his castle. But it is a waste of time. He paid some good money for her—more than she was worth."

Erec had enough. Without pausing, he sliced this sex trader's throat, killing him, blood pouring out everywhere, as the man slumped down in his seat, dead.

Erec looked down at the dead body, at the unconscious henchmen, and felt revolted by this entire place. He couldn't believe it existed.

Erec walked through the room and began to sever the ropes connecting all the women, cutting the thick twine, freeing them one at a time. Several jumped up and ran for the door. Soon the entire room was loose, and they all trampled for the door. Some were too drugged to move, and others helped them.

"Whoever you are," one woman said to Erec, stopping at the door, "bless you. And wherever it is you are going, may the lord help you."

Erec appreciate the gratitude and the blessing; and he had a sinking feeling that, where he was going, he was going to need it.

CHAPTER TEN

Dawn broke, spilling through the small windows of Illepra's cottage, falling over Gwendolyn's closed eyes, and slowly waking her. The first sun, a muted orange, caressed her, waking her in the near silence of dawn. She blinked several times, at first disoriented, wondering where she was. And then she realized:

Godfrey.

Gwen had fallen asleep on the floor of the cottage, lying on a bed of straw near his bedside. Illepra slept right beside Godfrey, and it had been a long night for the three of them. Godfrey moaned throughout the night, tossing and turning, and Illepra had tended to him incessantly. Gwen had been there to help any way she could, bringing wet cloths, ringing them out, placing them on Godfrey's forehead, and handing Illepra the herbs and salves she'd continually asked for. The night had seemed endless; many times Godfrey had screamed out, and she'd been sure he was dying. More than once he had called out for their father, and it had given Gwen a chill. She felt her father's presence, hovering over them strongly. She did not know whether her father would want his son to live or to die—their relationship had always been so fraught with tension.

Gwen had also slept in the cottage because she did not know where else to go. She felt unsafe returning to the castle, to be under the same roof with her brother, and she felt safe here, in Illepra's care, with Akorth and Fulton standing guard outside the door. She felt nobody knew where she was, and she wanted it that way. Besides, she had grown fond of Godfrey these last few days, had discovered the brother she had never known, and it pained her to think of his dying.

Gwen scrambled to her feet, hurrying over to Godfrey's side, her heart pounding, wondering if he was still alive. A part of her sensed that if he woke in the morning, he would make it, and if he did not, it would be over. Illepra roused and hurried over, too. She must have fallen asleep at some point in the night; Gwen could hardly blame her.

The two of them knelt there, by Godfrey's side, as the small cottage filled with light. Gwen placed a hand on his wrist and shook him, as Illepra reached up and placed a hand on his forehead. She closed her eyes and breathed—and suddenly, Godfrey's eyes opened wide. Illepra pulled her hand back in surprise.

Gwen was surprised, too. She did not expect to see Godfrey open his eyes. He turned and looked right at her.

"Godfrey?" she asked.

He squinted, closed his eyes, and opened them again; then, to her amazement, he propped himself up on one elbow and looked at them.

"What time is it?" he asked. "Where am I?"

His voice sounded alert, healthy, and Gwen had never felt so relieved. She broke into a huge smile, along with Illepra.

Gwen lunged forward and embraced him, giving him a big hug, then pulled back.

"You're alive!" she exclaimed.

"Of course I am," he said. "Why wouldn't I be? Who is this?" he asked, turning towards Illepra.

"The woman who saved your life," Gwen answered.

"Saved my life?"

Illepra looked down to the floor.

"I only helped a small bit," she said, humbly.

"What happened to me?" he asked Gwen, frantic. "The last I remember, I was drinking in the tavern and then…"

"You were poisoned," Illepra said. "A very rare and strong poison. I've not encountered it in years. You're lucky to be alive. In fact, you're the only one I've ever seen survive it. Someone must have been looking down on you."

At her words, Gwen knew that she was right, and she immediately thought of her father. The sun streaked into the windows, stronger, and she felt her father's presence with them. He had wanted Godfrey to live.

"It serves you right," Gwen said with a smile. "You had promised to forsake ale. Now look at what happened."

He turned and smiled at her, and she saw the life back in his cheeks, and she felt flooded with relief. Godfrey was back.

"You saved my life," he said to her, earnestly.

He turned to Illepra.

"Both of you did," he added. "I don't know how I shall ever repay you."

As he looked at Illepra Gwen noticed something—it was something in his look, something more than gratitude. She turned and looked at Illepra, and noticed her blushing, looking down to the floor—and Gwen realized that they liked each other.

43

Illepra quickly turned and crossed the room, turning her back to them, busying herself with a potion.

Godfrey looked back to Gwen.

"Gareth?" he asked, suddenly solemn.

Gwen nodded back, understanding what he was asking.

"You're lucky you're not dead," she said. "Firth is."

"Firth?" Godfrey's voice rose in surprise. "Dead? But how?"

"He hung him from the gallows," she said. "You were supposed to be next."

"And you?" Godfrey asked.

Gwen shrugged.

"He has plans to marry me off. He sold me to the Nevaruns. Apparently they're on their way to take me away."

Godfrey sat up, outraged.

"I shall never allow it!" he exclaimed.

"Neither shall I," she answered. "I will find a way."

"But without Firth, we have no evidence," he said. "We have no way to bring him down. Gareth will be free."

"We will find a way," she responded. "We will find—"

Suddenly the cottage filled with light as the door opened and in marched Akorth and Fulton.

"My lady—" Akorth began, then turned at the site of Godfrey.

"You son of a bitch!" Akorth cried out in joy to Godfrey. "I knew it! You cheated just about everything in life—I knew you'd cheat death, too!"

"I knew no mug of ale would take you to your grave!" Fulton added.

Akorth and Fulton ran over, and as Godfrey jumped up from bed, and they all embraced.

Then Akorth turned to Gwen, serious.

"My lady, I'm sorry to disturb you, but we spotted a contingent of soldiers on the horizon. They are rushing for us even now."

Gwen looked at him with alarm, then ran outside, all of them on her heels, ducking her head, and squinting in the strong sunlight.

The group stood outside, and Gwen looked out at the horizon and watched a small group of Silver riding for the cottage. A half dozen men charged at full speed, and there was no doubt they were racing for them.

Godfrey reached down to draw his sword, but Gwen lay a reassuring hand on his wrist.

44

"These are not Gareth's men—they are Kendrick's. I am sure they come in peace."

The soldiers reached them and without pausing dismounted from their horses and knelt before Gwendolyn.

"My lady," the lead soldier said. "We bring you great news. We have pushed back the McClouds! Your brother Kendrick is safe, and he has asked me to send you a message: Thor is well."

Gwen burst into tears at the news, overwhelmed with gratitude and relief, stepping forward and embracing Godfrey, who embraced her back. She felt as if her life had been restored within her.

"They shall all return today," the messenger continued, "and there will be a great celebration in King's Court!"

"Great news indeed!" Gwen exclaimed.

"My lady," came another, deep voice, and Gwen looked over to see a lord, a renowned warrior, Srog, dressed in the distinctive red of the west, a man she had known since youth. He had been close to her father. He knelt before her, and she felt ashamed.

"Please, sir," she said, "do not kneel before me."

He was a famous man, a powerful lord who had thousands of soldiers answering to him, and who ruled his own city, Silesia, the stronghold of the West, an unusual city, built right into a cliff on the edge of the Canyon. It was nearly impenetrable. He was one of the few that her father ever trusted.

"I have ridden here with these men because I hear that great changes are astir in King's Court," he said knowingly. "The throne is unsteady. A new ruler—a firm ruler, a true ruler—must be placed in his stead. Word has reached me of your father's desire that you should reign. Your father was like a brother to me, and his word is my bond. If that is his wish, then it is mine. I have come to let you know that, if you should rule, then my men will swear allegiance to you. I would urge you to act soon. The events of today have proven that King's Court needs a new ruler."

Gwen stood there, taken aback, hardly knowing how to respond. She felt deeply humbled, and a sense of pride, but she also felt overwhelmed, in over her head.

"I thank you, sir," she said. "I'm grateful for your words, and for your offer. I shall ponder it deeply. For now, I wish only to welcome home my brother—and Thor."

Srog bowed his head, and a horn sounded on the horizon. Gwen looked up and could already see the dust cloud: a great army was appearing. She raised one hand to block out the sun, and her heart soared. Even from here, she could feel who it was. It was the Silver, the King's men.

And riding at their head was Thor.

CHAPTER ELEVEN

Thor rode with the army, thousands of soldiers heading as one back towards King's Court, and he felt triumphant. He still could hardly process what had happened. He was proud of what he had done, proud that when things seemed at their lowest point in battle, he had not given into his fear, but stayed and faced those warriors. And he was in shock that he had somehow survived.

The entire battle had felt surreal, and he was so grateful he'd been able to summon his powers—yet he was also confused, since his powers did not always work. He did not understand them, and worse, he did not know where they came from or how to muster then. It made him realize more than ever that he had to learn to rely on his human skills, too—on being the best fighter, the best warrior, he could be. He was starting to realize that to be the best warrior he could be, he needed both sides of himself—the fighter, and the sorcerer—if that's even what he was.

They rode all night to get back to King's Court, and Thor was beyond exhausted, but also exhilarated. The first sun was breaking over the horizon, and the vast expanse of sky opened before him in shades of yellows and pinks, and he felt as if he were seeing the world for the first time. He had never felt so alive. He was surrounded by his friends, Reece, O'Connor, Elden and the twins, by Kendrick, Kolk and Brom, and by hundreds of members of the Legion, the Silver, and of the King's army. But instead of being on the outskirts of it, now he rode at the center, embraced by all of them. Indeed, they all looked at him differently since the battle. Now, he saw admiration in the eyes of not just his fellow Legion members, but also in the eyes of the real, full-grown warriors. He had faced the entire McCloud army by himself, and had turned back the tide of war.

Thor was just happy that he did not let any of his Legion brothers down. He was happy that his friends had escaped mostly unharmed, and he felt a sense of remorse at his Legion brothers who died in the battle. He did not know them, but he wished he could have saved them, too. It had been a bloody, ferocious battle, and even now, as Thor rode, whenever he blinked, images flashed in his head of the fighting, of the various weapons and warriors who had come at him. The McClouds were fierce people, and he had been lucky; who knew if he would be so lucky if they met again. Who knew if he would be able to summon those powers again. He did not know if they would ever come back. He needed answers. And he needed to find his mother. He needed to know who he truly was. He needed to seek out Argon.

Krohn whined behind him, and Thor leaned back and stroked his head, while Krohn licked his palm. Thor was relieved that Krohn was okay. Thor had carried him off the battlefield and had slung him over the back of his horse behind him; Krohn seemed able to walk, but Thor wanted him to rest and recover for the long journey back. The blow of the club Krohn took was mighty, and it looked to Thor that he might have broken a rib. Thor could barely express his gratitude to Krohn, who felt more like a brother to him than an animal, and who had saved his life more than once.

As they crested a hill and the vista of the kingdom spread out before them, there came into view the sprawling, glorious city of King's Court, with dozens of towers and spires, with its ancient stone walls and its massive drawbridge, with its arched gates, its hundreds of soldiers standing guard on the parapets and on the road, rolling farmland encasing it, and of course King's Castle in its center. Thor thought immediately of Gwen. It was what had sustained him in battle; it was what had given him reason and purpose to live. Knowing that he was set up out there, that he was ambushed, Thor suddenly feared for her fate, too. He hoped she was okay back here, that whatever forces had put into play his treachery had left her untouched.

Thor heard a distant cheer, saw something glimmering in the light, and as he squinted his eyes at the hilltop, he realized that a great crowd was forming on the horizon, before King's Court, lining the road, waving flags. The people were coming out in force to greet them.

Someone sounded a horn, and Thor realized they were being welcomed home. For the first time in his life, he did not feel like an outsider.

"Those horns, they sound for you," Reece said, riding beside him, patting him on the back, looking at him with a new respect. "You are the champion of this battle. You are the people's hero now."

"Imagine, one of us, a mere Legion member, turning back the entire McCloud Army," O'Connor added with pride.

"You do great honor to the entire Legion," Elden said. "Now they will have to take all of us a lot more seriously."

"Not to mention, you saved all of our lives," Conval added.

Thor shrugged, filled with pride, but also refusing to allow any of this to get to his head. He knew he was human, frail, vulnerable, like any of them. And that the tide of battle could have gone the other way.

"I just did what I was trained to do," Thor responded. "What we were all trained to do. I'm no better than anyone else. I just got lucky on this day."

"I should say that it was more than luck," Reece responded.

They all continued at a slow trot, down the main road leading to King's Court, and as they did the road began to fill with people, pouring out from the countryside, cheering, waving banners, the royal blue and yellow of the MacGils. Thor realized that this was becoming a full-fledged parade. The entire court had come out to celebrate them, and he could see the relief and joy in their faces. He could understand why: if the McCloud army had come any closer, they could have destroyed all this.

Thor rode with the others through the throngs of people, over the wooden drawbridge, their horses' hooves clomping. They passed through the arched stone gate, through the underpass, the sky going dark, then out the other side, into King's Court—where they were met by cheering masses. They waved flags and threw candies, and a band started up, sounding cymbals, banging drums, while people broke into dance in the streets.

Thor dismounted with the others as it became too thick to ride, and he reached over and helped Krohn down from the horse. He watched carefully as Krohn limped, then walked; he seemed okay to walk now, and Thor felt relieved. Krohn turned and licked his palm several times.

The group of them walked through King's Plaza, as Thor was hugged and embraced from every side by people he did not know.

"You have saved us!" an older man called out. "You have liberated our kingdom!"

Thor wanted to respond, but he could not, his voice swallowed by the din of hundreds of people cheering and shouting all around them, the music rising up. Soon, casks of ale were rolled out onto the field, and people burst into drinking, song and laughter.

49

But Thor had only one thing on his mind: Gwendolyn. He had to see her. He scanned all the faces, desperate for a glimpse of her, sure that she would be here—but he felt crushed to see that he could not find her.

Then he felt a tap on the shoulder.

"I believe the woman you're looking for is that way," said Reece, turning him and pointing the other way.

Thor turned and his eyes lit up. There, walking quickly towards him, wearing a huge, relieved smile and looking as if she had been up all night, was Gwendolyn.

She looked more beautiful than he had ever seen her, and she hurried towards him and ran right into Thor's arms. She jumped up and embraced him, and he hugged her back, tightly, spinning her in the crowd. She clung to him and would not let go, and he could feel her tears pouring down his neck. He could feel her love, and he felt it right back.

"Thank god you are alive," she said, overjoyed.

"I thought of nothing but you," Thor said back, holding her tight. As he held her in his arms, everything felt right in the world once again.

Slowly, he let her go, and she stared up at him and they leaned in and kissed. They held the kiss for a long time, the masses swirling all around them.

"Gwendolyn!" Reece called out in delight.

She turned and embraced him, and then Godfrey stepped up and embraced Thor, then his brother Reece. It was a big family reunion, and Thor somehow felt as if he were a part of it, as if these were all his family already. They were all united by their love for MacGil—and by their hatred for Gareth.

Krohn stepped forward and jumped up onto Gwendolyn, and she leaned back with a laugh and hugged him as he licked her face.

"You grow bigger with each passing day!" she exclaimed. "How can I thank you for keeping Thor safe?"

Krohn jumped up on her again and again, until finally, laughing, she had to pat him down.

"Let's leave this place," Gwen said to Thor, being pressed from every side by the thick masses. She reached out and took his hand.

Thor reached out and took hers back, and was about to follow—when suddenly, several warriors of the Silver came up behind Thor and picked him up into the air, high above their heads, placing him on their shoulders. As Thor rose into the air, a great shout came from the crowd.

"THORGRIN!" the crowd cheered.

Thor was spun around and around, as a mug of ale was thrust into his hand. He leaned back and drank, and the crowd cheered like wild.

Thor was set down roughly, and he stumbled, laughing, as the crowd embraced him.

"We head now to the victor's feast," said a warrior Thor did not know, a member of the Silver, who clapped him on the back with a beefy hand. "It is a feast for warriors only. For men. You will join us. There will be a spot reserved for you at the table. And you and you," he said, turning to Reece, O'Connor and Thor's friends. "You are men now. And you will join us."

A cheer rose up as they were all grabbed by members of the Silver and dragged away; Thor broke free at the last second and turned to Gwen, feeling guilty and not wanting to let her down.

"Go with them," she said, selflessly. "It is important that you do. Feast with your brothers. Celebrate with them. It is a tradition among the Silver. You cannot miss it. Later tonight, meet me at the back door of the Hall of Arms. Then we will be together."

Thor leaned in and kissed her one last time, holding it as long as he could, until he was tugged away by his fellow soldiers.

"I love you," she said to him.

"I love you too," he said back, meaning it more than she would ever know.

All he could think of, as he was dragged away, as he watched those beautiful eyes, so filled with love for him, was that he wanted, more than anything, to propose to her, to make her his forever. Now was not the right time, but soon, he told himself.

Perhaps, even tonight.

CHAPTER TWELVE

Gareth stood in his chamber, looking out the window at the breaking light of dawn as it rose over King's Court, watching the masses gather below—and he felt sick to his stomach. On the horizon there sat his worst fear, the very picture of what he dreaded most: the king's army returning, victorious, triumphant from its clash with the McClouds. Kendrick and Thor rode at its head, free, alive—heroes. His spies had already informed him of everything that had happened, that Thor had survived the ambush, that he was alive and well. Now these men were all emboldened, returning to King's Court as a solidified force. All of his plans had gone terribly awry, and it left a pit in his stomach. He felt the kingdom closing in on him.

Gareth heard a creaking noise in his room, and he spun and shut his eyes quickly at the site before him, stricken with fear.

"Open your eyes, son!" came the booming voice.

Shaking, Gareth opened his eyes, and was aghast to see his father, standing there, a corpse, decomposing, a rusted crown on his head, a rusted scepter in his hand. He stared back with a reprimanding look, as he had in life.

"Blood will have blood," his father proclaimed.

"I hate you!" Gareth screamed. "I HATE YOU!" he repeated, and pulled the dagger from his belt and charged forward for his father.

As he reached him, he sliced his dagger—though hit nothing but air, and stumbled through the room.

Gareth spun, but the apparition was gone. He was alone in the chamber. He had been alone the entire time. Was he losing his mind?

Gareth ran to the far corner of the chamber, rummaged through his dressing cabinet and extracted his opium pipe with trembling hands; he quickly lit it, and inhaled deeply, again and again. He felt the flush of drugs wash over his system, felt himself lost temporarily in the drug high. He had been turning to the opium more and more these past days—it seemed to be the only thing that helped chase away the image of his father. Gareth was tormented being here, and he was starting to wonder if his father's ghost was trapped in these walls, and if he should move his court somewhere else. He would like to raze this building anyway—this place held every memory of his childhood that he hated.

Gareth turned back to the window, covered in a cold sweat, and wiped his forehead with the back of his hand. He watched. The army neared, and Thor was visible even from here, the stupid masses flocking to him like a hero. It made Gareth livid, made him burn with envy. Every plan he had put into motion had fallen apart: Kendrick was freed; Thor was alive; even Godfrey had somehow managed to escape the poison—enough poison to kill a horse.

But then again, his other plans had worked: Firth, at least, was dead, and there was no witness left to prove he'd killed his father. Gareth took a deep breath, relieved, realizing things were not as bad as they seemed. After all, the convoy of Nevaruns was still en route to take away his sister, Gwendolyn, and drag her off to some horrible corner of the Ring and marry her off. He smiled at the thought, starting to feel better. Yes, at least she would be out of his hair soon enough.

Gareth had time. He would find other ways to deal with Kendrick and Thor and Godfrey—he had a myriad schemes to kill them off. And he had all the time and all the power in the world to make it happen. Yes, they had won this round, but they would not win the next.

Gareth heard another groan, spun, and saw nothing in this chamber. He had to get out of here—he couldn't stand it anymore.

He turned and stormed from the room, the door opening before he reached it, his attendants careful to anticipate his every move.

Gareth threw on his father's mantle, crown and scepter, as he marched down the hall. He turned down the corridors, until he reached his private dining room, an elaborate stone chamber with high arched ceilings and stained-glass windows, lit up in the early morning light. Two attendants stood waiting at the open door, and another stood waiting behind the head of the table. It was a long banquet table, stretching fifty feet, with dozens of chairs lined up on either side of it; the attendant pulled Gareth's out for him as he approached, an ancient, oak chair that his father had sat on countless times.

Gareth sat, and he realized how much he hated this room. He remembered being forced to sit in here as a child, his entire family lined up around it, being rebuked by his father and mother. Now, the room was profoundly lonely. There was no one in here but him—not his brothers or sisters or parents or friends. Not even his advisors. Over the past days, he had managed to isolate everybody, and now he dined alone. He preferred it that way anyway—there were too many times he had seen the ghost of his father in here with him, and he had become embarrassed to cry out in front of others.

Gareth reached down and took a sip of his morning soup, then suddenly slammed his silver spoon down on the plate.

"The soup is not hot enough!" he shrieked.

It was hot, but not piping hot as he liked it, and Gareth would not tolerate one more mistake around him. An attendant ran over.

"I am sorry, my liege," the attendant said, bowing his head as he rushed to take it away. But Gareth picked up the plate and threw the hot liquid in the attendant's face.

The attendant grabbed his eyes, screaming, as he was scolded by the liquid. Gareth then took the plate and lifted it high over his head, and smashed it over the attendant's head.

The attendant screamed, clutching his bloody scalp.

"Take him away!" Gareth screamed to the other attendants.

They looked at each other warily, then reluctantly took away the bloody attendant.

"Send him to the dungeons!" Gareth said.

As Gareth sat back down, trembling, the room was empty save for one attendant, who walked over to Gareth meekly.

"My liege," he said, nervous.

Gareth looked over at him in a seething rage. As he looked over, Gareth could see his father, sitting erect at the table, a few chairs away, looking back at him and smiling an evil smile. Gareth tried to look away.

"The Lord you summoned has arrived to see you," the attendant said. "Lord Kultin, from the Essen province. He waits outside."

Gareth blinked several times, as he began to process what his attendant was saying. Lord Kultin. Yes, now he remembered.

"Send him in at once," Gareth ordered.

The attendant bowed and ran from the room, and as he opened the door, in strutted a huge, fierce warrior with long black hair, cold black eyes, a long black beard. He wore full armor and a mantle, wore two long swords, one on either side of his belt, and he kept his hands resting on both of them, as if ready to defend—or attack—at any moment. He looked as if he were in a rage himself, but Gareth knew he was not—Lord Kultin had always appeared this way, ever since the time of his father.

Kultin strutted up to Gareth, stood over him, and Gareth waved his hand at an empty seat.

"Sit," Gareth said.

"I will stand," Kultin said back curtly.

Kultin scowled down at Gareth, and Gareth could hear the strength in his voice, and knew that this Lord was unlike the others. He was fierce, filled with bloodlust, ready to kill anyone and anything at the drop of a dime. He was exactly the type of man that Gareth wanted around.

Gareth smiled, pleased for the first time this day.

"You know why I have summoned you?" Gareth asked.

"I could guess," Kultin answered, terse.

"I have decided to elevate you," Gareth said. "You will be elevated beyond even the King's Men, beyond even The Silver. From now on, you will be my personal guard. The King's Elite. You and your five hundred warriors will be given the choicest meat, the choicest lodging and the venerable Silver Hall. The very best of everything."

Kultin rubbed his beard.

"And what if I don't wish to serve you?" he scowled back, challenging him, tightening his grip on his sword.

"You served my father."

"You are not your father," he replied.

"True," Gareth said. "But I am far richer than he, and I pay far more handsomely. Ten times what he paid you. You and your men will live in King's Court. You will answer to me personally—there will be no one above you. You will bring riches back to your province beyond what you'd ever imagine."

Kultin stood there, rubbing his beard, and finally reached down and pounded a fist on the table.

"Twenty times," he replied. "And we will kill anyone you like upon your command. We will guard you with our lives, whether you deserve it or not. And we will kill anyone who comes near you."

"*Anyone*," Gareth insisted. "King's soldiers or not. The Silver or not. If I tell you to kill them, you will do so."

For the first time, Kultin smiled.

"I don't care who I kill. As long as the price is high enough."

CHAPTER THIRTEEN

Thor sat at the long banquet table in the Hall of Arms, surrounded by his Legion brothers, his close friends, by scores of the Silver, Kendrick across from him, Kolk and Brom nearby, and he felt more at home than he ever had in his life. The day had been a whirlwind. Before today, they had still looked at him as something of an outsider, or at best, as just another Legion member. But after today, he could see from their every glance, from the way they addressed him, that they looked at him as one of theirs. As an equal. These men, whom he had always admired, were giving him the respect he had strived for his entire life. There was nothing he'd ever wanted more than just to be here, to sit with these men, to fight by their side, and to be accepted by them.

Thor felt more weary than he'd ever had, having been awake for nearly two straight days, his body covered in bruises and cuts and scrapes, having not stopped for he did not know how long; physically, a part of him just wanted to collapse, to go to sleep and not wake for a week. But he caught a second wind, and these men and boys were more festive than he'd ever seen them. A great tension had broken, and relief filled the room. It was more than relief: it was joy. The joy of victory. The joy of saving their homeland. And it all had to do with Thor.

One after the other, members of the Silver came by, draped an arm around Thor, patted him on the back, shook him roughly, clasped forearms, and called him "Thorgrinson." It was a title of respect, one usually reserved for adults, implying that Thor was a famed warrior. It was a title usually reserved for an elite warrior. If ever the Legion boys had used that title amongst themselves, it had been in jest; but now, these men used it with Thor with seriousness.

As another mug of frothing ale was put into Thor's hand, he took a long drink, feeling it go to his head; then he reached out and took a huge chunk of the venison laid out before him. He was starving, but first he bent over and handed this chunk to Krohn, who happily snatched it from his hand. Thor took another piece for himself, and he chewed and chewed, starving. The food was delicious.

Serving girls, barely clothed, passed by the rows of men, refilling their mugs of ale and goblets of wine, and as one walked by, one of the warriors grabbed her and yanked her down onto his lap. She giggled. Another servant girl came close to Thor, and a warrior grabbed her and tried to thrust her into Thor's lap—but Thor held up his hands, and gently prodded her away.

"Don't you like the women?" the warrior asked Thor.

"I like them just fine," Thor said. "But there is one in particular who I am saving myself for."

"Just one?" the warrior pressed, disappointed. "Take two or three. Don't fall for just one. You're too young. Take as many as your hands can grab," he said, and with that, he grabbed the girl himself, who screamed with delight, and carried her over his shoulder, off to a far corner of the room, to a pile of soft rugs.

"Don't listen to him," came a voice.

Thor looked over and saw Reece, sitting beside him, who reached up and placed a hand on his shoulder.

"Gwen would be proud," Reece said. "I am proud. That was exactly the kind of response I would want from a brother-in-law."

Thor smiled at the thought.

"If I were to propose to her, would you really accept me into your family?" he asked.

"What kind of questions that is that?" Reece asked. "You already are my brother. In every sense of the word. My *true* brother."

Thor felt honored. He also felt the same way about Reece.

"Be good to her," Reece added. "That's all I ask. She's tough, but sensitive. Don't take a second wife. And don't look elsewhere."

Reece went back to his drinking, and before Thor could respond, Kolk suddenly stood, across from Thor, and banged his mug on the wooden table several times, until finally the room quieted. All that could be heard was the crackling of the fire, roaring at the far end of the hall, and the growling of the dogs who fought with each other for a spot beside the flames.

"Men of the Legion!" he called out in his booming voice. "Men of the Silver! The King's soldiers! Today was a day of glory day for the MacGils! And we would be remiss if we did not acknowledge the exploits of one warrior: Thorgrinson!" he called out, raising his mug to Thor.

The entire room suddenly stood, raising their mugs.

"Thorgrinson!" they shouted, breaking into a cheer.

Thor stood and felt hands patting him on the back, tugging at him roughly. He was embarrassed, but elated at the same time. He hardly knew what to make of all this. Kolk. The warrior who had always rebuked him. He had never expected this.

Kolk banged his mug again, and everyone sat back down, and the room fell silent.

"Thor's courage today typified everything we want in a member of the Legion, everything we want in a member of the Silver. Honor must be rewarded, at all costs. So from this day, Thorgrin, you are promoted to Captain of the Legion. You will answer only to me, and the rest of the Legion will answer to you. You have in your command now hundreds of the finest young warriors our kingdom has to offer. To Thorgrinson!" he shouted again.

"To Thorgrinson!" the room shouted.

As they all sat back down, Thor sat there, stunned, hardly able to breathe, not knowing what to make of all of this. He, the youngest of the Legion members, promoted to Captain of them all. A part of him felt he didn't really deserve it. All he had done what was he had been trained to do.

The room settled back into its festivities, and Thor heard a whining beside him. He looked down and saw Krohn, resting his head in his lap, and realized he felt left out—and hungry. Thor reached out and grabbed another hunk of venison, even bigger, an entire leg, with the bone, and Krohn snatched it from his hands and carried it happily across the room. Krohn found a spot beside the fire, walking boldly right between the pack of wolfhounds. Although they were all bigger than he, as Krohn walked down the center, they all parted ways, none of them daring challenge him. Already, Krohn exuded an energy unlike any other animal. Thor could see him growing bigger and stronger every day, more powerful, more mysterious.

"It is an honor well-deserved," Reece said, standing and embracing Thor. Thor stood and embraced him back, and received embraces from Elden, O'Connor, and the twins. One after the other, Legion members shook his hand and clasped his forearm, all showing deference to him, clearly all pleased to have him as their Captain.

"A battle won by mere witchery and tricks," came a dark voice.

Thor turned to see standing behind him his three real brothers, Drake, Dross and Durs. His heart skipped a beat as he saw them, standing just a few feet away, looking down at him coldly, unsmiling. He hadn't seen them in ages, and had nearly forgotten about them. He could see in their eyes that they still held hatred for him, and it brought back fresh memories of his childhood, of his feeling unworthy, feeling small next to them.

"You did not fight like a warrior," said Drake, the eldest. "You did not fight like one of us. If you did, you never would have won."

"You are not deserving of the honors they heap on you," added Dross.

"Despite what these men think, we know the truth about you. You are still just our younger brother," said Durs. "Still just a poor sheepherder. The smallest and least deserving of all of us. You cheated your way into the Legion, and you cheated your way into the honors you won today."

"And what do you all know of cheating?" O'Connor said back, stepping up and defending Thor.

"And what makes you all so superior?" Elden added, at his side. "Just because you are older?"

"That's right," Drake said. "We are older. And bigger. And stronger. We could beat you all to a pulp one-on-one, any day."

"So why don't you?" Reece countered. "Let us arrange a one-on-one combat, and see who wins."

Dross laughed derisively.

"I don't need to listen to you," he said. "You are too young and ignorant to even talk to me. I'm a far greater warrior than you will ever be."

"Oh no, but you do need to listen to Thor," Reece countered. "He's your Captain now. Did you not hear Kolk? You'll have to listen to Thor's every word from now. How does that make you feel?" Reece smiled.

The three brothers scowled down.

"We will *never* listen to you," Drake spat to Thor. "We will *never* take an order from you. Ever. As long as we live."

Thor was taken aback by their anger towards him.

"Why do you hate me?" Thor asked. "You always have, ever since I could remember."

"Because you're not worth anything," Durs sneered.

With that, the three of them turned and walked off into the crowd, disappearing. Thor felt his heart pounding, felt a pit in his stomach.

Reece reached up and laid a hand on his shoulder.

"Don't worry about it. They're not worth the ground you walk on."

59

O'Connor turned to him.

"Some people hate for no reason," he added. "That's just who they are."

"Others are just filled with envy, for everyone and everything," Elden added. "They need someone or something to blame, so they decide that you are the reason they don't have what they want in life, and they hate you for their own failed lives. It is the easy way out for them—to blame you instead of being truthful and blaming themselves. It is just bullying—in another form."

Thor understood. But it still stung him to the core. He did not know what he had done to deserve such animosity from his own family. Not just now, but his entire life. Why had he had to be born into this family? Why had they had to be there, always, at every turn, to ruin things for him at his happiest moments?

"My friend," Reece said.

Thor looked up.

"There is something across the room that might cheer you up," he laid a hand on Thor's shoulder and turned him in the direction of the opposite side of the chamber.

There, standing in the doorway, smiling across the room at him, was Gwendolyn. Thor's heart leapt.

"It seems she waits for you," Reece said, smiling.

Thor had completely forgotten. With all the excitement, he had forgotten to meet her at the back door.

Thor hurried across the hall, whistling for Krohn, who raced to catch up. He saw Gwen smile wide, then duck out the back door, and Thor's heart raced as he realized that finally, after everything, they could have time to be together.

CHAPTER FOURTEEN

Thor held Gwen's hand with anticipation, as she led him through the moonlit night, down winding paths that turned through the gently rolling hills outside of King's Court. Krohn walked at their side, and as they nearly crested a hilltop, Gwen came around behind Thor and smiling, placed her hands over his eyes and made him stop.

"Don't look," she said, leading him forward, one step at a time.

Thor smiled, holding his hands out in front of him.

"Where are we going?" he asked.

"I want you to see something," she said. "But wait until we reach the top of the hill. Just a few more steps. Don't open your eyes until I tell you. Promise?"

Thor smiled wide. He loved Gwen's playfulness; he always had.

"I promise," he said.

Slowly, Gwen removed her hands. Thor waited, until finally she said: "Okay."

Thor opened his eyes and was breathless at the site: stretched before him as far as the eye could see were rolling meadows, filled with the most beautiful and exotic night flowers he had ever seen. He had never even known that flowers like these existed. Under the moonlight, these flowers were alive, blooming, and even more so, they were actually glowing, lighting up the night. There were entire fields of glowing yellows and violets and whites, swaying in the nighttime breeze, making the fields look alive, as if they were holding thousands of swaying candles. It was the most breathtaking thing he had ever seen.

"Glow flowers," she said, coming up beside. "Aren't they beautiful?"

She took his hand, as they looked out at the fields and he learned in and kissed her.

They held the kiss for a long time, and finally they clasped hands, and continued on the trail, through the glowing field of flowers, side by side, Krohn leaping into the flowers beside them.

They had been walking for what felt like forever when Thor asked, with a smile: "Where are we going?"

She smiled back.

"Some place very special to me," she replied. "It is a place I hold dear to my heart, a place that few people know about."

They walked for a while in silence, with no sound but the whistling of the wind, and the occasional night bird's song, along with Krohn's breathing beside them as they went. Every now and again Krohn would bound into the flowers, pouncing on some animal they could not see, then come victoriously back to the trail, trotting along beside them.

"I prayed for you," Gwen said, softly. "I thank god that you were delivered back safe to me. The thought of you being gone was too much for me to bear."

"I'm sorry to have left you," Thor said. "I wish I did not have to."

"It's funny," Gwen said, "but ever since I met you, I'm finding it hard to think of anything else. You have a way of getting into my veins. It's hard to concentrate when you're gone. But it's hard to concentrate when you're near me."

Thor's squeezed her hand harder, overcome with love for her, amazed to hear that she felt the same way about him as he did her. He was burning with a desire to ask her to marry him. He was starting to wonder if now was the right time and place. He was about to, and cleared his throat, but then felt himself getting nervous, afraid she might say no.

He steeled himself. He opened his mouth to speak, and was about to ask her.

But suddenly they rounded a bend, and they stopped as there came into view a small but magnificent structure, built in the shape of a miniature castle, intimate and quaint. It was nestled in the hills, high up, with a commanding view of the meadows, surrounded by thousands of glowing night flowers.

"My mother's house," Gwen said.

"Your mother's?" Thor asked.

"She and my father found it harder to take each other as they grew older. She had this place built for herself, mainly, to get away from him. From all of us. She liked to be alone. Not anymore. Now, ironically, she's confined to the castle—at least until she is better. So this place sits empty. Few people know of it. I would come here, sometimes, when I was young, to get away from it all, when she was not here. I wanted to share it with you," she said, squeezing his hand.

Thor was amazed this place existed. The site of it took his breath away, so quaint, the ancient stone nestled into the hills, its façade covered with clinging, glowing flowers. It looked magical.

Gwendolyn led him across the meadow, up to the structure and in through its small, arched door. She lit a torch as they entered, and used that to light others, lighting up room after room as they went. It was cozy in here, the stone rooms not too large. Gwen lit a fire in the fireplace, mounted the torch on the wall, and she and Thor lay on the pile of furs close to the flames. Krohn came up and sat a few feet away, near the fire. He faced the door, on guard, protecting them.

As Thor and Gwen sat beside each other, Gwen reached over, clasped his fingers between hers, and they leaned in and kissed. Thor felt her hand trembling, and he felt nervous himself. He caressed her cheek, and they held the kiss for a long time.

As Thor lay there with her, feeling overwhelmed with love for her, there were so many things he wanted to say. Most of all, there was something he wanted to ask. Something he *needed* to ask. He wanted to be with her forever, and he wanted her to know it.

"There is something I need to ask you," he said, finally, his heart pounding.

But Gwen reached up, placed a single finger on his lips, and quieted him. She leaned in and kissed him.

"Now is not the time for words," she said softly, smiling.

Thor did not resist as she kissed him again and again. Soon they were in each other's arms, rolling in the furs, beside the crackling of the fire. It had already been a day beyond his wildest dreams, and being here, in Gwen's arms, topped all of it. There was no place in the world he wanted to be more in this moment. He only prayed this night would never end.

*

Gwen swam in the Lake of Sorrows. It was a beautiful, sunny day, and the water was clearer than she had ever seen it. As she swam she looked down, and beneath her there passed schools of fish, of the most brilliant colors she had ever seen—bright blue and pink and yellow—swimming all around her. They swam past, and she looked towards the bottom, and saw that the sands below were all lined with gold. Gold was everywhere, lining the lake floor, and it sparkled as she went, sending a million reflections of light through the water.

Gwen decided to dive down, deeper and deeper, determined to grab some, to bring it back. But the deeper she went, the farther away the bottom became. Soon, it disappeared completely.

Gwen blinked, and when she opened her eyes, she found herself standing atop a hill. She was in a desolate landscape which she recognized immediately as Argon's. But as she looked, his cottage was nowhere in sight; in fact, there was nothing as far as the eye could see. There was only the howling of the wind over the rocks.

She suddenly felt movement inside her stomach, and she looked down and was shocked to see that her belly was swollen, sticking all the way out. She was pregnant.

She reached down and felt her stomach with both hands. As she did, she was startled to feel a kick.

She suddenly heard Argon's voice:

"You carry within you a great being," he said.

Gwendolyn looked down and welled with tears, knowing what he said to be true. With both hands she caressed her stomach, wanting to send it love, feeling the power radiating from within her. It kicked back.

Gwen opened her eyes and looked all around, breathing hard, wondering where she was. As her eyes slowly adjusted, she saw that she lay in Thor's arms, in the pile of furs, in her mother's castle, beside the dying embers of the fire. She turned and saw the first light of dawn breaking through the window, saw Krohn lying asleep, close by, and realized it was all a dream.

Gwen rose, gently extricating herself from Thor, who was sound asleep, and walked over to the open air window. As she did, she looked down and rubbed a single hand over her stomach. Nothing had changed.

Yet somehow, she felt different inside. She felt an energy coursing through her. She couldn't explain it, but somehow she felt as if she had changed forever.

And in that moment she knew, she just knew, that she was carrying Thor's child.

CHAPTER FIFTEEN

King McCloud fumed as he marched across the plaza before his castle, riddled with his injured and defeated soldiers. Everywhere, his men lay about, moaning, bleeding; those that weren't hurt, sat on the ground, dejected. It was enough to make him sick. Never mind that they had just had a hundred days of unprecedented victories, of spoils, of a reach into the MacGil side deeper than any of his ancestors. Now all that these men would remember would be their defeat, the loss of their spoils, of their slaves, their injuries, their lost brethren. And all at the hands of the boy.

It was a disgrace.

McCloud scowled as he marched, kicking soldiers randomly who sat on the ground, shoving others, slapping the wounded, trailed by his small entourage of advisers, none of whom dared speak to him. They knew, wisely, that that would be a mistake.

McCloud ran over and over again in his mind the cause of their defeat, what had gone wrong, what he could have done differently. Perhaps he should have stopped before the last city; perhaps he should not have ventured so deep. If he had turned back sooner, he could have returned to the McCloud side of the Highlands on his own terms, as a conquering hero, a greater king than all the McClouds before him.

But he had pushed it, had taken one city too many, had risked one battle too many. He had miscalculated the MacGil's defenses. He had been sure that the new MacGil son, Gareth, was a weakling, unable to muster a defense. Perhaps the troops had fought despite Gareth. He didn't understand it.

Most of all, he did not understand that boy, Thor. He had never encountered anyone in battle like that, anyone so powerful. He had simply no way to defend against it.

As McCloud marched through the camp of men, he knew that revolt would be inevitable. Sooner or later, his own men, who had once praised him so, would rally and rise up against him, would try to oust him. Instead of being known as the greatest of the McCloud kings, he would go down in history as the failed McCloud king. And that was something he could not allow.

McCloud had to preempt it. He would get tougher, more vicious with his men, so vicious that they would not even think of revolt. Then he would form another scheme, and strike the MacGils again, even harder than before.

But looking at the sorry state of his army, he did not know how that was possible. He felt a rage towards them. They had let him down—and no one lets him down.

McCloud turned the corner and marched through yet another row of dejected soldiers, and he saw before him his son Bronson's new wife, the MacGil daughter, Luanda, bound with twine, on the ground with the other slaves. In her, he finally found an object for his hatred.

It all came back to him: McCloud had been enjoying that girl immensely when Luanda had interrupted him, had snuck up on him—and now it was time to take his bad mood out on her. He saw in her the very emblem of disobedience of his own men. His own son's daughter, trying to kill him, and in the midst of his greatest victory. It was too much for him to bear. Her behavior would embolden the other men, and now, more than ever, he needed to send a message to all of them.

McCloud stormed over to Luanda, lying on her back, eyes opened wide with fear, feet and hands bound, and he reached out with his dagger. She flinched as he approached, thinking he would cut her—but he had other plans. He reached down and sliced the ropes binding her. She was startled to be freed her, and seemed confused—but he didn't give her time to think about it.

McCloud reached out and yanked her to her feet by her chest, then grabbed her by the shirt and lifted her off the ground, scowling up at her. She scowled back down, and then to his surprise, she spat in his face.

Her boldness and courage startled him. Without thinking, he reached back and smacked her hard enough to make all the men around him turn and watch what was going on. A growing crowd of soldiers formed, as she stopped struggling in his arms, getting the message, her face already black and blue from the time he had punched her. He held her high above his head and turned slowly, facing the crowd of soldiers in the dusty square.

"Let this be a message for all those who dare defy my command!" he boomed. "This woman dared to raise a hand against her King. Now she will know the full wrath of my justice!"

A cheer arose and McCloud carried her across the square, bent her over a large wooden log, grabbed her wrists and yanked them behind her back and tied each to the log. She stood there, bent over the log, helpless. She screamed and struggled, but it was no use.

McCloud turned and faced the thick crowd of soldiers.

"Luanda dared to defy me. She will be a message for all women who dare to defy their men, and for all subjects who dare to defy their King. I hereby sentence her to public attack! Let any man who wants to, step forward and have his way with her!"

A great shout rose up among the soldiers, as several of them stepped forward, hurrying towards her, angling to see who would be first.

"NO!" shrieked Luanda, as she struggled against the ropes, buckling like mad, trying to break free.

But it was no use. He had tied her securely.

Three soldiers came up behind her, elbowing each other to get their first, and the one closest to her pulled down his pants, then stepped forward to grab her.

Suddenly, there came the sound of someone running through the crowd, and a moment later, to McCloud's chagrin, there appeared his son, Bronson, still in his armor, wielding a sword. He charged through the crowd, sword raised high, and brought his sword down on the first attacker's wrist as he reached out to touch her.

The man shrieked as Bronson cut off his wrist, blood pouring from the stump.

Bronson faced the other two men about to attack Luanda, and swung around and chopped off one of their heads with his sword, then lunged forward and plunged his sword through the third one's chest.

The three soldiers lay there on the ground, dead, and Bronson wasted no time in swinging his sword and freeing Luanda. She cowered behind him, holding onto his back, as the crowd came closer to them.

"Any of you come closer," Bronson called out, "and it will be the death of you! This is my wife. She shall not be punished, or tortured, by anyone. You will have to get through me first."

McCloud's wrath flared up, a greater wrath than he had ever felt. Here was his own son, defying him in front of all the men—and all for the sake of a woman. He would have to teach him a lesson in front of everyone.

McCloud drew his sword himself with a great clang, and rushed forward with a shout, pushing his men aside roughly, and facing off with his son. He charged his boy.

"It's time I teach you respect!" McCloud screamed.

He charged and brought his sword down right for Bronson's face, hoping to slice him in half, and his bride with him.

But the boy was quick. He had trained him too well. Bronson blocked his blow with his shield, then parried with his sword. McCloud blocked it, and the two went, back and forth, exchanging blow for blow. The elder McCloud was bigger and stronger, and he managed to slowly drive his son back, farther and farther, as the great clang of swords and shields went on.

The elder McCloud swung a great blow, aiming to chop off his son's head—but he overestimated. The sword went flying over his head, and Bronson leaned back and kicked his father hard in the gut, sending him down to the ground. The blow surprised McCloud, his pride hurt as he hit the ground.

He looked up to see his son standing over him, his sword pointed down at his throat. His son could have killed him when he missed with that blow, but he had kicked him instead. It was not an opportunity he would have given his son if the roles had been reversed. He was disappointed in him. He should have been more ruthless.

"I do not want to hurt you," Bronson said to his father. "I only want you to let Luanda go. Order your men that no one is to touch her, and the two of us shall leave this camp, and be done with this kingdom. I shall not hurt you. Nor any more of your men."

There came a thick, tense silence, as a growing crowd, hundreds of soldiers now, closed in, listening to every word as father and son faced off.

The elder McCloud's mind raced, humiliated, seething with rage, and determined to put an end to his son once and for all. A scheme entered his mind.

"I YIELD!" he shouted.

A gasp spread through the crowd.

"THE GIRL IS NOT TO BE TOUCHED!" he shouted again.

Another gasp arose, and as McCloud watched, he could see, slowly, Bronson's shoulders relax, his sword drop just a bit.

The elder McCloud forced himself to smile, a big toothy grin, laid his sword down on the ground, and reached up with an open palm, as if to ask his son to give him a hand up.

Bronson hesitated for just a moment; it appeared as if he were debating whether or not to trust his father. But Bronson had always been too naïve, too trusting. That was his downfall.

Bronson relented. He reached down with an open palm, switching hands with the sword, to give his father a hand up.

McCloud saw his chance. He reached over, grabbed a handful of dirt, and swung around and threw it in his boy's eyes.

Bronson screamed out, raising both hands to his eyes, stumbling back, and McCloud jumped to his feet, kicked his son hard in the chest, knocking him to the ground, and pounced on him.

"Soldiers!" he screamed out.

In a moment's notice several of his loyal soldiers appeared, pouncing onto Bronson, holding back Luanda, who tried to come to his rescue.

"Bring him to the post!" McCloud commanded.

They dragged Bronson, struggling, sand still in his eyes, to a huge wooden post, and bound one of his arms roughly to it. McCloud then grabbed his son's free arm and tied it to a wooden beam, stretched out before him.

Bronson looked back at his dad, helpless, fear in his eyes.

"Men, gather around!" McCloud screamed.

The thick mob of soldiers gathered within feet of them, and McCloud took his sword, and raised it high overhead.

"No, father, don't do this!" Bronson screamed.

But McCloud grimaced, wielded his two-handed sword high above his head, and brought it down with all the strength in his body.

Bronson shrieked, as the sword cut through the flesh of his wrist. Blood squirted everywhere, as his hand fell limply to the ground.

Luanda, behind him, shrieked and shrieked, and she broke free of her attackers and pounced on McCloud, grabbing at his hair. He turned and elbowed her hard, right in the nose, breaking it, and knocking her flat, unconscious.

"THE IRON!" he screamed.

Within moments, a scolding hot iron poker was put into McCloud's hand, and he reached back and jabbed it into his son's stump.

Bronson shrieked even louder, louder than he ever thought possible, as the smell of burning flesh filled his nostrils. McCloud held the poker steady against the stump, until the bleeding stopped. He didn't want his boy dead. He wanted him alive. He wanted him maimed. He wanted him to suffer, and to remember this event. He wanted all of his men to remember. And to fear him.

"I promised you that the girl was not to be touched," he said to his son, who stood there, limp, hunched over, breathing hard. "And I am good to my word. She will not be touched—she will be killed!"

McCloud leaned back and roared with laughter, hardly able to catch his breath. This day was not as bad as it seemed. No. It was not so   bad   at   all.

CHAPTER SIXTEEN

Thor strolled with Gwen hand in hand through the meadows in the early morning light, Krohn by their side, on the way back from her mother's castle. It had been a magical night, beyond his wildest dreams. He had never awakened before feeling so peaceful, so content, so at one with the world. He felt as if he had found his place in the world, beside Gwen, and he never wanted to be anywhere else. He didn't care where she led him, where they might go, as long as they were together.

Thor also felt immensely relaxed after finally having had a good night sleep. It had been days on his feet, of battle, of riding, and he felt as if it were the first time he had slept in a month. He had strange dreams all night long, of battle, of soldiers, of swords and shields—and even of his having a child. If Krohn hadn't awakened him, licking his face in the early morning, he felt as if he might have slept all day.

As they strolled, Thor wondered what the future might look like with Gwen. He had his duties to fulfill for the Legion, yet he also wanted to spend time with her. He wondered how they could build their life together. He knew he wanted to be here, in King's Court, but in the back of his mind he knew that as long as Gareth was king, that was not possible. There was too much danger here for them both.

As they strolled hand in hand, a nice fall breeze picking up, the world alive with every shade of fall flower, Gwen smiling beside him and Krohn nipping at their heels, Thor wanted more than ever to ask Gwen the question. Would she would marry him? But once again, he hesitated. The time did not seem quite right. He was waiting for a magical, perfect moment, and for some reason, he just was not sure if this was it. He also became too nervous, his heart pounding and his throat going dry, every time he thought of asking her. He was too scared of being rejected, and a part of him didn't know if he could summon the courage to do it. What if she said no? What if his asking her ruined their relationship forever? A part of him didn't want to take that chance.

As they rounded the final hill, walking in silence, King's Court came into view in the distance, and they both stopped in their tracks. Something was wrong. Thor could see from here that scores of The Silver, the Legion and the King's army were pacing about in an agitated way. They were all milling outside the Hall of Arms, and Thor could feel something brewing. He could not understand what was happening: when he had left last night, they had been in the middle of the feast and had been jovial. He expected to return this morning to see them all still sleeping, recovering. But they were all awake, on their feet, alert, most of them armed and anxiously hurrying inside.

"Something's wrong," Thor observed.

"Yes, it is," she said. "Let's hurry."

The two of them broke off at a trot, Krohn running beside them, across the plains, through the arched stone gate, and into King's Court. They strutted across the dusty plaza and entered the crowd of men, merging with them as they poured into the Hall of Arms.

As they entered, Thor was surprised to find the hall packed with soldiers. He spotted all his friends in the Legion, and dozens of the Silver. He spotted Kendrick, Kolk, Brom, Atme, and dozens of famed warriors. The mood inside was agitated. Many warriors sat at the table, heads in their hands, as if nursing a hangover, while others paced the room, arguing with each other. There was a tense energy in the air, a murmur, as if they had all been in the midst of a heated debate.

"But it is not just!" yelled one soldier to the other. "Never in the history of the MacGils has there been anything like this!"

Thor walked with Gwen and cut a path through the center of the room to Reece and Godfrey and Kendrick, who sat huddled together, with several Silver members clustered around them. They turned and looked up at their sister, making room.

"What has happened here?" she asked Kendrick.

Thor had a sinking feeling that whatever it was, it was not good. He could not believe how the mood had changed since he had left this hall just hours ago.

"It is our dear brother, Gareth" Kendrick said, morose. "He has displaced the Silver from the Silver Hall."

"What!" Thor yelled out, unbelieving.

"It's true," Kendrick said. "The Silver have lived in that hall for a thousand years, for every MacGil king. Now they are being relegated to the minor army barracks."

"It is an insult that will not be tolerated!" a soldier added.

"But why?" Thor asked. "Why would Gareth do this? How could he get away with it?"

"He won't get away with it," Brom responded sternly, slamming a fist on the table.

"It seems he has brought in another band of warriors," Kendrick said. "Lord Kultin, from the Essen province. He has hired them as a private king's guard, his own personal fighting force. He is showering them with the best of everything, including the Silver's Hall. It is a slap in the face. To all of us."

"But can he do such a thing?" Thor asked.

"He is King," Reece responded. "He can do whatever he wishes."

Thor shook his head, shocked, as the others fell into a disturbed silence, muttering all around them. He could hardly believe that Gareth would have the audacity to do such a thing. He wondered what it meant for them all. Would there be a civil war? Clearly, a line had been crossed.

"Well, at least the Silver will finally see what we have known for a long time now," Gwendolyn spoke up. "That our brother is not to be trusted. That he strives to cause division amongst our kingdom. That he caused Kendrick to be jailed unfairly. And that he was responsible for the death of our father."

The hall grew quiet at Gwendolyn's final words, as all the warriors turned and looked at her.

"The death of your father?" one of the soldiers asked.

"Those are serious charges, my lady," Brom said. "Have you any proof?"

"We had proof, Godfrey and I," she responded. "We had a witness to the crime. The man who wielded the blade, and Gareth's advisor, Firth. But now he hangs from the gallows. Gareth made sure of that."

"Then you have no proof," Kolk said.

"Not anymore. Gareth has managed to do away with whatever proof we could find. But he would not have tried to poison Godfrey, and he would not have tried to kill me, if he didn't know we were close to revealing him."

"Still, it remains circumstantial," Brom said. "The Council is very strict. We cannot oust a King without proof of wrongdoing—we would be considered traitors to the Ring. Unfortunately, our law leaves no room for compromise. Proof is required, however unjustly a King may act."

"But there is more than the fact that he assassinated our father," Kendrick chimed in. "He is also endangering us, our men, the Ring, leaving us open to attack. That is why the McClouds' breached the Highlands: they sensed our vulnerability. One can argue that we have

73

a right, a responsibility, to revolt, and to institute a new rulership, on behalf of the best interests of the Ring."

"That may be true," Kolk argued, "but still we cannot take any action while he is lawful King. We need proof of his assassination attempt. Then we can oust him."

"I think I can find proof," Godfrey said.

The room turned and looked at him.

"If I can prove who poisoned me, the other night in the tavern," he continued, "then that may lead back to Gareth. Surely, an assassination attempt on his own brother, a member of the royal family, would be grounds to oust him as king."

"Yes it is," Brom replied. "But we would need proof. And a witness."

"I can find it," Godfrey said. "I'm sure I can."

"Then find it, and be quick about it. And in the meantime, we will do what we can to help rebuild and refortify from our fragile state," Kendrick added. "We are weakened since the McCloud attack. I will lead a group to our eastern defenses and help fortify them, in case of another attack. They have been badly damaged in the raid and we will need a contingent of men to fortify our cities and to prevent another McCloud raid."

"I will help by dispatching the Legion," Kolk chimed in. "They can help rebuild the other villages destroyed by the McClouds."

"In the meantime, we will find proof, and find a legal way to oust Gareth," Gwen said.

"You better be quick about it," Brom said. "Because my men will not suffer Kultin and his savages in Silver Hall for long. I fear that if we don't find a way to legally oust Gareth soon, then we will have a civil war on our hands."

The room muttered in approval.

"Speaking of traitors," Kendrick added, "we must first oust the traitors within our own ranks."

Kendrick turned towards the door and nodded to Atme, who suddenly slammed closed the huge door of the Hall of Arms. It reverberated with a hollow thud and he barred it, not allowing any soldiers to leave. The room grew silent with a thick tension.

"Forg!" Kendrick called out. "Come forward! The time has come for you to account for your actions on the battlefield yesterday."

A shout rose up, as several members of the Silver grabbed Forg and dragged him forward, cutting a path through the crowd, to the center. He was held in place by four knights, as he struggled to break free.

"What is the meaning of this?" Forg yelled, indignant. "I'm a loyal member of the King's Army. I did nothing wrong!"

"Didn't you?" Kendrick asked. "Thor and several of his Legion friends were led into an ambush by the McClouds. You set them up to be killed."

Kendrick stepped forward, pulled a dagger from his belt and held it to Forg's throat, as the room grew silent.

"I'm only going to ask you this once. Answer truthfully, and it might just save your life. Was it Gareth who commanded you to do so?"

A thick silence fell over the room, as Forg swallowed hard, sweating.

Finally, he nodded, and lowered his head.

"He did," he admitted.

An outraged gasp erupted through the hall.

"He admits his treachery!" several knights called out.

"Forgive me my Lord," Forg pleaded, desperation in his eyes. "It was a command from the King. And I was too weak not to heed it."

"Yet it was a command to kill one of our own," Kolk said, stepping forward. "To set up noble Legion members for death at the enemy's hands. It was a command for treachery and betrayal. And you executed it. You know what the punishment is for betrayal of a Legion member."

Forg swallowed hard.

"Please, my lords, have mercy!"

"Thor," Kendrick said, turning to him. "It falls on you to pronounce a death sentence on Forg. It is you whom he betrayed."

The entire hall grew silent, as everyone turned to Thor.

Thor's heart pounded as he watched the man before him, waiting to be killed. A great fury washed over him, as he considered how this man had endangered his Legion brothers.

Yet at the same time, to Thor's surprise, he felt compassion for him, too. After all, it seemed that Forg had once been a good knight; he had simply been unable to stand up to tyranny, to do the right thing when the time came, in the heat of the moment. Thor hated the idea of his being executed—and especially at his own expense.

Thor stepped forward and cleared his throat.

"It is true," Thor called out, "Forg is deserving of death for what he did. But I would ask you all to have mercy on him."

A surprised gasp spread through the room.

"Mercy?" Kolk asked. "Why?"

"He may be deserving of death," Thor said. "But that does not mean we should give it to him. He made a mistake. Gareth is the evil one behind all of this. I would rather not have this knight's blood shed on my behalf. He made a mistake. And we survived, after all. Most of us, anyway."

"Thorgrinson," Kendrick said, "our law prohibits us from allowing a traitor to stay within our ranks. Something must be done with him."

"Then banish him," Thor said. "Send him away from your hall. Let him join Gareth's men, or let him leave the Ring. But don't kill him."

Kendrick looked long and hard at Thor, and finally he nodded.

"I can see that you hold much wisdom, despite your young age."

Kendrick turned to Forg, grabbed him by the chest, and scowled into his eyes.

"You are very lucky on this day," Kendrick said. "If I see your face before me again, I will kill you myself."

Kendrick reached over, tore the army's pin from Forg's vest, spun him around and kicked him hard, sending him stumbling through the hall. Forg hurried through the room and Atme opened the door, let him out, and slammed the door behind him.

Slowly, the room burst back into life, and as it did, Brom stepped forward.

"We still have not addressed the most important issue here today," he boomed.

The room fell silent as all turned to him.

"The gods be willing, one day, sooner or later, Gareth will be ousted. When that day comes, we will be left with no ruler of the Ring. Which MacGil shall succeed him? Kendrick, you are firstborn, legitimate or not. The men look up to you. Is it a role you will accept?"

Kendrick shook his head adamantly.

"My father's dying wish was that Gwendolyn should rule. We all witnessed it."

A gasp spread throughout the room.

"A woman?" one of the knights called out.

76

"It is true!" Reece said.

"It is!" Godfrey called out, too. "We were all at that meeting. It was our father's wish. He skipped over all of us and chose her. As her siblings, we accept it. In fact, we all approve of the choice."

"If you all honor MacGil," Kendrick said, "then you will honor his final wish. You will institute and defend Gwen as ruler of this kingdom."

All the soldiers in the room turned and looked at Gwen, and a heavy silence filled the room.

Thor looked over at her, and saw her lower her head in humility.

"If it was good enough for MacGil, then it's good enough for me," Brom boomed, breaking the stunned silence.

"And I!" Kolk added.

"And I!" echoed all the soldiers in the room.

"But Gwendolyn, would you accept?" Kendrick asked her.

An expectant silence followed, as she lowered her head. Several moments of silence followed.

"I know that you would be a fair and wise ruler," Kendrick added. "Much better than Gareth."

"You are what our father wanted," Godfrey added, "and you are what the Ring needs."

Finally, Gwen cleared her throat.

"It is not something I wish for, or something that I seek, my Lords," she said. "It is true, when father pressed me, I did agree to him that I would accept it. But I did so grudgingly. I would much rather that one of you rule in my stead."

Kendrick shook his head.

"We do not always get what we wish," he said. "Sometimes you must do what is best for the kingdom. And with every ounce of who I am, I know that it is you who should rule."

"Aye!" called out several soldiers, in agreement.

The room was thick with silence, as they awaited Gwen's response.

"Gwen, say yes," Godfrey urged, as she wavered. "The people need someone to rally around. The nobles, the Lords, everyone in all the provinces—they need to know that someone is in place, someone they can get behind, when Gareth should fall. For the kingdom's sake, say yes."

Gwen looked down to the ground, feeling her father's spirit with her strongly, then finally looked back up.

"I will agree," she said, finally.

The room erupted into a cheer, and Thor could hear how happy and relieved everyone was to have an alternate to Gareth. He felt elated himself, and beyond proud of her.

Before the cheer had even died down, before he'd had a chance to congratulate her, suddenly, the door to the hall burst open again, and in rushed a messenger, frantic.

"My Lord!" he said bowing in Kendrick's direction. "Outside this hall waits a contingent of men—a hundred men strong, fierce warriors all of them. Nevaruns! They say they have come to take their bride away!"

"Bride?" Kendrick called out.

"They say they have come to claim Gwendolyn!" the messenger said.

The hall burst out in an outraged gasp.

"Gwendolyn, is this true?" Kendrick asked her.

She frowned.

"It is but another devious plot set into place by our brother. He did not succeed in assassinating me, so now he thinks he can marry me off, to get me out of his hair. He has no right. He is not my father."

Thor suddenly drew his sword, and began marching out the hall.

"Whether he has a legal right or not, I don't care," Thor said. "There is only one right that I will heed, and that is the right of swords. If these men want to take Gwendolyn away, they will have to go through me!"

"And me!" Reece yelled, drawing his sword.

There came the sound of hundreds of swords being drawn in the hall, as all the soldiers got behind Thor.

Thor led the way, across the hall, out the open door, hundreds of soldiers following as they went outside to greet the contingent.

Before them, waiting, were a hundred of the fiercest warriors Thor had ever laid eyes upon, mounted on horseback, their leader on the ground, standing before his horse. He was twice as tall and as broad as any man Thor had ever seen. He had bright red skin, and scowled, with two long fangs protruding from his mouth, like tusks, and several rows of sharp, rotted teeth. The skin on his face was red, his eyes were hardly bigger than slits, a dark yellow, and his bald head was shaped in a point. He and his men all wore yellow and green armor.

"I have come to claim my bride," he growled down at Thor. It sounded like the snarl of an animal.

Krohn, standing beside Thor, snarled, the hair on his back standing, ready to pounce at the man.

"You are mistaken," Thor answered back, bravely, trying to use his most confident voice. "There is no bride for you here. Gwendolyn does not wish to leave, and she will not leave this kingdom without the spilled blood of all our men."

The man scowled down at Thor, his fist tightening on the hilt of his sword, his face turning even redder.

"I was promised a bride by your King!" the man snarled, gripping and releasing the hilt of his sword, as his soldiers pranced anxiously behind him.

"He has promised you something you cannot have," Thor answered. "Your fight is with our King, not with us. And not with Gwendolyn."

"My fight is with no one!" he yelled. "Because that bride is mine. And I am taking her! Now out of my way, little one!"

The Nevarun took several steps towards Thor, raised his sword high, as he did, Thor felt a burst of rage flash through him, unlike any he had ever felt. As the man came close, Thor raised his left palm and thrust it towards him, and Thor watched as a yellow ball of energy went flying from his palm, struck the man in the chest, and sent him flying back, dozens of feet, landing hard on the ground.

The crowd froze, watching.

Slowly, the Nevarun shook his head and got back to his feet. He turned and looked down at Thor with surprise. And with hatred. But this time, he did not dare come near.

"You are a demon!" the Nevarun said.

"Call me what you will," Thor said, no longer embarrassed of who or what he was. He was beginning to feel more at home with himself. "You will not touch Gwendolyn."

The Nevarun stood there, unsure, grabbing and releasing his sword, as he snarled with each breath.

After what felt like an eternity, finally, he turned to his men, muttered something in a language that Thor did not understand, then jumped up and remounted his horse.

"You have insulted the honor of the Nevaruns. We do not forgive. One day, you will pay—you will all pay—by blood. And when we take your bride, which we will, we will return her as a corpse!"

79

The Nevarun spat, then he and his contingent turned and rode off, speeding back down the main road out of King's Court.

Thor slowly lowered his sword, shaking inside but not wanting to show it. Reece came up and patted him on the shoulder, as did several others.

Gwen came up beside him. She laid a hand on his cheek, leaned in and kissed him. And with that kiss, all felt right again in the world. He would never let her go. Never.

CHAPTER SEVENTEEN

Erec galloped on Warkfin, kicking him with all he had, racing against time as images of Alistair flashed through his mind. He galloped from Baluster late into the night, charging and charging across the outskirts of the city, heading west, until finally the first sun began to break in the sky and in the distance he spotted the outline of a small castle, high up on a hill, surrounded by a formidable moat, a drawbridge, stone walls, and guarded by dozens of soldiers. They wore a distinctive armor, different than the armor of the north—a green, shiny armor, covered in scales, and helmets with noses that came to a point. There were probably two dozen knights guarding the entrance, unusual for a lord. Erec realized that the slave trader had been telling the truth: this was indeed a powerful man.

Erec raced down the road in the early morning, right for the drawbridge, and as he neared the large spiked gate was slowly lowered, as several knights stepped forward, holding their javelins high, wary of Erec's approach. Erec could see at a glance that he was vastly outmanned, yet still felt confident that he could find a way through if need be. But he not did not want to begin with a confrontation. He still had faith in his fellow man, and being the noble fellow that he was, he wanted to give this Lord the benefit of the doubt and believe that he had made an honest mistake; perhaps, when he had purchased Alistair, he had not realized she had been stolen from him. He wanted to give him a chance to make wrongs right before he resorted to an armed confrontation.

As Erec charged up to the bridge, several soldiers blocked his path. He could have killed each of them with the four throwing weapons on his belt; but instead he stopped before them, trying to hold his patience.

"Announce yourself!" one of the soldiers yelled out.

"I am Erec, son of Arosen, champion to King MacGil of the Western kingdom of the Ring," Erec announced, sitting erect, using his authoritative voice. "I demand an audience with your Lord."

"And who is it that wishes to speak to me?" came a booming voice.

Erec looked up, and above the drawbridge, in the upper tower of the castle, standing on a small balcony, he saw the lord of the castle, a man dressed in red and white silks and high green boots that stretched up to his knees, wearing a cape and a small crown. It was obvious from his appearance that this man thought that he was more than he was. He seemed to imagine himself a king; yet he was but a lesser lord, one of thousands that answered to King MacGil and the King's Army. From his bearing, he did not seem to realize it.

"You might know me as the King's right-hand man and as the champion of the Silver," Erec announced. "My brothers in arms number in the thousands, and upon my calling, they will come from all corners of the Ring to take up my cause. I have never summoned them, because I take it upon myself to resolve my own differences. I say this not to threaten you, but merely to make my point that it would be best to resolve our differences without confrontation."

"And what differences might I have with you?" called out the Lord. "I know who you are. And your armor belies you."

Erec cleared his throat, encouraged. Perhaps this lord could be reasoned with, after all.

"There is a woman you bought from a slave trader but a day ago," Erec said, the words nearly catching in his throat as he thought of Alistair. "I have no doubt that you did not realize who it was that you were purchasing. But she is a very special woman. She was kidnapped, taken against her will, from Savaria, and brought here illegally."

"And how do you know all of this?" asked the lord.

"Because she is my wife," Erec answered.

There came a surprised gasp among his men, as the lord looked down in silence.

"I will give you the benefit of the doubt," Erec continued, "and assume that you could not know this when you bought her. Now that you do, I ask that you release her, so that I can take her away from here, and we can avoid confrontation. Whatever money you paid to the slave trader, I will pay it back to you, and double."

"Will you?" called out the lord. "And if I refuse?"

Erec was shocked at his response; it was one he had not expected. He glowered, his heart sinking in anger.

"Why would you refuse?" Erec called out, surprised.

"I will refuse," the lord yelled back, "because I choose to. Because no one tells me what to do. Perhaps your wife was taken illegally. But then again, perhaps you should have been more careful as

82

her husband. It hardly speaks well of the King's best knight if he cannot prevent his very own wife to be taken before his eyes."

The lord laughed, and his men laughed with him, and Erec began to feel a flush of rage rising through his body.

"While MacGil may have thousands of warriors—so do I," the lord called out. "There is no lord that matches me in wealth, and I've used it wisely. I've paid off warriors from every neighboring province from here to the Canyon. And I've paid them handsomely. Anyone who confronts me will face an army unlike any they have ever known. Even a fighter such as you would be crushed in an instant.

"So let this stand as a lesson to you," the lord continued. "Next time be more vigilant for those you care for. You are a pathetic excuse for a knight, to come here and expect me to make up for your mistakes. I may have bought her illegally, but now she is mine. And I will *never* let her out of these gates. Not if you asked, and not if the king himself asked. She is my property now, to do with as I wish. And so you know, your timing is fortuitous: I have her being cleaned up right now by the servant girls, and she will be brought to my bedchamber momentarily for the first time. Knowing who you are, and knowing who she is, I will now look forward to it much more."

The lord leaned back and smiled, crossing his arms triumphantly, looking down at Erec.

Erec was overwhelmed with a rage unlike any he had ever known. This man represented to him everything that was evil in mankind, the very opposite of chivalry, of everything he strived to be.

Faster than any of his men could react, Erec pulled a short spear from his saddle, a thing of beauty, with a well-honed mahogany shaft and a silver tip, reached back, and hurled it with all his might at the lord.

The spear flew through the air, faster than an arrow, and before the Lord could move, the spear went through his throat, all the way through and out the other side, lodging in the wooden wall behind him.

The Lord stood there for a second, a huge hole in his throat, blood gushing out, and raised his hands to his throat, eyes opened wide in shock and pain. He stood there for a few seconds, looking down at Erec in disbelief, and then slumped forward, over the balcony, and his body plunged down to the ground, tumbling end over end, until he landed face first with a splat.

He lay there, at the entrance to his own castle, dead.

In the stunned silence, none of his soldiers moved, all of them frozen in shock, hardly conceiving what had happened so quickly.

Erec did not wait for them to react. He already burst in motion while the lord's body was plunging in the air. He took in the entire security situation at once, and decided that he would not waste his time or energy with the soldiers outside the gate. His main objective was to get Alistair and get out of there, and his first order of business was getting beyond that tall spiked gate. He galloped forward, reached into his saddle, grabbed a long chain with a spiked ball at its end, and spun it overhead and hurled it. It went flying high above the gate and caught on a pole, the spiked ball wrapping around it. Erec grabbed hold of it, jumped up off his horse, and swung on the chain, like a pendulum. He went flying by, several feet above the heads of the soldiers, and right towards the gap above the metal gate.

He flew through the narrow gap between the top of the gate and the arched stone, and landed safely on the other side of the bars, inside the courtyard. The soldiers outside charged for him, but they were stuck, unable to get through.

Erec fell through the air and landed in a role, rolling seamlessly onto his feet and getting his bearings, immediately prepared to attack the soldiers within the courtyard.

The first of several green knights attacked, and Erec knelt down and plunged his sword into the man's stomach, finding a weak point between where the armor met his waistline—and the man keeled over, dropping a flail, dead.

Erec reached down, grabbed the man's flail, stood and spun it around, smashing the studded ball into another attacker's face, knocking him flat on his back. Erec kicked the third attacker in the chest, sending him backwards before he could bring down his ax. He then took a short spear from his belt and hurled it at another attacker, piercing him at the weak point in his armor between his knee and thigh. He then grabbed a small throwing axe from his belt, spun in the other direction and hit the final attacker at the weak point between his shoulder blade and chest, sending him to the ground with a shout.

Erec surveyed the courtyard: five bodies not moving, and for the moment, no more attacking him.

He wasted no time. He took off at a sprint across the courtyard and rushed inside the small castle.

He stood there in its dark and narrow corridors and looked all about, disoriented.

"ALISTAIR!" he screamed out, desperate.

There came no response—except for another attacker, coming around the bend, attacking him with but a moment to spare. This man lunged at Erec from behind with open hands, grabbing for his throat, preferring hand-to-hand combat. Erec grabbed the man's wrist, bent over and flipped him over his shoulder. He then stepped forward and stepped on the man's neck.

Another attacker came from behind, and Erec spun and elbowed him in the gut, then grabbed him and threw him headfirst into the wall. The two bodies lay on top of each other in the narrow corridor.

Erec wasted no more time. He chose a direction and turned and ran down the corridor, leading into the heart of the castle. He hoped Alistair was being kept in this direction.

"ALISTAIR!" he leaned back and shrieked again.

"Erec!" came a faint cry.

At first, he could not tell from where it came; but after a moment, the cry came again, louder this time.

"Erec!" came her cry. "Up here!"

Erec turned, saw a flight of spiral stone steps, and ran for them. As he charged, three soldiers came charging down them, all in green armor, swords drawn. Erec reached into his pouch, grabbed a handful of the small, smooth rocks he reserved for his sling, and threw them across the bottom of the stairs, before the feet of these men. They had no time to react, and the three of them stumbled, tumbling end over end, their armor crashing as they hit the ground right before Erec.

Erec stepped aside and let them tumble right past him, not wanting to waste precious time and energy on a confrontation when he didn't need to, as their own momentum and weight brought them tumbling down, unconscious at the base of the steps.

Erec ran past them, charging up the stairs, up flight after flight. Behind him, in the distance, he could hear the metal gate of the castle beginning to be crashed in by the host of soldiers. He didn't have much time.

"ALISTAIR!" he screamed out again.

"Erec!" she shrieked back.

Then there came a scream. Her scream. She was in distress.

Erec's heart pounded and he ran twice as fast.

He reached the top landing and finally heard where the screams were coming from. He turned to his right and charged down the hall, saw an open door at the end and raced for it, hearing the sounds of struggle.

He burst into the room and saw Alistair, her hands bound behind her, and saw an attendant, one of the lord's men, grabbing her roughly and pushing her towards the open window.

"You will pay for what he did to my master!" the attendant said to her.

The attendant ran with her, racing for the open window, and Erec could see that the man was preparing to hurl her out the window, send her plunging to her death. He could also see that he was too far across the room to reach her in time. He could kill the man afterwards, but he could not save her. She was going to die.

Erec did not hesitate. He racked his brain and came up with an idea. He knew it would risk Alistair's life to try it, but he had to try: he reached into his waist, grabbed his throwing dagger, leaned back, and prayed to all the gods that he did not miss. If he was off by a hair, the dagger would kill Alistair instead.

Erec leaned forward and threw it, and he watched, his heart stopping, as it flew end over end. He held his breath.

To his great relief, it pierced the man in his throat, and just missed Alistair.

The man let go of her and reached up to his throat, screaming, blood spilling everywhere as he slumped down to the floor.

Alistair stopped right before the window and turned and faced Erec. He ran to her, took out another dagger and cut the ropes binding her hands.

She embraced him, crying hysterically, wrapping her arms tight around him. It felt so good to have her back in his arms.

Erec opened his eyes and looked over her shoulder, and to his surprise he saw the attendant suddenly rise from the floor and get back to his feet, pulling the dagger out of his throat, somehow getting a second wind. He raised the dagger high and charged forward, aiming to bring it down on Alistair's back.

With a second to spare, Erec threw her out of the way, stepped forward and grabbed the man's wrist mid-blow. He then yanked the man's arm behind his back, grabbed him, took three steps forward and threw him face-first out the open window, giving him the same death that he had intended for Alistair.

The man went hurling through the air, screaming, tumbling end over end, until finally he landed on the ground below with a thud, just a few feet from his master.

As Erec looked out the window, he saw a site he did not like: dozens of knights were charging across the bridge, for the castle, pouring in from all over the countryside. They were already beginning to pry it open, to make their way inside. Clearly, this lord had powerful vassals, and they were showing up as they had sworn to.

"There's another way out," Alistair said, coming up beside him, watching his gaze. "I noticed it when they brought me here. There is a back way."

"Show me," Erec said.

They ran down the corridor, all the way to the opposite end of the castle, and she led them to a corner room, where they looked down out the open window. Erec saw the back of the castle, leading to an open meadow, with no knights in view. She was right. The back entrance was also blocked by an iron gate. Erec realized that if they could get down another way, beyond the gate, they could flee for the countryside and avoid a confrontation with scores of knights. He might win such a confrontation, but there was no way he could keep Alistair and himself safe at the same time. He had to choose the way of least confrontation if he wanted her to survive.

Erec reached down into his waist and pulled out the long bunch of wire he kept tied up. It was a long wire, maybe twenty feet, with a spike at the end of it, which he kept for special occasions, to trip up opponents' horses. He'd never used it for a purpose like this, and he realized it would not even be long enough to reach the ground—and that it would be a long, hard fall. But he had no choice.

Erec scanned the stone walls outside the window, spotted a metal flag post embedded in the wall, wrapped the metal ball around it, and threw the wire out. It dropped down the castle wall, landing about ten feet short of the ground, and landed on the other side of the castle, beyond the metal gate. If the fall didn't kill them, it could get them out.

There came the sound of soldiers coming down the hall, and he knew they didn't have much time.

"But what about our hands?" Alistair said. "That wire will cut right through them."

Erec had been thinking the same thing; he scanned the room for something, anything, to protect them.

"Take this," Alistair said.

She took off her fur cloak, and Erec gratefully took it and wrapped it around his hands, again and again.

"Get on my back," he said.

She jumped onto him, and with her on his back, he stepped on the window ledge, grabbed the wire, tested it, and lowered them down the castle wall.

They slid faster than he could control, too fast, and he could not stop the sliding. They went flying down, to the point where the wire ended, and then fell another ten feet through the air.

They landed hard on the ground—too hard—and Erec turned at the last second to cushion Alistair's fall and take the brunt of it himself. As she landed on top of him, he felt a rib cracking.

He was winded, and he got to his hands and knees, seeing stars, and turned and looked at her.

"Are you okay?" he asked.

She nodded back, and he could see that she was dazed, but unhurt, to his great relief.

Erec heard a crash of metal, and knew the army had broken into the castle, and was charging inside up the stairs for them.

Erec got up and whistled, a distinctive whistle, one that only Warkfin would hear and understand.

Moments later, Warkfin came charging around to the back of the castle, and Erec stood and threw Alistair up, then mounted himself. She held on tight to his chest, as he kicked Warkfin to a gallop.

They charged away from that place, the sounds of the warriors crashing into the castle becoming more and more distant, as they rode.

Feeling Alistair's hands wrapped around his chest brought him more comfort than he had imagined possible.

She was safe. Finally. She was safe.

CHAPTER EIGHTEEN

Andronicus held a flaming torch as he galloped out in front of his army, then leaned over and lit the thatched roofs of the McCloud houses as he rode through the village. In a matter of minutes he had managed to light the entire village on fire, and he galloped through the streets, circling again and again, through the roaring flames, as the screams began to rise up all around him. He smiled with satisfaction. This would teach that McCloud king. This would teach these McCloud villagers to hide inside their homes, to think that they would ever be safe from him or his men. He would destroy every last one of them before he left this town. Not a single soul would survive. That had always been his motto.

In all the countries, in all the territories of the world that he had conquered, Andronicus had always followed one simple rule: crush and kill and destroy everyone and everything in sight. Leave no survivors. Take no prisoners. Burn everything down to the ground, so that there would be no one left to try to resurrect the old way. There would only be the new way. *His* way.

And it had worked. They had conquered city after city, country after country, and his empire had grown to millions. His soldiers were in the millions, and his slaves were millions more, all of them obedient to a fault. He could dispatch armies simultaneously to any corner of the world to crush anyone who dared to rise up against him. Nothing gave him more joy.

Now it was time to make this McCloud king pay. McCloud had made the grave mistake of crossing Andronicus, of refusing to cooperate with him when he'd had the chance. Of course, Andronicus's offer had been a duplicitous one, and if McCloud had allowed him to cross the Canyon, he would have taken his first chance to destroy all that was McCloud's. But at least he would not have done so right away. He would have given McCloud a little bit of time to think he was free, before he ambushed and butchered him and his family.

But McCloud had not gone along with it, and that put Andronicus in a rage. Now, to send a message to the rest of his empire, he would not just destroy McCloud and his loved ones, but torture them first. He smiled as he imagined dismembering them slowly, carrying their body parts to all four corners of the empire. Yes, he would shrink their heads and preserve them, and maybe even replace his current necklace with McCloud's shrunken head. He reached out and fingered the shrunken heads dangling at the base of his throat, and he enjoyed the thought immensely. He already started to imagine the type of chain he would bore through McCloud's head.

Andronicus' men caught up to him, fifty paces behind, charging with a scream into the village of flames and slaughtering the villagers who ran out of their homes. Andronicus looked back and smiled, as he could already see blood filling the streets. It was gearing up to be a fabulous day.

This was the tenth McCloud village they had ravaged today, and the second sun had barely risen in the sky. They had landed earlier in the morning on the McCloud shore, Andronicus leading a fleet of ten thousand ships. As his feet had touched down on the sand, he'd marveled that he was back here in this place, on the outer shores of the Ring, twice under a single moon. This time, though, he had come prepared for war, not for talk. He had brought along the McCloud prisoner who held the key to breaching the Canyon. This time he would not meet with McCloud. This time he would lead his men across the fifty mile wasteland of the McCloud's outer territory, ride right to the Canyon itself, and use the McCloud prisoner to show him how to breach it. His men would cross the Canyon, onto the other side, and he would surprise McCloud and burn his court down to the ground. He looked forward to the look of surprise on McCloud's face when he saw Andronicus in his own backyard, across the Canyon. It would be priceless.

And when Andronicus finished destroying the McClouds, he would then turn to his real target: the MacGils. Once inside the Ring, he would cross the Highlands, bring his million man army to MacGil's front step, and wipe out any memory there ever was of King's Court. When he was through, it would be a distant memory, a pile of rubble. He could already see the smoke and ashes and fumes in his mind's eye, could already see the MacGil land, once so choice, nothing but a desolate ruin, a sign for all those who dared to fight him. The thought made him smile.

Andronicus charged, not pausing any longer to terrorize this village, but focusing instead on the looming Canyon. His men caught up, charging beside them, and they raced across this desolate wasteland, populated with random McCloud villages, foolish frontiersman who had been dumb enough to live outside the Canyon. It served them right. They should have lived inside the Canyon. Did they all really think they would be safe here forever from the reach of the great Andronicus?

They rode west for hours, getting closer to the Canyon, ravaging several more villages along the way. As the second sun grew long in the sky, finally, they rounded a hilltop, and Andronicus saw it: the great Canyon. It was as awe-inspiring now as it was when he had seen it as a boy. It perplexed him to no end, this wonder of the world, with its magic energy shield which had kept his people at bay from the Ring for generations. It was the one place left on the planet that his army could not breach, and it vexed him to no end.

Now, finally, he had the information he needed to cross it. He would accomplish what all of his ancestors before him had failed to do. He would enter the one last untouched, pristine part of the planet, and have his men soil every inch of it. He would crush it until it was entirely under his dominion. He could already savor the rush of power he would feel when he was done. There would be no place left on the planet he had not conquered.

Andronicus's men rode up beside him and they all stopped as they finally reached the edge of the Canyon. They dismounted, and Andronicus took several steps forward, looking down at the vast divide. It was enormous, awe-inspiring, even for him, who had been everywhere in the world, who had seen everything, every natural wonder. This one was unique. An eerie, yellow mist hung in the Canyon, which seemed to stretch forever, and even from here Andronicus could feel the great energy force of the shield. He reached up a hand, into the air, towards the edge, and held it there. He knew that it was protected by an invisible wall and that if he extended his hand any further it would eviscerate him. It was like an invisible bubble blocking them out.

If it weren't for the shield, he and his men could simply kill the McCloud warriors stationed on the bridge of the Eastern Crossing, or hike to the bottom of it, or build their own bridge. He imagined a thousand ways they could breach it. But he remembered when they had tried in the past, when they had set up camp for a full moon cycle, and had tried every imaginable way. Each time, as soon as they crossed the threshold, the energy shield eviscerated them, killing his men instantly and leaving no way to cross it.

This time would be different.

"Bring him to me," Andronicus snarled, not looking back as he held out a hand, unraveling his three long claws.

Moments later his men hurried forward, and he saw the McCloud prisoner, bound, squirming, fear in his eyes, as they pushed him to Andronicus' grip. Andronicus reached out and grabbed him with his three claws by his shirt, and pulled him close.

"Now is your chance, human," he said to him. "You vowed to show us how to breach the Canyon. We are here. What is it?"

The human stood there, wide-eyed, looking from McCloud down into the abyss of the Canyon, shaking. Andronicus started to sense something wrong, and he did not like what he was sensing.

"I'm sorry," the human yelled out. "I lied! I have no idea how to cross it. I just wanted to get out of jail. You had me down there so many years. I couldn't stand it. I was desperate. I would say anything. I'm sorry!" he said, weeping. "I'm sorry!"

Andronicus looked down at this human with disbelief; then his disbelief changed to fury, a fury deeper than any he had ever felt. He had been tricked. By a human. He had rallied his entire army, had crossed the Ambrek sea, had looked forward to and reveled in this moment—all to be lied to by a pathetic little human.

Andronicus let out a unearthly shriek, and reached over, picked the human up high above his head, and using his incredible strength, he tore him in half. Blood squirted everywhere, all over Andronicus' head and face, down his chest, as the human, torn into halves, shrieked and shrieked. He was still alive, the two halves of his body still squirming, as Andronicus reached back and threw them, hurling the body parts into the abyss of the Canyon.

The human shrieked as the two halves of his body tumbled end over end—but then all grew silent, as his body eviscerated as it crossed the invisible line of the energy shield. He disintegrated into ashes.

Andronicus leaned back and shrieked, a shriek of despair, of frustration, one that shook the entire kingdom of the Ring. He would find a way in, if it was the last thing he had to do.

CHAPTER NINETEEN

Thor walked with Gwendolyn on the path leading out of King's Court, through the arched Northern Gate, and onto the road that led towards the Kolvian cliffs, Krohn walking happily beside them. It had been a whirlwind since they had left the Hall of Arms, and Thor was still trying to process everything that had happened. There was the shock of Gareth's new fighting force, loyal to him only; the shock of the Silver splintering off, having to stay in the regular army barracks; the divide between the kingdom, which he could feel growing greater over time; the traitor, Forg; Gwen being named the next ruler if Gareth should fall; and most of all, the Nevaruns who had arrived to try to steal Gwen away. Thor tried not to think of what might have happened if he and the other men hadn't had been there when they had arrived. Would Gwen be gone from him even now? Was there no low to which her brother Gareth would not stoop to send her away?

Thor was so grateful that he had been there to stop them, and so grateful he'd had the support of his fellow soldiers. He felt so proud of her that they all wanted her to rule, and indeed, he felt that there would be no better ruler than her.

But he also felt that their time together was precious now, with the Legion preparing to be dispatched again to help rebuild the towns ravaged by the McCloud raid. He knew it was only a matter of time until he was summoned, sent forth with the others, and he wanted every minute he could have with Gwen.

Most of all, there was the question that still burned front and center in his mind: would she marry him? As they walked through the fields, making their way slowly past the cliffs, hand in hand, Thor's heart was pounding, his throat dry. He was ready to ask her; he wanted to ask her; and at every turn, he asked himself if this was a good place to ask the question that would change their lives forever. He felt ashamed that he did not have a jewel or a ring or anything of worth to give her; all he had was his love. And he was still afraid that she might say no. Then what would become of their relationship? Was he over-reaching? Did she still think that he was beneath her somehow? Did she ever truly believe that?

Thor wanted to think that she did not, that she would say yes, but a part of him was still unsure.

Still, the time had come to ask, and at every turn, he wanted to. But he just could not tell when the perfect moment was.

"You seem preoccupied," Gwen said, as they walked.

Thor snapped out of it.

"Do I?" he asked.

"Yes, you do," she said.

"I'm sorry," he said. "Tell me where you are taking me."

"I already told you," she said, a smile at the corner of her lips. "You really aren't present, are you?"

He blushed.

"I'm sorry. Please, tell me again."

"I wanted to bring you to a place that is important to me. You said you wanted to know more about me. And this place tells it all. It is where I spend most of my time when you are away. It means everything and more to me. And I wanted to share it with you."

"I am honored," he said. "What is it?"

Gwen's smile broadened.

"You'll see when we get there."

She squeezed his hand harder, and they stepped up their pace, Krohn yelping beside them, as they continued through the fields, and up the gradual terrain of a vast hill, covered in flowers.

"Our time together is short," Thor said, clearing his throat, sweating as he began his warm up to proposing. "Soon, I will be dispatched, with the rest of the Legion, to help rebuild."

"I know," she said, her face darkening. "But the rebuilding won't take long. You'll be back in a matter of days."

"When I return, I am hoping things will change," he said, nearly stammering.

"How so?" she asked.

He cleared his throat several times, blushing. He felt like a fool for being so embarrassed, so fearful in this arena.

"There is a question I've been wanting to ask you," he finally managed to say.

Her smile broadened.

"And?" she asked. "What might that be?"

Thor opened his mouth to speak several times, but each time, his throat went dry. He reddened, embarrassed. He'd never asked a girl to marry him before, and he did not know the right way to do it.

"Um…" he said then began again, "um… I was wondering……"

Gwen finally laughed.

"I haven't seen you at such a loss for words since I first met you," she said laughing and laughing.

Thor blushed even more, now not sure if he should proceed. He felt as if he had already ruined the moment.

They reached the top of the hill at that moment, and as they did, a building came into view before them. They both stopped, staring at it, and Thor was taken aback in wonder. It was one of the most beautiful structures he had ever seen. It was shaped in a perfect circle, built low to the ground, may be only twelve feet high, and built of ancient, worn stone, a glowing white. Its roof was completely flat, covered in a shining gold plate which reflected in the sun. Its door was low and arched, made of the same reflective gold.

"It's beautiful," Thor said. "What is it?"

"Have you never been here before?"

Thor shook his head, feeling ashamed, ignorant.

"It's the House of Scholars," she explained. "It contains the most precious and rare volumes of our kingdom. It houses the Royal Library—which are, in my view, the greatest treasures our kingdom has."

Gwen held his hand and led him to the door, and as she did he knew the time had passed to ask her. He was kicking himself; he would have to ask her later.

They reached the building and Gwen opened the door naturally, as if she owned the place. Thor walked inside, Krohn following.

As they entered, Thor was in awe. While the outer wall was made entirely of stone, the inner wall was made entirely of glass, and in its center lay a circular grass courtyard, with a single tree, a rare flowering fruit tree, in its center. Sunlight flooded in through the glass, lighting it up from the inner courtyard.

All along the inner walls, as far as the eye could see, were spines of books—ancient books, big, thick, with leather and silver and gold bindings, the most exotic and precious volumes he had ever laid eyes upon. They glistened, looked like works of art.

"This place is magnificent," Thor said. "Have you read all of these books?" he asked, in awe.

Gwen threw her head back and laughed.

"I wish," she said. "I have certainly tried. It is where I spend the better part of my days. My siblings always made fun of me for being a bookworm. But it is a big part of my life."

Suddenly, something occurred to Thor.

"That is why your father chose you to rule," he said. "He thought you were the smartest."

Gwen looked back, blinking, as if considering that for the first time. She shrugged.

"I don't know. My siblings are pretty smart, too."

But Thor could see that she was just being humble. Seeing her in this place, how at-home she was here, he saw her in a new light; he saw for the first time how learned she was, could see the intelligence shining in her eyes, and suddenly it all made sense. He could see that Gwendolyn had her own source of power. Knowledge. Wisdom beyond what Thor could ever hope to attain. It was inspiring. And he would never have expected it from her, given how beautiful she was, and given that women were rarely given such a scholarly education in this kingdom.

"You are late for the day's lesson," came a voice.

Thor turned to see an old man walking towards them, his face covered in wrinkles, his head covered in gray hair, wearing the royal purple and green robes of the Royal Council. He walked with a limp, slowly, hunched over just a bit, using a cane to help him go, the golden tip echoing as it touched down on the stone floor. He smiled warmly at Gwen, his face folding into a million lines.

Gwen cleared her throat.

"Thor, meet Aberthol. He is the Royal Scholar. He was of counsel to my father, and to his father before him."

"And to his father before him," Aberthol added in his hoarse voice, smiling. "But not to the new MacGil king," he added, growing serious. "Not anymore, anyway."

Gwen looked back at him, in shock.

"Really?" she asked.

He nodded.

"Not as of yesterday. It was too much. I could suffer no more of his indignities. He has surrounded himself with a new Council anyway. Young folk. All of whom seem bent on ill-advising him. I still sit at the council meetings, but it is just a formality now."

Aberthol shook his head sadly.

"Your father would be turning over in his grave," he said. "This does not bode well for the Ring. It does not bode well at all. When knowledge and wisdom are replaced with ignorance and haughtiness, it is only a matter of time until the court collapses—and the kingdom with it. For after all, what are a court and a kingdom built on, if not on knowledge and wisdom? All else—arms and soldiers and wealth and power—all else follows that. Wisdom is the foundation of any kingdom. Never forget that Gwendolyn."

She nodded back to him, and he studied her.

"I hear that you will rule," he added.

Gwen opened her eyes wide in surprise.

"How did you hear that?" she asked.

He smiled back.

"I'm not without my resources," he said, "even for an old man. Word travels quickly in King's Court. Too quickly. Yet in this case, it is word I am happy to receive. I always knew you would make a great ruler. Even greater than your father."

Gwen blushed and looked down to the floor.

"I am not ruler of anything yet," she said. "My brother still reigns. And there is no sign of his stepping down."

Aberthol shrugged.

"An apple with a rotten core can only last so long," he said. "Either he will fall, or the kingdom will first. Both cannot endure. Discard your humility. Begin your preparations. Our Ring needs you. Now is not the time for meekness. Now is the time for a show of strength. Embrace your role. Allow your fellow countrymen to take strength in you. Do as your father wished for you to do. It is no longer about you. Is about *them*. The people. The ones without a ruler."

Gwen nodded.

"I will do whatever I could to help our people," she said.

Aberthol turned and looked at Thor. He opened his heavily lined eyes just enough to really look at him.

"And you are the newcomer," he said. "MacGil took a liking to you. I can see why. There is intelligence in your eyes. It will serve you well. Don't ever forget it. Don't think you can rely on arms alone. Or sorcery. It is *intelligence* that is your backbone."

Thor lowered his head.

"Yes, sire," he said calmly.

"You are disadvantaged," he said to Thor. "You were raised a villager, with no access to the Royal Library. But then again, few people in the Ring are. Learn from Gwen. Let her teach you. Embrace what she has to offer. Be lucky that you found this place now, not later in life. Contemplate all the knowledge in here. Learn the history of the Ring and know it well. Without knowledge, without history, you are nothing but an empty shell."

With that, Aberthol turned and walked past them, brushing by them, his cane tapping as he went.

"Always remember, Gwendolyn," he said, not turning back as he continued to walk, "these books will save you."

Thor turned and looked at Gwen, overwhelmed. Her eyes were shining back at his.

When Aberthol was out of earshot, she said softly, "Sorry about him—he can be intense. He doesn't waste time on trivialities. He never has."

"Don't be sorry," Thor said. "He said enough in a few minutes to make me think for a lifetime."

Gwen laughed, reached down and took his hand, and led him down the hall. She led him around the broad circle, past stacks of books, then to a narrow, circular stone stairwell, which led down, underground, into the bowels of the place.

Thor followed her, amazed that there was another story underground. As they walked, the staircase kept going, and they passed floor after floor of books, descending deeper and deeper underground, probably a good ten stories. Thor was shocked. This place was vast. Labyrinthine.

"All of these books," Thor said, catching his breath to keep up as Gwen skipped down the steps as if she were home. "I was overwhelmed by the number of books simply on the first floor. But the number of floors here never seems to end."

Gwen laughed.

"Yes, the library is deep. But remember, we are dealing with seven hundred years of MacGil Kings. The knowledge is as vast and deep as the family history—as the Ring itself. This building also houses ancient texts from all corners of the Empire, going back thousands of years, of which we are the guardians. We are the holders of the ancient truth. This is one of the reasons why the Empire is so intent on crushing us. They want to wipe out the history. To rewrite it. As long as we preserve it here, they never can."

They reached the final floor, and Thor followed Gwen as they proceeded down a stone corridor, lit every few feet by torches. Gwen took one off the wall and turned several times down various corridors, until they reached a small back room.

As they entered she lit several torches along the walls, until the small, cozy room was brightly lit. She affixed her torch to the wall and led Thor to a comfortable seat, big enough for two, at an ancient oak table in the center of the room, covered haphazardly in stacks of books. Thor could hardly get over this place. There were enough books on this table alone to last him a lifetime, and from the way Gwen began to organize them, it seemed as if she were familiar with them all.

Gwen reached over and opened an oversized book, displaying ancient maps. Thor leaned over beside her and ran his hand along the fine, crinkled pages, along the raised ink, tracing the trails of rivers, of mountains. This map was like a work of art.

"Do you know the ancient language?" Gwen asked. "The lost language of the Ring?"

Thor shook his head, embarrassed.

"Don't feel bad," she said. "There's no reason why you should. Most don't. It is taught to the royal family as a matter of course. Other than that, it is often the domain of scholars and kings. I would like to teach it to you, if you'd like to learn."

"I would love to," Thor said, excited at the idea. Thor loved knowledge, he always had, but he had never been granted access to it in his humble village; he had especially never had access to learning anything like the ancient language, which he knew to be the language of Kings for hundreds of years. The idea of learning it thrilled him.

"That is good," she said, "because most of these books are written in it. Without that, it's hard to go back past a few hundred years. The treasures it unlocks are endless."

Gwen turned the heavy pages until they came to another map. This one was even more intricate, drawn in all different colors, with markings that popped off the page. The land it outline looked very beautiful. He had never seen a book like this in his life.

"What is this place?" he asked.

"The other night, when you were telling me about your mother," Gwen said, "you got me curious. I can't bear riddles; I always need to get to the bottom of things. When you told me that you never met her, and that you didn't know who or where she was, it peaked my curiosity. I've been doing research for you into the Land of the Druids."

Thor's heart skipped a beat as he leaned closer.

"I found these ancient maps," Gwen said. "I think this is the land where your mother lives."

Thor leaned over, fascinated, looking at the maps with a whole new sense of meaning. He saw the ancient letters, and although he could not understand the ancient language, he assumed that it described the Land of the Druids. He ran his finger over every line, the blue of the ocean, the red of the cliffs. He spotted on the map a blue castle, glowing blue, perched at the top of a cliff, surrounded by a vast and empty sea. There was a long stone walkway leading to it, which curved into nothingness. Thor could feel the magic coming off of this place.

"The Castle of Lira," Gwen said. "Rumored to be an ancient and holy place. It lies in the center of the Land of the Druids. I think this is where your mother lives."

Thor ran his finger over it, and he could feel an intense energy rushing through his arm, and suddenly he knew she was right. He felt with every ounce of his being that this was indeed where she was. He felt a burning desire, stronger than he ever had, to meet her. He *had* to meet her.

"What does it say of the Druids?" Thor asked, excited.

Gwen slid over another book. This one was short and thick, and had no pictures. She flipped through the pages, heavy and crinkling, reading a text which Thor did not understand, and stopped halfway through, turning pages faster than he knew was possible, combing her finger along the edges until she stopped.

"The Druids are a kind and gentle people," she began to read aloud. "But they can also be fierce. Their powers come not from arms, or armor, but sorcery. Druids are different from other sorcerers, however. Their powers are more mysterious, aloof. They are one with nature. It is quite common for a Druid to attract all sorts of animals, who will be more than a close companion. Animals are like an extension of the Druid. Because the Druid is at one with harmony and nature, more advanced Druids can control nature, can command animals, insects, all forces of nature around them."

As Gwen read, Thor felt an electric jolt, thinking back to the battle against the McClouds, his ability to summon those bees, without even meaning to. He felt the truth in what she was reading.

"The power of a master Druid is nearly infinite. At the height of his power a Druid can be stopped by no one and nothing, in nature or on earth. But few Druids ever reach this level of power."

Thor thought about that, and realized that his power was imperfect. It did not always come when he summoned it, and it did not always work. He also seemed to get tired quickly after using it. He wondered if that was because he was human, too. Did that riddle him with imperfections? He felt that it did.

As Gwen closed the book, Thor could not feel certain anymore of who or what he was, or what his place in the world was. Was he a Druid? Was he a human? He felt as if he were caught between two worlds, a half-breed perhaps, not a true Druid, yet not a true human. He wondered if Gwen thought any less of him for that.

"I hope you don't think of me as different," he said to her.

She shook her head.

"No, of course not," she said softly.

"Because all I want is to be like you," Thor said. "To be human. To be normal. I'm grateful for whatever powers I have, but I never asked for them. I just want to fight fair and square, like any other warrior. I just want to train and become great, based on my own efforts. I feel as if I am cheating when I summon a power."

Gwen shook her head.

"You are doing nothing wrong," she said. "This is who you are. You are meant to be who you are for a reason. All destiny has a purpose. To not fully embrace who you are—that would be wrong. That would be rejecting the fates. We are born with our special powers for a reason. And we are born with our limitations for a reason, too. They make us stronger."

Gwen reached over and grabbed another book, a beautiful thick book, covered with a gold and silver plate, and slid it over to Thor. Thor reached out and held it with both of his hands, looked down at the incredible craftsmanship, the emblem of the falcon, of the MacGil family, and he felt a tremendous energy coming off of it.

"What is it?" he asked.

"The *Chronicle of the Ring*," she answered. "It was written nearly a thousand years ago. It not only charts all the history of MacGils, it also tells the story of the Great Divide. Back when the Ring was one kingdom. Before the Highlands. Before the McClouds. It goes back even to before the Canyon. When the Empire was one. When there was no divide."

Thor stared at the book in wonder.

"But it also goes forward, into the future. They say it was written by a council of scholars and mystics and sorcerers. This council knew everything, saw everything. And they set it all down in this book. They talk about things that happen even today. They talk of seven generations of MacGil Kings. They predict that the seventh would bring a great evil upon the Ring. They do not mention Gareth by name, but they describe him in action."

Thor looked at the book with a new respect. He pulled back its heavy lid, and flipped through its pages, crinkling as he went, running his hand along the ancient, handwritten script which he could not understand.

"What else does it say?" he asked.

"It talks of the eighth MacGil ruler," she said. "It says that he will bring destruction to the Ring unlike any we have ever known. Yet he will also bring great change and the Great Peace. It is a mysterious prophecy. All the others are clear, but this one is vague. I do not understand it. Neither does Aberthol. If Argon does, he is not telling us. I have checked all the sources, and I can get no clarity. Our best guess is that this book is unfinished."

Gwen reached over, closed the book, and looked deeply into Thor's eyes, with an intensity unlike any he'd ever seen. Her eyes shone with scholarship.

"Do you understand what this means?" she asked. "If I am to rule, I will be the eighth MacGil ruler. That is me. I do not wish to be the harbinger of destruction. This prophecy, it scares me. I can't help but feel as if I'm a cog in the wheel of destiny, as if I'm destined to bring some great doom on my people, no matter how hard I try. Unless of course, I am killed, and the eighth MacGil ruler is someone else."

Thor sat there, trying to follow her quick wit, her bouncing between books with a dexterity unlike any he'd ever seen, her depth of knowledge. He tried to process it all. He was about to ask her more questions, when suddenly a horn sounded from high up above, from the top floor of the building, echoing down the spiral staircase, all the way down to this chamber.

Suddenly Gwen stood, looking alarmed.

"Aberthol," she said. "He never sounds the horn unless it is pressing, unless someone has arrived here for me."

She hurried from the room, and the two of them climbed up the flights of stairs, circling all the way to the top, then continued down the corridor and out the front door, Krohn following.

Thor raised his hands to the harsh sunlight, squinting, as he made out the figures before him. He was surprised to see his friends—Reece, O'Connor, Elden, the twins—along with several Legion members, on horseback, waiting for him.

"Sorry to break this up," Reece said, "but Kolk's orders. We need to go. The Legion has been dispatched for rebuilding. Squadrons are already beginning to line up, and you are captain now. They won't leave without you."

Thor felt his stomach drop at the thought of leaving Gwen, but he nodded back to the others.

"I'll be there momentarily," Thor said. "Go ahead without me."

Reece nodded in understanding, and corralled the others, and they turned and galloped away, back down the hill.

Thor turned to Gwen and saw the distress in her eyes. It was their final moment, before he left. He needed to ask her the question. Now, more than ever. But he saw the sadness in her eyes, and he did not feel that the time was right.

"Will you be safe here, alone?" Thor asked.

She nodded gravely.

"I'll be fine," she said. "Don't worry about me."

"But you can't stay in the castle," Thor said, concerned. "Not with Gareth there. It is not safe."

She shook her head.

"I will stay at my mother's castle. No one knows of it. I'll await your return there."

"When I return, if you have not found a way to depose Gareth, we will flee this place together. I will bring you to a place of safety."

"There is nothing to worry for," she said. "Gareth tried to ship me off, and he failed. There's no way he can harm me now. Too many soldiers are aware of his treachery. I will be fine. And you will be back in a short period of time."

"Let me, at least, leave Krohn with you," Thor said.

Krohn, beside them, whined, and jumped onto Gwen, licking her.

"He will watch over you here, in my absence," Thor added. "And when I return, we will be together. Forever this time."

Thor leaned in and kissed her, and she kissed him back. He felt transported by that kiss, and he held it as long as he could. A cool fall breeze rushed over them, and he wanted this moment to last forever.

Slowly, he pulled back. There was a tear in Gwen's eyes.

"I love you," Thor said.

"I love you too," she answered.

CHAPTER TWENTY

Gwen stood there, outside the House of Scholars, and watched as Thor disappeared yet again, riding into the horizon with his Legion members. Once again, she felt a pit in her stomach. She did not feel the same sense of desperation she'd felt when he'd left for the Hundred; it was different, since at least this time he would be coming home soon, and this time he was not risking his life in a dangerous place, but merely helping villages rebuild close to home. He would also be surrounded by loyal friends, and she felt confident he'd be safe; and she, for her part, had Krohn by her side, had her mother's castle to hide in, and had the other soldiers behind her, who were now at least aware of the depth of Gareth's treachery.

Yet still, she could not help but feel overwhelmed with a sense of sadness, of longing. In some ways, it was harder this time. She loved him more. More than she had ever loved anybody. She loved him with a love that was hard to explain, that even she did not understand. He was so kind, and sensitive, and loyal, and protective, and proud. It hurt her when he was gone. She wanted him close all the time. And as she reached down and felt her stomach, she sensed that she carried his child. With every move she took, every gesture she made, her body felt different. She felt an energy welling within her, an ever-present feeling. She felt a sense of peace. And that made her miss him all the more.

And even though he was leaving for a peaceful mission, these were troubled times, and one never knew what could happen, even close to home, even on a peaceful mission. A part of her feared for him. And a part of her still feared for herself: she had come too close to being taken away by the Nevaruns, and it had rattled her. Gareth's treachery never seemed to amaze her, and while she felt supported by the show of arms from the Silver, and the King's men, she also feared her brother. She was still in danger here. Staying in her mother's castle would provide her with some security for now—but not for the long run. She and Godfrey would have to find a legal way to oust Gareth soon—or else, she realized, she would have to leave this place for good.

More than ever, Gwen needed to see Argon, to know what the future would hold; but she knew that seeking him out would be a waste of time. He appeared when and if he wanted to, and if he didn't, she would never find him.

So instead, Gwen walked across the hilltop, watching Thor as he disappeared, farther and farther. Krohn whined beside her and leaned against her leg, virtually sticking to her side; she looked down and smiled, and he licked her hand as she stroked his head. She felt reassured beyond words to have him there; it was like having a piece of Thor with her. He was morphing into a full-grown leopard, and while he was still just a puppy in her eyes, she could see from the frightened looks of others that he was a savage beast in the eyes of others.

She looked back up and wiped a tear as she watched Thor's contingent fade into the horizon, swallowed in a cloud of dust.

"A horizon of faded dreams," came a voice.

Gwen did not need to turn to know whose voice it was. She felt overwhelmed with relief. Argon.

Gwen turned slowly and saw him standing there, beside her, a few feet away, wearing his robes, holding his staff, looking out over the horizon as if watching Thor leave with her; she did not know how he got there. He was such a mystery to her. But she felt comforted by his presence.

She turned away, watching the horizon beside him, and smiled.

"Thank you for being here," she said. "You must have sensed my desire to see you."

"I always answer when a King summons me," he said. "If it is a true summons. And a true King."

She looked at him, startled by his words, but he continued to watch the horizon, expressionless.

"Are you saying that I will rule?" she asked.

"You know the answer to that yourself," he responded.

"What of my brother, Gareth?" she pressed.

Argon's face darkened, a slight frown at the corner of his lips.

"His reign appears to be eternal. But it will not be. He who takes the throne by blood must pay its price by blood. There is always a price for everything."

He turned and stared back, and the intensity in his eyes forced her to look away.

"Do you remember, when you made that vow?" he asked. "To give up your life for Thor's?"

She nodded, a tear forming at the corner of her eyes. She did not want to die now. Not now.

"Vows bear a heavy price," he reminded. "Before you pay it, much has to happen. There will be a great future for you. But there will be a little death first," he said. "Steel yourself and be strong. You will need strength now. More than you've ever had in your life. If you can survive what's to come, you can survive anything."

Gwen trembled inside, and felt her skin run cold.

"Your words frighten me," she said.

"But you must learn to fear," he said. "Rulers must be fearless. But they also must fear."

"Please," she pleaded, "tell me what it is I should fear. Give me some warning."

"If I did, your destiny would change. That cannot be. Not for your sake. And not for the sake of the Ring. You know your history. Need I remind you? The seven sun cycles. The seven moon alignments. It happens once every thousand years. And when will it happen again?" he asked.

Gwen racked her brain, thinking through all the volumes of history she had ingested, all the ancient prophecies she had read.

"The sun and moon event you speak of happens in the next sun cycle," she said. "But weeks away."

Argon nodded, satisfied.

"Yes, very good. Very good indeed. You will be a far wiser ruler than your father. In fact, it has been generations since the MacGils have had a ruler like you. So then you know what lies ahead."

Gwen frowned.

"But I thought those ancient prophecies were just parables, metaphors. I did not think they were meant to be taken literally. I was taught they are open to interpretation."

"And who is to say which is the right one?" Argon asked.

Gwen's eyes opened wide.

"Are you saying that it's all true? That the Ring will come to an end in a matter of weeks? That the ancient prophecies will come to be?"

Argon turned and stared into the horizon for a long time, then finally, he sighed.

"The Ring will come to an end as we know it. We live in a time of great change. Greater than you can imagine. Everything you once knew will be different. There will be a time of tremendous darkness. And a time of great light. If one can survive the darkness."

Gwen's mind reeled as she tried to process the gravity of his words.

"It will be up to you to lead your people through the darkness," he said. "Ready yourself for the task."

Argon turned to go, and Gwen reached out and grabbed his shoulder.

"Wait!" she called out.

But she felt a burning in her hand and quickly yanked it back, the energy coming off of him so intense she could not tolerate it.

"Please! Before you go, tell me one thing."

He turned and stared at her.

"The answer is yes," he said, before she opened her mouth. "You carry Thor's child. And it will change your life."

Before she could ask him more, suddenly, he disappeared.

She turned, looking everywhere for him, but saw nothing, save for a single bird, screeching high up in the air, flying farther and farther away.

Gwen turned and looked out into nothingness, over the great expense of the Ring, and she wondered. She reached up and felt her stomach.

Thor's child.

It was real.

CHAPTER TWENTY ONE

Thor rode with a dozen Legion members at a relaxed trot on the well paved road, already a half day's ride from King's Court. Riding beside him were Reece, O'Connor, Elden and the twins, along with a half-dozen Legion members Thor had just met. They had been dispersed by Kolk to rebuild villages around King's Court, and the Legion had been broken into groups of ten, and Thor had been named to lead this group to the village of Sulpa, less than a day's ride south, hit hard by the McCloud raid.

It was an odd feeling for Thor to be heading back down this familiar road, which also led to his hometown. It was especially eerie to be traveling on it after his discussion with Gwen about his mother. He wondered if the universe were giving him a sign.

They reached a major intersection, a fork in the road, and Thor lead his men to the left, forking from the road that would have led directly to his hometown. His destiny was bringing him a different way. As they turned away, towards Sulpa, Thor could not help but glance back, over his shoulder, at the old, familiar road. He thought of home, and wondered what his father was doing there now. He wondered if he missed Thor. Probably not. He probably pined for his three other sons; he probably assumed that they were the stars of the Legion. He would be surprised to hear how well Thor had done. Thor was sure he wouldn't even believe it.

Thor drove it from his mind; instead he thought of Gwendolyn. Her touch lingered with him, and as they had parted only hours ago, he still felt as if she were right there with him. He was distracted, found it hard to think of anything else. It hurt to have left her there, and he also felt the absence of Krohn, whom he had not been apart from since he had found him. Thor felt as if he'd left a big part of him back there, in King's Court. And even though Krohn was with Gwendolyn, he couldn't help but fear for her safety. He resolved to finish this mission quickly and return to her soon as he could.

Thor was kicking himself for not mustering the courage to ask her the question. Why was it so hard? He resolved that when he returned, the first thing he would do, whether the time was right or not, would be to ask her, no matter what the circumstances. He just had to force himself to. He was beginning to realize that no time was the perfect time. If she said no, then she said no. But at least he had tried, and had faced his fear.

"What's the name of this place again?" O'Connor called out as they rode.

Thor snapped out of it.

"Kolk said it is named Sulpa," Thor said. "A small village, but in a strategic location, between the valleys."

"Apparently, they were hit pretty hard," Reece added.

"Well I don't see why we need to go and clean up after their mess," Elden said. "We certainly have better things to do. Like training."

"Every town is a link in the chain," Reece answered. "We don't want any weak links. Besides, these are our people. We owe it to them."

"No we don't," Conval said. "We are warriors. Not homebuilders. We only owe it to the kingdom to protect it from threats. And to kill our attackers."

"Part of protecting the kingdom is keeping it strong," Reece answered. "We protect it not only by fending off attackers, but by fortifying our towns for attack."

The boys rode on in silence for a while, and as they did, the landscape began to change. The beautiful green hills gave way to a landscape that turned desolate and dusty. It was like walking through a desert. The contrast between the two terrains was stark. Thorn bushes, ten feet high, rolled in the wind, and stuck to everything. The road faded in the dirt, and it became hard to keep sight of where they were going. Thor didn't like the look of this.

"Is this the only way there?" O'Connor asked.

Thor held out the map Kolk had given him, and stared at it again.

"That's what it says," he answered. "Kolk warned us. He said there'd be a barren stretch. The village is surrounded by desert. Then it turns fertile again."

Thor looked around at the apprehensive faces of his brothers, who were spread out from each other, and he realized that now it was time for him to assume his role as leader, make them feel as if they were being confidently led, and put them at ease.

"Just stick close together and we'll be fine," Thor commanded. "One never knows what might come out at us in these parts."

The others, respecting Thor's command, listened to him immediately and tightened their formation, all of them riding much closer together. They all became more alert, on edge, as an odd, high-pitched wind howled through the open desert. Thor had heard stories about this wasteland. He didn't want his men to be another victim of it.

They rode for hours in silence, and as the second sun grew long in the sky, on the horizon there appeared the first glimpse of fertile land again. Thor exhaled with relief. They had made it without incident.

"Mind if I stop?" Reece asked.

The others turned and looked at him and Reece gestured over to a small cave, nestled in a huge boulder in the empty landscape.

"Got a go," he said, "I can't hold it any longer."

Thor shrugged.

"Do what you have to," he said.

Thor sat there, on his horse, impatient in the heat of this place, as a large thorn bush went rolling past him with a loud, rustling noise. He flinched. He was too on-edge. This place was eerie. All around him his men bore arms, on guard. He was relieved to see that he was not the only one being cautious.

"So what do you think will become of the Ring?" Elden asked Thor. "Do you think Gareth's men will—"

A shriek cut through the air, and Thor immediately dismounted, as did the others, drew his sword, and sprinted for the cave. The shriek came from inside. It was Reece's.

Reece came flying out of the cave, running at full speed, and as he did, Thor spotted a strange animal stuck to his arm. Reece flailed, shrieking, and Thor finally realized what it was: a Forsyth, the largest and deadliest spider in the Ring. Black and furry and covered in red spots, it had twelve legs, and its body span stretched over Reece's entire arm, from his forearm to his shoulder. It clung to him, not letting go, despite Reece's frantic efforts to brush it off.

Thor ran to Reece and grabbed the insect with both hands, yanking its furry arms with all its might, trying to pry it off. But it did no good.

Thor drew his dagger and plunged it into the head of the beast.

The beast screamed, then let out an awful hissing noise, and reached up with one of its tentacles to try to grab Thor's hand. Thor slashed the beast again and again, and his brothers came running up and slashed it, too. Finally, it let go of Reece and turned to the others, opening its small mouth and spitting out a liquid right for them.

Thor dodged it, but the liquid grazed the arm of one of his Legion brothers, and he screamed and clutched it, smoke rising from his sleeve as the acid ate away at it.

The beast dropped to the desert floor and scurried away. A few Legion hurled daggers at it, but it went too fast for them to hit. In moments, it was gone.

Reece clutched his arm, bent over in agony, and Thor draped an arm over his shoulder.

"You okay?" Thor asked.

Reece bit his lip and shook his head. "I don't think so," he said.

Thor looked down and saw the wound—and was aghast. There was a large, circular spot on Thor's arm, and the wound was deep, oozing green puss and blood. O'Connor, beside him, tore a piece of linen from his shirt with his teeth and wrapped it around Reece's arm to staunch the bleeding.

"The venom of a Forsyth is toxic," Elden said grimly, analyzing the wound. "It will spread through his system. It will paralyze him. If we don't get him help soon, he's finished."

Thor looked over at Reece, who looked more pale than he'd ever seen and who started to shake.

Before Thor could react, suddenly there came a noise, a distinct clicking noise, and he looked over with the others and his heart stopped.

From out of the cave there slowly crawled another Forsyth, pausing at the entrance, then slowly creeping towards him.

Thor and his brothers slowly backed up, one step at a time, Thor helping Reece.

"On your horses!" Thor commanded. "Let's get out of here. Now!"

It was the first time Thor had ever commanded his fellow Legion members, and strangely enough, it had come to him naturally. He did not seek a leadership role, but it felt comfortable to him, and he felt that he could help the others, who were paralyzed with fear, by taking charge for them.

As it crept closer, they all mounted their horses—all except one. A Legion boy, a couple of years older than Thor, who Thor did not know, the one whose arm had been sprayed. He defied Thor's orders and stayed put.

"I will not run from an insect!" he yelled.

He reached into his waist, took out a short spear, and hurled it at the beast.

But before he could even release the spear, the Forsyth sprang into motion. It was the fastest thing Thor had ever seen, and in a split second it was in the air, lunging for the boy.

The boy, to his credit, reacted quickly—all of his training in The Hundred must have sank in. He leapt up onto his horse a second before the thing got his leg; it missed him, but it kept flying and instead clung to the leg of his horse.

The horse neighed and pranced and kicked its legs, as the beast wrapped itself around him and would not let go.

After a moment, the horse let out an awful shriek, then stiffened and fell over on its side, the boy still on it.

The boy struggled, but could not dismount in time; he found himself falling with the horse, the horse landing on top of him and crushing his leg. The boy shrieked in agony.

Thor jumped off his horse, dagger in hand, ready to plunge it into the Forsyth, but before he could reach it, an arrow sailed past him, through the air, and landed right into the center of the beast. It let out an awful scream, and acid sprayed everywhere; luckily, the acid was blocked by the horse, and it ate away at the horse's skin instantly.

Thor looked back to see O'Connor holding his bow.

"Nice work," Thor said to him. "Give me a hand!"

The others all rushed over to him, helping to pry the boy, moaning in pain, out from underneath the horse. Conven slung him over his shoulder, and draped him across his horse.

Before they could all remount, suddenly, a noise rose up, and Thor's heart stopped as he looked over to see a dozen more of those things appear at the entrance of the cave. They all paused, then slowly began to inch forward.

Before Thor could issue another command, Elden let out a battle cry and burst into action. He charged forward fearlessly, right for the mouth of the cave. Thor wondered what he was doing—it seemed like suicide—until he saw him lift his huge war hammer high overhead with both hands, and smash it into a boulder perched atop the entrance to the cave.

There came a great rumbling, and boulders rolled down and covered the mouth the cave, crushing several of the Forsyths and blocking the others.

They all looked to Elden with gratitude and pride.

"Nice work," Thor said. "You saved our lives."

Elden shrugged and slid the hammer back into his horse's saddle.

Without waiting another moment, Thor draped Reece, now limp, over the back of his horse, and they all remounted and rode, intent on getting Reece help and on getting as far away from this place as possible.

*

Thor and his contingent rode into Sulpa at a gallop, their leisurely journey having now become a race against time. With each passing second Thor felt increasing panic for Reece, who rode with him on his horse, behind him, clutching onto Thor's shoulders weakly. Thor prayed that it was not too late for his best friend, whose hands were now icy cold to the touch. He shook violently behind him, and Thor knew how toxic the venom must be, spreading through his system. He hoped with all he had that someone in this village had medicine to help him.

As they rode, the desert landscape gave way to a small oasis: they were back on rolling green hills, the sand giving way to fields of grass, and a well-paved road appeared which led them over a gurgling stream, across a small drawbridge, unmanned, and into a small village. It was surrounded by a stone wall, demolished in places by the McCloud raid, and the village, with its several dozen cottages, looked large enough to hold only a few hundred people. Thor could tell from here that most of the buildings had been damaged. The streets were filled with debris and even one or two houses were still smoking, smoldering slowly.

There was no sentry standing guard as they rode through the open gate, which was smashed off its hinges, and headed right into the town square. But this village was beautiful: in stark contrast to the wasteland around it, it had vibrant green grass, gurgling streams, beautiful fruit orchards. Sulpa was an idyllic oasis in the midst of a vast and unforgiving terrain. Thor was not that well-traveled, and he had no idea that places like this existed in the Ring.

As they charged into the town square, a dozen of the town's elders hurried out to greet them, concern in their eyes. These were smart people, and they spotted Reece's condition before Thor even stopped, before he even had to say anything. They fixed grave looks of concern on him, and seemed to immediately recognize what he was suffering from.

"How long ago was he bit?" one elder called out.

"Not ten minutes ago," Thor responded.

"There might still be time. He must to the healer's house, and quickly. Follow us."

The elders turned and ran through the narrow streets, and Thor and the others rode after them. The village was small, and after a few blocks the men came to a stop before a small cottage built of an ancient stone, with an arched door. The elders slammed the knocker as Thor dismounted, carrying Reece in his arms. Reece was completely limp, and Thor could not believe how sick he had become so quickly.

The door opened, and a beautiful young girl, maybe sixteen, stood in the doorway, wearing a flowing white robe, with straight black hair and sparkling blue eyes. Her eyes immediately fell to Reece and flashed with concern; she ran to him without saying a word.

She reached up, lay a palm upon his forehead, scanned his body, and saw the bite festering on his arm.

"Inside!" she said urgently.

She turned and hurried back inside, and Thor raced after her, carrying Reece. Behind him, the other Legion members took positions outside the door, the house too small to fit them all.

"Set him down there!" she ordered, frantic, gesturing to a stack of hay in the corner of the room. Thor hurried and set Reece down, and as soon as he did, the girl crossed the room with a sharp knife.

"Hold his arms!" she commanded, great authority in her voice, an authority that surprised him. "Grab his wrists!" she added, "and hold them firmly! Do you understand? He will fight you. Even in his weakened state. Do NOT let him flail. Do you understand?"

Thor nodded back, nervous, and she wasted no time. She leaned forward, took the knife, and in one quick motion cut deeply into the wound that was already festering, half of it black. She cut in a small area, right at the center, and Reece suddenly shrieked as she did, trying to sit up. He buckled like crazy, and Thor, sweating, did his best to hold him down. It took all of Thor's might. He had never seen his friend like this.

She held a pan beneath his arm, and black liquid began oozing from the wound, filling nearly all of it. Gradually the oozing stopped, and Reece began to calm, breathing hard, moaning in agony.

She threw the pan of black ooze out an open window, set down the knife, hurried over to a stand, took a red ointment, and quickly rubbed it into the wound. It hissed, and Reece screamed once again. Thor did his best to hold him down, though it was not easy.

She wrapped a fresh bandage around Reece's wound several times, then tried to calm him by laying an open palm on his chest, reassuringly, slowly easing him onto his back.

She held a palm to his forehead, pried open both eyelids, and examined his eyes. She let go and his eyes closed. She waited patiently, and after several seconds, his eyes fluttered, then opened. Thor was shocked: he looked exhausted, but alert.

"I feel better," Reece said weakly, his voice hoarse.

"That is the poison leaving you," she explained. "We may have just caught it in time."

Reece licked his lips, chapped and dry.

"Am I seeing things, or are you the most beautiful girl I've ever seen?" he asked, sounding nearly delirious.

The girl blushed and looked away.

"You're seeing things," she replied. "Either that, or making fun."

Reece grew serious.

"I swear I am not, my lady," he said, eyes open, more alert, looking at her with urgency. "I must know your name. I think I love you."

She reached up, took a small vial of liquid, opened Reece's mouth and poured it in.

"My name is Selese," she said. "You don't love me. You love my medicine. Now drink," she said, "and forget all of this."

Reece gulped down the liquid, and a moment later, his eyes closed, unconscious.

Selese looked at Thor.

"Your friend will live, it seems," she said. "But I doubt he'll remember much of this. He was delirious."

But Thor was of another mind. He had never seen Reece so smitten, and he knew he was not one to take love lightly. He felt that, despite his sickness, Reece's feelings for her were genuine.

"I would not be so sure of it," Thor said. "My friend does not speak lightly. I would not be surprised if he has found his love."

CHAPTER TWENTY TWO

Godfrey walked with Akorth and Fulton down the back streets of King's Court, on guard, keeping a loose hand on the dagger on his belt as he went. His eyes shifted, and he was increasingly paranoid in light of the week's events. Godfrey no longer underestimated the tyranny of his brother's reach, and felt he could be assassinated at any moment. He had become closer to Akorth and Fulton than ever, grateful to them for helping save him, and while they were hardly warriors, they were at least two more bodies, two more sets of eyes to stay vigilant.

Godfrey turned the corner and saw the sign for his old tavern, hanging crookedly, swinging in the afternoon, drunks spilling out of it, and he felt a sense of repulsion. A wave of anxiety overwhelmed him. He no longer felt comforted being here; now he just associated the place with his near death. He told himself that he would never walk through its doors again.

But he trudged forward, despite his fears, right through the open door, because he was determined. He was determined to bring Gareth down, whatever the cost, whatever the personal danger. There was too much at stake for him now, too much blood that had been drawn. He couldn't just let this go and disappear quietly in the night. He had to find out who had tried to poison him, not for his own sake, but for the sake of them all. If he could prove the assassination plot, then legally it would be enough for the Council to depose Gareth. All he needed was a witness. One credible witness.

But in this part of town, he knew, credibility was a rare commodity.

Gareth and his friends entered the tavern, and several of his old compatriots stopped and looking his way. Their expressions told him that they were surprised to see him alive; they looked as if they were watching a walking ghost. He did not blame them. He also felt certain that he would die the night before, and that it was a miracle he had survived.

Slowly, the room came back to life, and Godfrey made his way over to the bar, Akorth and Fulton beside him, and they took up their old seats. The barkeep looked at Godfrey warily, then ambled over to them.

"I didn't expect to see you back here so soon," he said in his deep, shaky voice. "In fact, I didn't expect to see you here at all. You seemed pretty dead last I saw you."

"Sorry to disappoint you," Godfrey responded.

The barkeep looked over, rubbed the stubble on his chin, then broke into a large smile, revealing crooked teeth. He reached out and clasped Godfrey's forearm, and Godfrey clasped him back.

"You son of a bitch," the barkeep said. "You really do have nine lives. I'm glad your back."

The barkeep filled mugs for Akorth and Fulton.

"None for me?" Godfrey asked, surprised.

The barkeep shook his head.

"I promised your sister. She's a tough one, and I'm not keen to break it."

Godfrey nodded. He understood. A part of him wanted the drink, but another part of him was glad for the encouragement not to.

"But you didn't come to drink, did you?" the barkeep asked, growing serious, looking back and forth between the three men.

Godfrey shook his head.

"I've come to find the man who killed me."

The barkeep leaned back, looking grave, and he cleared his throat.

"You're not saying I had anything to do with it?" he asked, suddenly defensive.

Godfrey shook his head.

"No. But you see things. You served the drinks. Did you see anyone last night?"

"Anyone who shouldn't have been here?" Akorth added.

The barkeep shook his head vigorously.

"If I had, don't you think I would've stopped him? Do you think I want you poisoned in my place? It upset me worse than you. And it's bad for business. Not many people want to come in and get poisoned, do they? Half my clients haven't returned since you keeled over like a horse."

"We're not accusing you," Fulton chimed in. "Godfrey is simply asking you if you saw anything different. Anything suspicious."

The barkeep leaned back and rubbed his chin.

"It's not so easy to say. The place was packed. I can't remember a stream of faces. They come in and out of here so quick, and half the time, my back is turned. Even if someone snuck up on you, the chances are I would've missed it."

"You're forgetting the boy," came a voice.

Godfrey turned and saw a drunk old man, hunched over, sitting alone at the end of the bar, who looked over at them warily.

"Did you say something?" Godfrey asked.

The man was silent for a while, looked back to the bar, mumbling to himself, and Godfrey thought he would not speak again. Then, finally, he spoke up again, not looking at them.

"There was a boy. A different boy. He came and left, real quick like."

Godfrey recognized the old drunk; he was a regular. He had drank at the same bar with him for years, but had never exchanged words before.

Godfrey and Akorth and Fulton exchanged a curious glance, then all got up and ambled their way over towards the end of the bar. They took up seats on either side of the old man, and he didn't bother to look up.

"Tell us more," Godfrey said.

The old man looked up at him and grimaced.

"Why should I?" he retorted. "Why should I stick my nose in trouble? What good would it do me?"

Godfrey reached down, pulled out a bag of thick gold coins from his waist, and plopped them down on the bar.

"It can do you a lot of good," Godfrey answered.

The old man raised one finger skeptically, reached over, and pried open the sack. He peeked inside at the stash of gold, far more than he had ever seen in his life, and he whistled.

"That's a high price. But it won't do me much good if I don't have my head. How do I know your brother's not going to send his men down here and poison me, too?"

Godfrey reached down and plunked a second sack of gold beside the first one. The old man's eyes widened in real surprise, for the first time.

"That's enough money to go far from here—farther than my brother's reach—and to never have a worry again," Godfrey said. "So now tell me. I won't ask again."

The man cleared his throat, his eyes fixated on the two sacks of gold, then finally, he grabbed them, pulled them close, and turned to Godfrey.

"He was a commoner," the old man said. "An errand runner. You know the type. I seen him before, once or twice, over at the

119

gambling den. You pay this boy, he'll run any kind of errand you want. He was in here that night. He came and went. Never seen him in here before, or since."

Godfrey studied the old man carefully, wondering if he was lying. The old man stared back, holding his gaze, and Godfrey concluded that he was not.

"The gambling den, you say?" Godfrey asked.

The old man nodded back, and Godfrey, wasting no time, turned and hurried from the tavern, Akorth and Fulton following.

In a moment they were out the door, hurrying down the street, twisted down the narrow alleyways as they heading towards the gambling den, just a few blocks away. Godfrey knew it was a den of sin, with cretins of all types. Lately the crowd there had grown even worse, and he stayed clear of it, for fear of getting into yet another fight.

Godfrey and friends pushed open the creaking door to the gambling den, and he was immediately struck by the noise. The small room must have held a hundred people, all busily engaged in gambling, hunched over tables, betting with odd coins, with every sort of currency. Godfrey scanned the crowd for a boy, for anyone under age, but saw no one his age, or younger. They were all older, mostly broken types, lifelong gamblers, all hope lost in their eyes.

Godfrey hurried over to the manager, a short, fat man, with eyes shifting in his head and who would not look him in the eye.

"I'm looking for a boy," Godfrey said, "the errand runner."

"And what's it to you?" the man snapped back at him.

Godfrey reached down, and pushed a sack of gold coins into the man's hand. The man weighed them, still not looking into Godfrey's eyes.

"Feels light," the man said.

Godfrey shoved another sack into the man's hand, and finally he grinned.

"Thanks for the gold. The boy's dead. Found his body washed up last night, in the streets with the rest of the sewage. Someone killed him. Don't know who. Or why. Means nothing to me."

Godfrey exchanged a baffled look with Akorth and Fulton. Someone had killed the boy who was sent to kill him. It was Gareth, no doubt, covering his tracks. Godfrey's heart fell. That meant yet another dead end. Godfrey racked his brain.

"Where is the body?" Godfrey asked, wanting to be sure this man wasn't lying.

"With the rest of the paupers," the man said. "Didn't want the body in front of my place. You can check out back if you like, but you are wasting your time." The man burst out laughing. "He's dead as death."

They all turned and hurried from the place, Godfrey anxious to get away from that man, from that place, and they hurried out the back door, down the road, until they reached the pauper's cemetery.

Godfrey scanned the dozens of mounds of fresh dirt, sticks and markers in the ground in the shapes of all the different gods they prayed to. He looked for the freshest one—but so many of them seemed fresh. Did that many people die in King's Court each day? It was overwhelming.

As Godfrey walked, turning down a row of graves, he spotted a young boy kneeling before one of them. The grave before him was fresher than most. As Godfrey neared, the boy, maybe eight, turned and looked at him, then suddenly jumped to his feet, fear in his eyes, and ran off.

Godfrey looked at the others, puzzled. He had no idea who this boy was or what he was doing here, but he knew one thing—if he was running, he had something to hide.

"Wait!" Godfrey screamed. He broke into a run after the boy, trying to catch up with him as he disappeared around the corner. He had to find him, whatever the cost.

Somehow, he knew this boy held the key to finding his assassin.

CHAPTER TWENTY THREE

Thor sat with his Legion brothers around a roaring bonfire in the center of Sulpa, his muscles weary from a long day of work. They had spent all day helping the villagers rebuild, rolling up their sleeves and getting to work as soon as he had left Selese's home. Reece was not strong enough yet to join them, and he'd spent the day sleeping and recovering in her cottage—and the tenth Legion member was recovering himself, from his crushed leg. That had left Thor, O'Connor, Elden, the twins and a few others, and they'd labored until the second sun grew long to help reinforce whatever simple defenses this village had, rebuilding walls, patching roofs, clearing rubble, putting out fires, reinforcing gates. To Thor it didn't seem like much, but to these villagers, he could see that it meant a great deal. Thor felt a great sense of satisfaction as he saw their grateful expressions, many of them finally able to return comfortably to their homes.

The fire crackled before him, and Thor looked around, and saw all of his brothers looking equally weary. He was thrilled to have Reece back, sitting beside him, looking a little bit weak, but recovering, and in good spirits. His day of recovery had went well, and he seemed back to his old self. It had been a close call.

"But when I woke, she had already gone," Reece repeated to Thor. "Do you think that means she doesn't like me?"

Thor sighed. Reece had been going on about Selese ever since he had left her cottage. Thor had never seen his friend like this; he was obsessed with this girl, and would talk of nothing else.

"I can't say," Thor said. "She certainly didn't seem to dislike you. She seemed more…amused by you."

"Amused?" Reece asked, defensive. "What is that supposed to mean? That doesn't sound positive."

"No, I don't mean it like that," Thor said, trying to back track. "But you have to admit, you were delirious, and you didn't even know her and you told her that you loved her."

Snickers rose up from O'Connor, Elden and the twins, listening in around the fire, and Reece reddened. Thor felt bad. He hadn't meant to embarrass his friend; he was just telling the truth as he saw it.

"Listen, my friend," Thor said, laying a hand on his shoulder. "There is no reason to think that she does not like you. Maybe you just came on a little bit strong and now she's not sure what to make of it. Maybe she didn't think you were being genuine. Maybe you should return to her in the morning, and see how she reacts."

Reece looked down at the dirt, toeing it.

"I think I ruined my chances," he said.

"It's never too late," Thor said.

"Are you kidding?" Elden asked. "We're in the middle of nowhere. What country girl wouldn't want to be taken away from here?"

"Some people like their villages," O'Connor said.

"This place is nice enough," Conven said, "but it is not King's Court. I'm sure she'd want to leave with you."

"You sure you want to take her?" Conven asked. "That is the question. You don't even know her."

"I know her well enough," Reece said. "She saved my life. She is the most beautiful girl I have ever seen."

The other boys exchanged wary glances.

"That was just the drugs," Elden said. "I'll bet if you met her under some other circumstance you wouldn't even look twice at her."

"That's not true," Reece said, reddening, growing angry, determined.

The group fell silent, and Thor could see in Reece's eyes a determination unlike he'd seen before. It surprised him. He thought he had known everything about his friend—but he had never seen this side of him. Then again, they had never really had much of a chance to be around girls, training all the time.

"Maybe she is involved with someone else," Reece said softly him to Thor, glum. "Did she say anything else about me? After I fell asleep?"

Thor couldn't stand it anymore.

"I'm sorry," Thor said, trying to add a sense of finality in his voice to wrap up the conversation. "I wish I'd asked her more. But I left in a rush to help the rebuilding effort. I haven't seen her since. Go to her in the morning. I'm sure she will answer all your questions. How can she not? After all, you are royalty. Do you really think she would turn you down?"

Reece looked at the ground, and shrugged. Thor could see the fear and hesitation in his eyes, and he realized that Reece was nervous. Thor thought back to the first time he had spoken to Gwendolyn, and he understood. He had never seen Reece afraid of anything, but looking at him now, he wondered if Reece would be able to muster the courage to approach her in the morning.

Thor understood, too well. He was hardly one to talk. He hadn't been able to muster the courage to ask Gwendolyn to marry him. In some ways, he was realizing, the courage needed to race into battle was nothing compared to the courage needed to face the rejection of a girl you loved.

More villagers appeared, distributing a fresh round of goko sticks, a red, chewy substance on the end of long sticks, which Thor and the others held over the fire. They hissed as they held them over the flames, burned bright, then burned out quickly. Thor blew on his, and ate. It was sweet and delicious. They had helped these villagers, but these villagers had treated them very well in return. He was still stuffed from the huge meal they had given them earlier.

As the group drifted off into a content silence, Thor lay back on one elbow and looked up at the night sky, at the sparkling red and yellow stars, so far away. His thoughts returned to Gwendolyn. He thought of their last trip, to the House of Scholars, thought of those books. He watched the distant stars and thought again of his mother, of that map, of the Land of the Druids. He wondered if he would ever make it there. He wondered why there had to be a sea between he and his mother, why he had never met her. He wondered again of his destiny.

Thor felt there a mystery at his fingertips, just out of reach of his thoughts. His thoughts swirled, as he tried to get to the bottom of it, thinking of his mother, his father, his upbringing, of the Druids. But it had been a long day, too long, and his mind was overcome with exhaustion; although he tried to fight it, the cool fall breezes were lulling him to sleep, and before he knew it, his eyes closed without him.

*

Thor walked slowly through the streets of his hometown, which sat desolate, doors opened, each home sitting vacant. The wind ripped through it, sending clouds of dust and huge thorn bushes rolling right at Thor. Thor raised his hands to his eyes and pressed on. He did not know what he was doing here, but he felt he needed to be here for some reason, that there was something he needed to see.

He turned down the corner of his old block, and in the distance he saw his house, which approached quickly. The door was ajar, and he walked inside.

Everything was exactly as he had left it. But it was empty now. His father was gone, and Thor sensed that he had left long ago.

Thor walked out the back door, towards the shed where he used to sleep, and as he did, he was surprised to see a woman standing in the doorway. She wore flowing blue robes and held a long, intricate yellow staff. A blue light shined from her face, so intense that he could not make out her features. He sensed that she was someone important his life. Perhaps, even, he dared to hope, his mother.

"Thorgrin, my son," she said, her voice so gentle, so soothing, "I await you. It is time for you to return home. It is time for you to know who you are."

Thor took a step closer to her, so curious to see her face, to know more. Her energy drew him in like a magnet, but the closer he got, the more intense the light became, and he raised his hands and found he could not get any closer.

"Mother?" he asked. "Is that you?"

"Come home, Thorgrin," she said, urgently. "Come home now."

She stepped forward and held his shoulders, and Thor felt an intense energy pouring through him, felt his own body infusing with light. He still could not see her face, and he reached up and shielded his eyes from the light, which felt as if it might burn right through him.

Thor sat up, breathing hard, looking all around him. He was surprised to realize he had been dreaming. It had felt so real.

Thor lay with the other Legion members on the ground before the dying fire, where he had fallen asleep. The others still slept. He turned to see dawn breaking over the horizon, the first sun flooding the sky with yellow and purple.

He stood and wiped the sweat from his brow as he pondered his dream. It had been so vivid; his heart was still pounding. He had really felt as if he had just encountered his mother. And her words to him kept repeating in his mind. They felt like a message. More than a message—they felt like a command.

Come home.

Thor felt an urgency, felt there was some great message awaiting him in his hometown. Some great secret waiting to be unlocked. The secret of who he was. Of who his mother was.

He walked over to the gurgling creak, knelt down and splashed cold water on his face, trying to shake it. But he could not. It clung to him, this persistent feeling that he needed to go there. Was he imagining it? Was it wishful thinking? Was it just a fanciful dream? It was so hard to know what was a dream, and what was a message. When did his own unconscious get in the way of his seeing a message clearly?

"Sometimes dreams are more than dreams," came a voice.

Thor knew that voice, and it sent a chill up his spine.

He turned slowly to see Argon standing there, holding his staff, dressed in his white robes, looking out at the breaking dawn. He did not even look Thor's way.

Thor was so relieved to see him; it was like seeing an old friend.

"Argon," Thor said. "Please, tell me. Was it all true? The dream? Does my mother wait for me?"

"Yes and no," he responded.

Thor wondered.

"Must I return to my hometown?" he pressed.

"You know the answer."

Thor did. He felt it. He had to go.

"But is she awaiting me there now? How did she get there? What is she doing there?"

"Some things you must find out on your own," Argon said. "It is up to you to make the journey."

Suddenly, Argon vanished. Thor turned every which way, looking for him, but he was gone.

Thor rubbed his face several times, wondering if he'd imagined the whole thing.

But he was certain that he had not. First there was the dream. Then, Argon. Thor felt it was a sign, one he could no longer ignore. He felt the same way he did on that fateful day when he'd left his village and first embarked for King's Court. The universe was telling him something. He had to go back to his hometown. Something was awaiting him there. Some secret he needed to unlock. Was that why fate had sent Thor here, to this remote village, which shared the same road as that to his hometown? He wondered. Had the universe been giving him signs all along?

Thor stood upright, ran his wet hands through his hair, and decided. He must go. He needed answers. His hometown was hardly a day's ride from here, and he could make it there and back before the sunset. His Legion brothers would be okay without him for the day. It was risky, because he would be leaving his post, and if the Legion commanders found out, he could be punished. But there wasn't much to do here today, anyway, aside from some more light rebuilding. It wasn't like they were at war, and Thor felt confident his friends would be safe.

Thor turned and headed for his horse, preparing to take off before the sun rose higher.

Suddenly, there came a voice.

"Where are you going?"

Thor turned and saw Reece, standing there, looking much more recovered, fully dressed. Thor stopped and turned to him.

"Reece," he said. "You look well. I'm glad to see you're feeling better."

"I am," he said, his energy returned. "Much. In fact, I'm going to go and pay a visit to the girl who helped me now."

Thor smiled.

"Not wasting any time, are you?" Thor remarked, looking at the dawn. "Good for you."

Thor admired his courage. He knew what it took.

Reece smiled sheepishly back.

"And you?" he asked, looking at Thor's horse. "You look as if you're going somewhere."

Thor cleared his throat, wondering how much to say. He could trust Reece more than anyone, and he decided to tell him.

"I had a dream," Thor responded. "It felt like a sign. I need to visit my hometown. I will return before the second sun sets. Can you cover for me?"

Reece nodded solemnly.

"Do what the fates tell you to do," he said.

Reece stepped forward and clasped Thor's forearm firmly.

"You saved my life yesterday. I shall never forget."

As they clasped arms, Thor felt more than ever that Reece was his true brother, closer to him than anyone he'd ever known. And as he thought of returning home, to the place where he was raised with three brothers who hated him, Thor felt more grateful for that than Reece would ever know.

CHAPTER TWENTY FOUR

Luanda stood chained to a stone wall in the McCloud dungeon, each of her wrists and ankles bound with iron shackles. Her body shook from exhaustion, fear and hunger. She wondered how she, a royal princess, the firstborn of the MacGil children, had found herself in this position, had sunk to such a low. It was hard to conceive. Just weeks ago she had imagined her life to come with such joy. She had imagined herself married off to a McCloud prince, imagined becoming queen of the McCloud kingdom. And now, here she stood, a prisoner in her own court, treated like a common criminal—and even worse.

The elder McCloud was an evil creature, the lowest of mankind. She had never encountered a more crude, more vile, more vicious man in her life. He terrorized everyone and everything around him, and even though she'd taken a chance and failed and ended up where she was, she still did not regret her attempt to end his life in that house, back in her home city, when she had attempted to save that poor girl from attack. It had been a mistake to think she could kill him, as Bronson had warned. And in retrospect, it had been stupid. Yet still, she did not regret it.

Luanda closed her eyes and there flashed through her mind the horrific image of Bronson's being attacked by his own father, of watching him lose his hand in his attempt to save her life. She felt overwhelmed with waves of guilt. She loved Bronson more than ever, admired him for finally taking a stand against his father, and appreciated his sacrifice more than he would ever know. She also felt a fresh repulsion for his father, stronger than ever.

She had to get herself out of this dungeon, and had to rescue Bronson, who was set to be executed, before he died at his own father's hand. And she had to get them out of this city, out of McCloud territory, somehow back over the Highlands, back to the safety of the MacGil side. She had to make it back to her father's court, and hope that they would take her back in.

But right now, all of that seemed like a far cry. Bronson might already be dead for all she knew, and as she stood there, shackled, there was no hope in sight for evading her jailers. In fact, she had more pressing things on her mind: her jailers, two cretins, had taken turns tormenting her throughout the night. One would grab her hair, the other would pull on her shirt; one would threaten her with a blade, another with a hot iron. They hadn't raped or tortured her yet. But their threats had been ongoing for hours, and they were escalating. She felt as if they were building up to something, and if all their threats were true, she knew she would be raped and tortured and left for dead before the sun rose. They were two disgusting little men, unshaven with greasy hair, wearing the uniform of the McClouds, and she felt they were good to their word. Her hours were numbered. She had to find a way out of here, and fast. It was time to make a move. She just didn't know what.

"I say we cut her slowly," one said to the other, an evil grin on his face, revealing rotten teeth.

"I say we burn her first," said the other.

They both laughed, amused at their own jokes, and Luanda tried to think fast, faster than she ever had in her life. Being a woman, no one had ever credited her for being smart—but she was smart, at least as smart as her father, as smart as any of the other MacGil children. Throughout her life, she had managed to find her way out of almost anything.

She summoned her inner strength, all the cunning she'd ever had—the cunning of generations of MacGil kings, whose blood ran through her. She closed her eyes and thought, willed for a solution to come to her.

And then, one did.

It was far-fetched, and probably wouldn't work, but she had to try.

"I will go along with whatever you say!" she suddenly cried out, her voice hoarse.

"We know that you will!" one of them shouted back. "You have no choice!"

They both broke into hysterical laughter.

"That is not what I mean," she said, her heart pounding. "If you unchain me," she added, "I will show you pleasures unlike any you've ever had in your life."

The two jailers looked at each other, a smile on their faces, debating. She wondered if they were buying it.

"What pleasures, exactly?" asked one, coming close, so close she could smell his rotten breath as he held a blade up to her throat.

"Pleasures beyond what any woman has ever showed you," she said, trying her best to sound convincing.

"That doesn't impress me," said the other dismissively, "I've spent my life in whorehouses. Do you think there's something you can show me that some common whore cannot?"

They both yelled out in laughter again, and the other took his metal poker and dipped it into the hot fire, until the tip of it glowed orange.

"Besides," he said, turning to her. "I prefer to torture you anyway. I get more pleasure from that. The king said you are ours to do with as we wish. And we most certainly shall!"

Gwen's eyes opened wide in terror as the hot poker came close to her face, so hot it made her sweat even from a foot away. She saw the malicious smile on the man's face, and knew that in just a moment, her face would be scarred forever.

"Wait!" she screamed out. "I don't just offer you pleasure! But riches! I am the daughter of a king, lest you forget! I will give you more money than you can ever imagine! Certainly more money than McCloud ever will!"

Her jailers stopped, intrigued for the first time.

"And how much is that exactly?" he asked.

"More than you can carry. Wheelbarrows fill. An entire house full, if you like."

"And how will you manage that?" the other one asked, stepping forward.

"I will send word to my father. He will ship me whatever I like. Did you not see our wedding? The jewels that I wore?"

The two attackers looked at each other, unsure.

"Your father is dead," said one.

"But his court lives on," she said, thinking quick. "My mother still lives. So do my siblings. They will send you any riches you want. if I pen a letter."

One of them stepped close, holding the blade tighter to her throat.

"Why don't we just kill you," he said slowly, "pen the letter in your name, and take the riches anyway?"

"Because you don't know my penmanship," she said, thinking faster than ever. "They would never believe it if it were not in my hand! Then you would have nothing! Surely it is worth more to you to have all that gold than to have me dead!"

They looked at each other, debating.

"What's to stop us from forcing you to pen the letter, then killing you? That way we get the gold, and we get to torture and kill you!"

She looked at them, terrified. She thought quick, and a solution came to her.

"I will do whatever you wish," she said. "I will put myself at your mercy. But I can't write with my hands shackled. Unshackle me, and bring me a quill and parchment, and you can choose what to do with me."

The two men looked at each other, then finally one nodded to the other, licking his lips.

"You are more stupid than I thought," said one, coming up a few feet behind her and unlocking each of her shackles with a key where they met the stone wall.

"Because now we will take your letter, and then I will reshackle you and rape and torture you all night!"

The two erupted into uproarious laughter.

As soon as the man finished unlocking her second shackle, Luanda burst into action. Each shackle was affixed to the wall by a three foot iron chain, with one shackle on her wrist and the other on the wall. As her jailer unlocked the one on the wall, leaving her wrist still shackled and connected to the chain, she knew she only had one chance at this.

She swung around with her wrist, still bolted to the shackle, swung the heavy iron chain overhead, and brought it down with all her might, aiming for the man's face as he stepped carelessly back in front of her.

They had underestimated her. They did not expect that she still had the reservoir of strength that she did, that she had the means to use it, that she had the knowledge and cunning of a king's daughter, one who had been trained her entire life by the King's best warriors.

And that was their last mistake.

Luanda summoned every skill she had, every ounce of bravery, as she swung the chain around and down for her jailer's face. She took aim, and her aim was true.

The chain came flying down, with the heavy iron shackle at the end of it, right for her jailer's nose. It was a perfect hit, and she struck him hard, smashing it across the bridge of his nose and sending him stumbling back several feet, landing on the ground, screaming in agony. He dropped the hot iron poker and reached up to hold his face.

131

Without hesitating, Luanda swung around with her other hand, and took aim for the other jailer's throat, as he made the mistake of turning his back on her and looking down at his friend. The chain wrapped itself cleanly around his throat, and she immediately reached up with her other hand, grabbed the other end, and squeezed.

The man bucked wildly, and she grabbed hold with everything she had as he resisted, squeezing harder and harder. He did everything he could to break free, but she strangled him with all her might. He reached up and tried again and again to release the chain from his throat—but her grip was too strong. She was holding on as if her life depended on it. And it did.

The other man was slowly rousing on the ground, slowly getting to his hands and knees, and she hoped and prayed she would have time to finish choking this man to death before the other approached her.

She squeezed harder and harder as the man cried out, gurgling, struggling, bucking like a wild animal. At one point he even reached back and elbowed her in the gut.

It hurt, but she didn't let go, and she didn't stop. Too much was at stake.

The other man finally gained his feet, reached up and grabbed the hot iron poker, and charged her. She didn't have enough time. The other man was still alive, writhing, in her hands. He just would not die.

She could not let go of him to defend herself. She racked her brain for a strategy.

As the other man charged her, hot poker out in front of him, she waited until the last moment, and then dodged him, squirming out of the way, and instead pulled the man she was choking out in front of her, using him as a body shield.

It worked. The man pierced his cohort instead of her, driving the hot poker all the way into his friend's heart as he shrieked while she choked him. Finally, his body went limp in her hands, the poker lodged in his chest.

The other one stood there, dumbfounded, staring at his friend's corpse.

Luanda did not wait. She dropped the corpse and in the same motion, reached around, swung her hand high and whacked her other attacker hard across the face with the iron shackle a second time. Her aim, again, was true, and she broke his nose a second time, knocking him flat on his back, moaning in agony.

She took no chances. She reached over, pulled the hot poker from the chest of the dead man, then reached up high, leaned over, and drove it through the chest of the other man.

He sat up, shrieking, blood gurgling from his mouth, staring wide-eyed at the ceiling, as if unbelieving.

Then, a moment later, he stiffened and collapsed, dead.

Gwen dropped to her knees, searched the man's belt, found the key, and unlocked the shackles at her feet, then at her wrists. She rubbed them, more sore than they had ever been, deep bruises left where she had been clasped.

She looked down at her two jailers, dead, a bloody mess. Filled with rage, she spit on them both.

She reached down and grabbed one of their daggers. Where she was about to go, she would need it. For she could not leave this place without her husband. And she would free him, even if it cost her her life.

CHAPTER TWENTY FIVE

Thor rode alone across the desert wasteland, galloping west as the first sun began to rise, and his heart welled with a great sense of expectation. He had been riding for hours, feeling a sense of guilt over leaving his brothers behind, but feeling more than ever that he was on a momentous trip, riding into his destiny. After his dream, and his encounter with Argon, he felt some great secret awaiting him in his hometown, and as he rode, he felt a tingling through his body, felt on the precipice of a great discovery.

Thor also felt a sense of dread. He hadn't seen his father since he had stormed out that fateful day, after their argument, and had never returned. He wondered what his father thought of him now. Would his father be remorseful? Would he regret that he had treated Thor so harshly? Would he regret that he had favored his brothers so much? Did he miss having Thor around? Would he apologize and welcome Thor back? Would he want him to stay? Would he be proud of Thor when he saw the warrior he had become, what he had achieved, against all odds?

Or would he be the same old hateful, begrudging father? The one who had always been in competition with him, who had always favored his brothers? Who had refused to recognize Thor's individuality, his positive traits, his unique talents? The one who had, at every turn, tried his best to keep Thor down? That was the father he had always known. That was the father he had grown to hate.

Thor had tried so many times to love him, to get close to him— but his father just kept pushing him away, finding a way to put barriers between them. Finally, Thor had given up.

As Thor thought it through, he concluded that his leaving probably had not changed his father much, if at all. Most likely, he was the same begrudging, stubborn, spiteful person. Most likely, he would not be happy to see Thor again. He would probably compare him, as he always had, to his three brothers, only seeing their greater height and larger size as proof that they were superior to him. His father was who he was, and nothing could change that. Not even Thor's love.

His father was a victim of his own personality. But that was no excuse: his father should have been strong enough to overcome his own personality at least enough to be kind to Thor. There came a point, Thor realized, when he could only forgive his father so much for his personality. After a certain point, his father had to take some personal responsibility.

Thor kicked his horse ever harder, as they sprung from the wasteland into the well-paved roads and grassy fields, heading closer to the home he once knew. It was weird to be coming back here, on this familiar road, heading home—this time, on a horse of his own, a fine animal, finer than any warrior, any full grown man, in his hometown owned. And to be bearing his own, superior weaponry, and wearing his own armor—and most of all, the emblem of the Legion. The small black pin of the falcon on his chest, gleaming in the sun, which Thor was more proud of than anything. A part of him felt as if he were returning a conquering hero; he felt as if he had left as a boy, and was returning as a man. An equal to his father. Although, of course, his father would never recognize that.

Thor turned onto the familiar roads, marveling that he was back here. On the day he'd left, he never imagined returning, for any reason. And when he had lived here, he had never imagined getting out. The whole experience of being here was surreal.

Thor turned onto the wide open road that led to his small village, remembering it like the back of his hand. As he surveyed the town before him, he was amazed: nothing had changed. There were the old women, still hunched over their cauldrons, boiling their dinner. There were the dogs, running about, the chickens, the sheep…. It was as if no one had even changed position. He recognized the faces, the same old women, the same old men, the same boys, everyone going about their same daily routine. It was like nothing had changed in the world for these people in all these months he had been gone. It was hard for him to fathom. Because he had changed so much, so fast.

Thor had been to so many places since he had left, had undergone so many new experiences, that it had changed his perspective: while this place had once seemed so big and important, it now felt small and quaint to him. Even insignificant. He could not believe that it had ever seemed important to him at all. What had once felt familiar, comforting, now felt small, confining. Thor appreciated now how big the world was out there, and he could finally see this town for what it was: just another insignificant farming town on the periphery of King's Court. Riding through here he felt claustrophobic, felt a desire to leave already; he could hardly even imagine remaining here for an afternoon.

Thor also felt a sense of anger being here—even a desire for vengeance. In this town he had always been known as the youngest, the weakest, the least ambitious, of his father's children; he had been known as the one least loved and least wanted, the one destined to stay at home, to tend the sheep. He had never really been taken seriously by anyone here. And no one had ever expected him to leave. Being here had made him feel small, less than himself. It was the very opposite of being in King's Court, of the way the Legion made him feel. Now, looking at it with fresh eyes, he found himself resenting this place deeply.

He slowed his horse as he headed down the main street, to all the wondering stares of the villagers. He could feel the glances, but he did not stop to talk to anyone, and did not meet anyone's eye. Instead he rode proudly down the center, then turned down the street for his house, the one he knew by heart. The one that lingered in his dreams. And his nightmares.

Thor found himself outside his old door, and he jumped down, his spurs jingling, tied his horse, and headed for it, weapons rattling on his hip. Thor noticed that the door to his house was ajar, and it was eerie to see. It brought his dream back with full force. He felt a tremendous heat rise through his body, and it told him that something momentous was about to happen.

Thor reached for the iron knocker, but as he did he heard a clanging coming from the back of the house, and he recognized the sound: it was his father, banging away at his forge, probably fixing one of the horse's shoes, as he often did. The sound fell regularly, and it was definitely his father's handiwork.

Thor turned and walked around the side of the house, steeling himself to set his eyes upon his father again. His heart was pounding. He felt more nervous than he had when riding into battle. A part of him couldn't wait to see him, couldn't wait to see if he was proud of him, couldn't help but hope; but another part of him dreaded it, and feared the worst.

Thor turned the corner and there he was: his father. He was hunched over his forge, wearing the same clothes he had seen on him when he'd left, hammering away at a horseshoe as if it were the most important thing in the world. Thor stood there, feeling cold with anxiety, looking at his father, remembering their last encounter. His heart beat faster as he wondered what his father's reaction would be upon seeing him.

Thor stood there, waiting patiently, not wanting to interrupt him—and a part of him not really sure what he was doing here after all. Had it been a mistake to come here? Had he been a fool to heed his dream?

Finally, his father took a break. He set down his anvil, leaned forward, and wiped the sweat dripping from his brow with the back of his hand. Then he turned—and as he did, he froze. He flinched upon seeing Thor, his eyes opened wide in shock.

There was a moment when Thor was filled with hope, with expectation. Would everything be different this time? A part of him hoped that it would. Maybe they could start again.

But as he watched, his father's face darkened, settling into a deep frown.

That frown told Thor all he needed to know. His father was not repentant. His father was not forgiving. His father did not want to start again. He was the same old dad.

"And look who has come crawling back home," his father seethed, looking Thor up and down as if he were an insect. "Dressed in all your fancy armor, are you? Did you think that would impress me?"

Thor felt himself shaking inside. He had forgotten how mean, how cutting, his father could be, and he had not wanted it to go down like this.

"Well, it does *not* impress me," his father continued. "Not in the least. The day you left here you were dead to me. How dare you come back?"

Thor felt his breath taken away by the harshness of his father's words. It made him realize, in comparison, how kind the new father figures in his life had been—MacGil, Kendrick, Erec. None of them were related to him, yet they had all been much kinder to Thor. It made him finally realize what a cruel, small man his father was— especially compared to other fathers—and how unlucky he'd been to be his son. It was odd to Thor, because for most of his life he had idolized his father, had thought he was the biggest and most important man in the world. But now that he had gotten out of this place, now that he had met the others, he realized that it had all just been an illusion.

He was beginning to feel a new feeling: that his father was nothing to him now. He was beginning to feel like a distant acquaintance who it displeased him to run into again.

"I have not returned to you, father," Thor said coolly and calmly, shaking inside but respectful, as he had always been. "I haven't come back here to stay."

"Then for what?" snapped his father. "Did you leave something behind? Or have you come to deliver some news of your brothers? It had better not be bad. They were finer men than you will ever be."

Thor tried to remain calm, tried to stay brave. He felt flustered now around his father, as he had always felt, and he could not think as clearly as he had before. He had always had a hard time standing up to him, had a hard time expressing himself in the heat of the moment. But this time he resolved for things to be different.

"No, I've not come to deliver news of your beloved other sons," Thor said. It felt good to speak the words, and he heard in his own voice a new strength, one he had never felt before when speaking to his father. It was the strength of a warrior. The strength of someone who had become independent, his own man.

His father must have sensed it, because he got to his feet, agitated, turned his back on Thor and began fiddling with his tools as if Thor didn't exist.

"What then?" he snapped, not looking Thor's way. "Because if you're coming to ask my forgiveness, you won't get it. The day you left, you lost a father. Unforgivable. I heard you barged your way into the Legion. Do you think that makes you a man? You stole your position. You got lucky. You didn't deserve it. You might fancy yourself some sort of warrior. But you're nothing. Do understand me?" he asked, turning red-faced, facing Thor in a rage.

Thor stood his place, beginning to well up with rage himself. He had seen this going so differently in his head. He had come here with plans to ask his father certain questions—but now, in the moment, those questions all fled from him. Instead, another question popped into his head.

"Why do you hate me?" Thor asked calmly, surprising himself that he had the courage to ask the question.

His father stopped and looked at him, stumped for the first time since he had known him. He narrowed his eyes at Thor.

"What kind of a question is that?" he asked. "Whoever said I hate you? Is that what they teach you in the Legion? I don't hate you. Like I said, you are nothing to me now."

"But you don't love me," Thor insisted.

"And why should I?" he retorted. "What have you ever done to deserve my love?"

"I'm your son," Thor responded. "Isn't that enough?"

His father looked down at him, long and intense, then finally turned away. Before he did, Thor detected a different expression, one he had never seen before. It was one of confusion.

"Sons don't deserve love just by being sons," his father said. "They must earn it. Everything must be earned in this world."

"Do they?" Thor retorted, not letting it go this time. In the past he had always given in to his father's arguments, his father's abrupt way of ending a conversation, of getting in the last word and refusing to hear anymore. But not this time. "And what exactly must a son have to do to earn his father's love?"

His father reddened, on the verge of exploding, clearly outwitted and fed up. He turned and charged towards Thor, reaching out to grab him by the shoulders with his strong, callused hands, as he had so many times in Thor's life.

"What is it that you are doing here?" he screamed in Thor's face. "What is it that you want from me?"

Thor could feel his father's anger coursing from his hands and into his shoulders.

But Thor's shoulders were bigger and wider now than when he had left, and his hands and forearms were more powerful, too, twice as strong as they had been. His father always thought he could end an argument by grabbing Thor's shoulders, by shaking him, by infecting him with his anger—but not anymore. As soon as his father's hands dug into his shoulders, Thor reached up, lifted his hands between them and knocked his father's hands away; then, in the same motion, he shoved his father with the heel of his hands, right in his chest, hard enough to send his father stumbling back a good five feet, and sending him so off-balance that he nearly fell.

His father looked back to Thor, shocked, as if wondering who he was. He looked as if a snake had bit him. His face remained red with rage, but this time, he stayed his ground and kept a healthy distance and dared not approach Thor—for the first time in Thor's life.

"Don't you ever lay a hand on me again," Thor said calmly and strongly. "It is not a warning."

Thor was being genuine. Something inside him would not tolerate this treatment anymore; something inside him warned him that if his father ever laid a hand on him again, he wouldn't be able to control his reaction.

Something unspoken passed between them, and his father seemed to understand. He stood there and lowered his shoulders just a bit, enough for Thor to realize that he wouldn't attempt it again.

"Have you come here to harass me then?" his father asked, sounding broken, sounding old, in that moment.

"No," Thor said, finally remembering. "I've come here for answers. Answers that only you can give me."

His father stared back, and Thor took a deep breath.

"Who was my mother?" Thor asked. "My *real* mother?"

"Your mother?" his father echoed, caught off guard. "And why would you want to know that?"

"Why *wouldn't* I want to know?" Thor asked.

His father looked down to the ground, and his expression softened.

"Your mother died in childbirth with you. I told you that already."

But he would not meet Thor's eyes when he said it, and Thor sensed he was not being truthful. Thor was more sensitive now, he could feel things more deeply, and he could feel that his father was lying.

"I know what you told me," Thor said, strong. "Now I want the truth."

His father looked up at him, and Thor could see his expression change once again.

"Who have you spoken to?" his father asked. "What have they told you? Who has gotten to you?"

"I want the truth," Thor demanded. "Once and for all. No more lies. Who was my mother? And why did you hide it from me?"

Thor's father stared at him, long and hard, and finally, after several moments of thick silence, he gave in. His eyes drooped, and he looked like an old man.

"I guess there is no point in keeping it from you anymore," he answered. "Your mother did not die in childbirth. It was a story I made up, to keep you from asking questions. Your mother is alive. She lives far from here."

Thor felt energized. He knew it to be true, but hearing it from his own father made it real.

"In the land of the Druids?" Thor pressed.

His father's eyes opened wide in surprise.

"Who told you?" he asked.

"She is a Druid, isn't she?" Thor asked. "Which means I am half-Druid? I'm not entirely human?"

"Yes," his father admitted. "It was not information I wanted spreading around this village."

"And is that why you were always ashamed of me?" Thor asked. "Because my mother was of another race?"

His father looked away, frustrated.

"Tell me, then," Thor pressed, "how did you know her? Why did you divorce her? Why was I not raised by her? Why was I raised by you?"

His father shook his head, again and again.

"You don't understand," he said. "It's more complicated than that."

"Tell me!" Thor demanded, yelling, fists bunched in rage, using a fiercer voice with his father than he ever had in his life.

For the first time in his life, he saw his father afraid.

His father looked back, and finally, slowly, said:

"You are not mine."

Thor looked back, trembling with rage, trying to understand his words.

"I am not your father," he added. "I never was. I just raised you as my own."

Thor's heart pounded in his chest as the words sunk in, the words of this man whom he had once thought to be his father. His felt his world shaking all around him. And suddenly, it all made sense. For the first time in his life, it all made sense.

This man was not his father.

"Then who is?" Thor asked.

"I honestly don't know," he said. "I never met him. I only met your mother once. Briefly. She left you, as a baby, put you in my arms. I had been with the flock, at the top of the mountain. And she had appeared, holding you. She had said that I was to raise you. That you had a great destiny, and that I was destined to be your caretaker. She was the most beautiful and powerful woman I had ever laid eyes upon. She was not of this world. I went weak at the sight of her. I would have done anything she'd asked for. I took you in my arms. And then she disappeared.

"I was left holding you, alone on the mountaintop, and as soon as she'd left, I'd wondered why I had taken you. When she had gone, my senses cleared. But I was stuck with you."

It hurt Thor to hear these words, but at the same time, for once in his life, it all rang true.

But this still didn't explain who his real father was. Or why this man had been chosen to raise him.

"Before she left, she gave me one command. She told me that on the day you found out about her, I was to give you something."

He turned and strutted across the small yard, to a shed, and Thor followed him inside.

He knelt down on its wood floor, used his big beefy palm to swipe it of dust, and revealed a hidden compartment. He blew on it, revealing a latch, then turned it and hoisted it with all his might. A foot thick, he slowly raised it, and ancient air came out, along with a small cloud of dust. It looked as if it hadn't been opened in years.

He reached in up to his elbow, fished around, then grabbed something and pulled it out. Thor knelt there, opposite him, and he held a small leather sack in his palm, covered in dust. He blew on it, and handed it to Thor.

Thor gently opened and reached into the sack. He felt a piece of parchment, rolled up, and took it out and unrolled it.

He could not believe it. It was his mother's handwriting. He felt a thrill as he read it:

My dearest Thorgrin:

On the day that you read this, you will already be a man. I am so sorry that I left you. But it was for a good reason. Fate has its own way of unfolding, and on the day that we meet, you will understand.

Inside this sack are two pieces of jewelry—both of which you will need to save your life. The first is a ring, which you must give to the one you love. The second is a necklace, which you must wear. It will lead you to your father. And to me.

I love you with everything that I am, and I weep every day I do not see you.

Your mother.

142

Hands trembling, Thor reached into the sack and first pulled out a ring. His breath was taken away: it was a large diamond ring, flawless, with rubies and sapphires all around the band. It was the most spectacular piece of jewelry he had ever seen. He then reached in and pulled out the necklace. The chain was bejeweled with diamonds and sapphires and rubies, and from it hung the emblem of a falcon, carved in black amethyst.

Thor reached back and put on the necklace, and he could feel its power throbbing immediately through his chest. He felt comforted by it. Protected. He felt, for the first time, as if he was close to his mother.

Thor tucked the scroll and the diamond ring safely inside his shirt, and as he put it away, his thought turned to only one person.

Gwendolyn.

Give it to the one you love.

"That is all I have for you," he said, standing.

Thor stood, too.

"So you see," he said, "you have no more business here. You have received what you've come to find."

Thor looked back up at this pathetic man, who had once loomed so large for him. He felt a deep sadness.

"Before I leave, tell me one thing," Thor said. "Did you ever have any love for me? Any at all?"

Thor needed to know. For his own sake. For some reason, it was important to him.

Slowly, sadly, the man shook his head.

"I wish I could say that I did," he said solemnly. "But my life was my three boys. They are who mattered to me. You were always a burden to me. To this entire family. If you want the truth, there it is."

Slowly, sadly, Thor nodded, realizing it was the truth, and grateful, at least for that. If this man could not give him anything else in life, at least he could give him that.

"Do not worry," Thor said, preparing to leave. "I shall never burden you—ever again."

Thor turned and walked out the shed, across the man's yard, back to his horse.

As he mounted it and began to ride away, out of this village for the last time in his life, he could have sworn he heard something behind him, could have sworn he heard the man call out. He could have sworn he heard the man call his name, longingly, apologetically, one last time.

But as the noise of the horses' hooves rose up, Thor could not be entirely sure.

CHAPTER TWENTY SIX

Reece's heart was pounding as he made his way across the small village of Sulpa, on his way to see Selese. He wiped his sweating palms on his pants yet again and realized he hadn't been this nervous in as long as he could remember. He had procrastinated from seeing her for the better part of the morning, joining his brothers as they rebuilt the town gate. As the first sun had grown high in the sky, he had continued to lose himself in the chain line, handing off large blocks of stone, passing them down the line, then helping his brothers mortar them in the wall. By the time the second sun had risen the wall had grown nearly four feet high, thanks to all of their labor, and when they all finally took a break, he realized the time had come. He could put it off no longer. He had been distracted the entire time with thoughts of her, and he had to confront his fear.

Reece finally broke off from the group and made his way through the dusty streets of the village, his palms sweated as he neared her cottage. She had done her job masterfully—the wound in his shoulder barely hurt anymore, and he felt as if he had never been infected. Yet he needed an excuse to approach her, and figured maybe somehow that could be it. After all, he could say that he was there for a checkup. And then if it did not go well between them, he would have an excuse to leave.

Reece breathed deep, doubling his pace, and strengthened his resolved. He knew he should have nothing to fear. After all, he was a prince, son to a King, and she was a mere commoner in a remote village on the outskirts of the Ring. She should be thrilled by his advances. But even in his delirium, he had sensed something in her eyes. She was willful. Noble. Proud. Independent. So a part of him wondered how she would react.

Reece stopped before her door, and hesitated. He breathed deep, and realized he was sweating, and wiped his palms again. His heart pounded as he stood there, and a part of him did not want to go through with this. Yet he knew that if he did not, he would think of nothing else.

Reece steeled himself, reached up, and slammed the knocker. Several passersby turned and looked at him, and he felt self-conscious, especially as the iron knocker echoed way too loudly.

He stood there, shifting, not knowing what to do with himself, as he waited and waited. Just as he decided she wasn't home, just as he was about to turn around and leave, suddenly, the door opened.

Reece's throat went dry. She stood there, proud, confident, staring back at him, her blue eyes aglow in the rays of the second sun. It took his breath away. She was even more beautiful than he had remembered. Her black hair dropped down on either side of her face, framing it, her cheeks were high, her chin proud, and she had the bearing of someone from a royal court. He could not understand what a girl like her was doing here, in this humble village. She seemed too big for this place.

Reece realized he was staring, and he cleared his throat and shifted, as she looked back, waiting. She was expressionless, maybe slightly amused. She was not making this easy on him.

"I…um…I," Reece began, stopping and starting, looking down, then up, "I have come to check on you."

She burst out laughing.

"To check on *me*?" she asked quizzically.

Reece reddened.

"I meant…um…to check on me."

She laughed harder.

"What!?" she asked. "You have come here to check on yourself?"

"I meant…um…," he said, reddening, "for you to check on me. I mean—on my wound."

She looked at him, her eyes aglow with laughter, and smiled from ear to ear. He felt like an idiot. He had already messed things up.

"Have you?" she asked skeptically, clearly not buying it. "And why would you do that? I told you yesterday that your wound was healed."

Reece reddened even further, toeing the dirt, looking down, not sure what to say. His entire life, being at the center of King's Court, he had encountered thousands of people, and had felt comfortable speaking to anyone. Girls had always sought him out, and he had always had to deter their advances—and he had never felt nervous before. He was not used to pursuing girls. And this one was different. There was something about her that kept him off-balance.

"I um…I…guess…well, it was hurting a bit," he said, not knowing what else to say.

She smiled, clearly not buying it.

"A bit?" she asked. "Well, if your wound was infected, it would hurt a lot. And it's healing, so a little bit of pain is normal. Aren't you a big strong warrior of the Legion?" she asked with a laugh.

Reece was flustered, not imagining it would go this way.

He turned to go, embarrassed, when suddenly she stepped out and laid two hands on his arm. She held up his arm and examined it with a professional eye, studying the wound. She ran a hand along it, then rolled back his sleeve.

Despite everything, the feel of her hand on his arm electrified him. It made it hard for him to think clearly.

"Your wound is just fine," she said. "I am proud of my handiwork, in fact."

"I came here to thank you," Reece said softly. "For saving my life."

"I thought you came because your wound hurt?" she asked, smiling, her eyes twinkling, clearly enjoying this.

Reece flushed.

"I didn't save your life," she added, finally rescuing him. "Your friends did. They got you here quickly. If they had waited any longer, nothing would have saved you."

Reece nodded back, not knowing what else to say. He was stumped—and was impressed by her humility.

"So was there something else you wanted?" she asked, still smiling.

She was not going to make this easy on him. He looked into her eyes, playful, intelligent, and he felt that she was too smart for him. She saw right through him, and she had from the second he walked up to her door. She clearly wanted him to say what was on his mind, and would not let him off the hook until he did.

"Well...um," he said, swallowing. This was not easy. He did not remember it being this difficult to speak to girls before.

"I suppose there was something else," he said. "I guess...I am wondering...what you think of me? I mean...of us?"

"Of us?" she asked, laughing.

Reece reddened. He just could not get his bearings around her.

"I mean—I guess—I was wondering—if—do—you have a boyfriend?"

Reece finally got it out, feeling relieved that he did. He hadn't felt this anxious in years. He had rather be back fighting that Forsyth than putting himself through this torture.

But now that it was out there, he looked up and met her eyes—now the ball was in her court. Now it was her turn to be flustered.

Selese blinked several times and looked away, then looked down and fidgeted with her hands.

"And what business is that of yours?" she asked.

"I mean you no offense, my lady," he said. "I was just wondering—"

"I do not have a boyfriend," she said.

Reece looked at her with renewed hope. But she still looked back at him proudly, standoffish.

"Nor do I wish to have one," she added.

He looked back, puzzled.

"And why is that?" he asked.

"Because I've not found a man suitable for me in this village."

"And what about from outside your village?"

"Travelers rarely pass through here. And when they do, I am too busy with my healing arts."

"Well...I am passing through here," Reece said.

She looked into his eyes, smiling.

"And?" she said.

Reece looked back, flustered. Why was she making this so hard? Was she not interested? It appeared as if she wasn't. He was becoming exhausted.

"I am the son of a King," he said, and immediately regretted it. He hated boasting; it was not who he was. But he was desperate and found himself flailing, and he did not know what else to say. It just came out.

"And?" she prodded. "What difference does that make?"

Reece did not understand her.

"To most women in this kingdom, that would make a great difference," he said. "All the difference in the world."

Slowly, she shook her head.

"I'm not most women," she said. "I am not impressed by titles, or land, or riches. I will leave that for other women."

He studied her, trying to understand her.

"What does impress you then?" he asked.

She seemed to think for a moment.

"Honesty," she said. "Loyalty. And maybe...perseverance."

"Perseverance?" he asked.

She smiled coyly.

"And what of your love life?" she asked.

Reece stumbled.

"I'm not presently engaged to any woman," Reece responded, trying to sound noble and proper. "If I were, I would not be speaking with you."

"Wouldn't you?" she asked, smiling, clearly enjoying this. "And then why would a King's son take an interest in a simple villager?"

Reese took a deep breath. It was time for him to tell how he felt.

"Because when I look into your eyes, my lady, I see far more than a simple villager. I feel something that I've never felt for any woman. When I look at you, I cannot look away. And it takes my breath away to see you. My lady, I am in love."

He was shocked and proud of himself. For the first time, he had stopped stumbling and had managed to get it all out, to say how he really felt. He could not believe the words had escaped. But they were all true. And now that they were out, it was her turn to react as she wished.

For the first time in their conversation, she seemed truly caught off guard. She blinked several times, and shifted, and he could see her cheeks flush.

"You speak strong words," she said. "How am I to know they are true?"

"My lady, I never lie," Reece replied, earnest.

She looked down and toed the sand.

"Words are just words," she finally said. "They don't mean anything."

"And what does mean something?" he asked.

She shrugged, silent. He could tell that she was guarded, slow to trust.

"And then how do I prove my love to you?" he pressed.

She shrugged again.

"You have your world, and I have mine," she said. "Sometimes worlds should stay that way."

Reece felt his heart falling, and couldn't help but feel as if she were telling him to leave.

"Are you asking me to go?" he asked, heartbroken.

She looked into his eyes. They were soulful, knowing eyes, and he felt himself getting lost in them. He could not tell what her expression said.

"If you wish," she replied.

Reece's heart dropped.

He turned and walked off, feeling crushed. He was confused; he wasn't sure if he had been rejected—but he certainly had not been embraced. Selese was a mystery to him; he wondered if he would ever understand her.

He increased his pace, heading back towards his Legion brothers, towards a world he did understand, and wishing he had never come here. If this was the girl who had saved his life, a part of him wished it had never been saved at all.

CHAPTER TWENTY SEVEN

Godfrey ran through the back alleys of the seediest part of King's Court, trying to keep up with the young boy as he weaved in and out of the crowds, running ever since the graveyard. Akorth and Fulton trailed behind him, struggling to catch up, breathing hard, not in as good shape as he—and Godfrey was not in great shape, so that wasn't saying much. Too many years in the alehouse had affected all of them, and chasing after this boy was a mighty struggle. As Godfrey heaved, he resolved to turn over new leaf, to stop drinking for good, and to start getting into shape. This time, he meant it.

Godfrey shoved a drunk out of his way, sidestepped a young man trying to sell him opium and pushed his way past a row of whores as this part of town became worse and worse, the alleys narrowing, filled with sewage and mud. This boy was quick and knew these streets well, twisting his way through shortcuts, around vendors—it was obvious that he lived somewhere close.

Godfrey had to catch him. Clearly, there was a reason this boy was running, why he had not stopped since they'd spotted him at the grave. He was scared. He was Godfrey's only hope of finding the proof he needed to find his assassin—and to bring down his brother.

The boy knew his way around here well, but Godfrey knew it even better. What Godfrey lacked in speed he made up for in wit, and having spent nearly his entire life drinking and whoring in these streets, having spent way too many nights here running from his father's guards, Godfrey knew these streets too well—better, even, than the boy. So when he saw the boy turn left down a side street, Godfrey immediately knew that that street hooked around, and that there was only one way out. Godfrey saw his chance: he took a shortcut between buildings, preparing to head the boy off at the pass.

Godfrey leapt out of the alley just in time to block the boy's path, who, looking back over his shoulder, never saw it coming. Godfrey tackled him from the side and drove him down hard into the mud.

The boy screamed and flailed, and Godfrey reached up and grabbed his arms and pinned him down.

"Why do you run from me?" Godfrey demanded.

"Leave me alone!" the boy shouted back. "Get off of me. Help! Help!"

Godfrey smiled.

"Do you forget where we are? There is no one around to help you here, boy. So stop shouting and speak to me."

The boy breathed hard, wide-eyed in fear, and at least he stopped shouting. He stared back at Godfrey, scared but also defiant.

"What do you want from me?" the boy asked, between breaths.

"Why did you run from me?"

"Because I didn't know who you were."

Godfrey looked down, skeptical.

"Why were you in that graveyard? Who do you know was killed? Who was buried there?"

The boy hesitated, then relented.

"My brother. My older brother."

Godfrey, feeling bad for the boy, loosened his grip a bit, but not enough to let him go yet.

"Well I'm sorry for you," Godfrey said. "But not for myself. Your brother tried to poison me the other night. In the Tavern."

The boy's eyes opened wide in surprise, but he kept silent.

"I know nothing of the plot," the boy said.

Godfrey narrowed his eyes, and knew for sure that this boy was hiding something.

As Akorth and Fulton arrived behind him, Godfrey got to his feet and grabbed the boy by his shirt, and picked him up with him.

"Where do you live, boy?" Godfrey asked.

The boy looked from Godfrey to Akorth and Fulton, and remained silent. He seemed scared to answer.

"He's probably a homeless bugger," Fulton volunteered. "I bet he doesn't even have any parents. He's an orphan."

"That's not true!" the boy protested. "I DO have parents!"

"They probably hate you, want nothing to do with you," Akorth goaded.

"You're a LIAR!" the boy screamed. "My parents LOVE me!"

"And then where do they live, if these parents exist?" Fulton asked.

The boy fell silent.

"I will make this very simple for you," Godfrey said, matter-of-fact. "Either you tell us where you live, or I will drag you to the King's Castle and have you chained to the dungeon, never to come out."

The boy looked at him, eyes widening in fear, then, after several tense seconds, he lowered his eyes to the ground, raised an arm behind him, and pointed.

Godfrey followed his finger to see a small attached house—more like a shack, leaning to one side, looking as if it might collapse at any moment. It was narrow, barely ten feet wide, and had no windows. It was the poorest place he had ever seen.

He grabbed the boy's arm, and dragged him towards his home.

"We'll see what your parents have to say about your behavior," Godfrey said.

"No, Mister!" the boy cried out. "Please don't tell on me to my parents! I didn't do anything! They'll get mad!"

Godfrey led him there, pleading and protesting, then kicked open the door and let himself inside, dragging the boy, Akorth and Fulton behind him.

The inside of this shack was even smaller than the outside. It was a one room home, and as they walked in, the boy's parents stood a few feet away, and turned and faced them, alarmed. The mother had been engaged in knitting, the father in tanning a hide, and they both stopped what they were doing, stood upright, and stared at the intruders, then looked down to their boy with concern.

Godfrey finally released the boy, who ran to his mother's side, hugging her tight around the waist.

"Blaine!" she said to the boy, worried, hugging him. "Are you okay?"

"Who are you?" the father demanded, angry, taking a step towards them. "What right do you have to charge into our home? And what have you done to our boy?"

"I did nothing to your boy," Godfrey answered. "I only brought him back home, because I want answers."

"Answers?" the father demanded, angrier, confused, walking towards him threateningly. He was an older man, with a large nose, covered in warts, and strong face—and he did not look pleased.

"Your other son poisoned me last night," Godfrey stated.

The father stopped in his tracks, as the mother burst out weeping.

"You speak of Clayforth," the father said. He looked down sadly, and slowly shook his head.

"They chased me home all the way from the grave mama," the boy said.

"I believe that Blaine knows something about my attempted murder," Godfrey said to the mother.

She looked at him with alarm, protective of her son.

"And what makes you say that? You know nothing of our son."

"He ran from us at the grave. He is hiding something. I want to know what it is. I don't want to hurt your boy. I just want to know why his brother poisoned me, and who was behind it."

"My boy knows nothing of such devious plots," his father snapped. "Clayforth was trouble, I admit. But not Blaine. He would never sink to business like that."

"But his brother would?" Godfrey asked.

The father shrugged.

"He's dead now. He has paid for his sins. It is what it is."

"It is NOT what it is," Godfrey corrected, his own voice rising. "I was almost killed last night. Do you understand? I am the son of a King. Do you know the sentence for attempted murder on royalty? Clayforth is dead, but that does not make amends. Blaine knows something. That makes him an accessory to the crime. By King's Law, he can be punished. Now you will tell me what you know, or I will bring the Royal Guard here!"

Godfrey stood there, red-faced, breathing hard, more worked up than he had been in a long time. He had had enough, and he wanted answers.

The father looked alarmed for the first time, and he turned and looked at his son, now unsure. Blaine clung to his mother's waist.

"Blaine," his father said to him, "is there something you know that you are not telling us?"

Blaine looked from his father to his mother, shaking his head nervously.

Godfrey sighed, thinking what to do. He finally reached into his pocket, pulled out a sack of gold, and threw it on the floor before them. Tons of gold coins spilled out over the floor of the small house, and the mother and father both gasped at the sight.

"King's Gold," Godfrey said. "The finest. Go ahead, count it. It's enough for you to live the rest of your lives and never have to work again. I don't want anything in return. It is yours to keep. All I want is the truth. All I want is for your son to tell me what he saw. I know that he knows something. I just want to know what it is. I will protect him. I promise."

The mother stroked her boy's hair, squatted down, and kissed him on the forehead.

"Blaine, if you didn't see anything, don't be afraid. We don't need this gold."

But the father marched over sternly and grabbed Blaine by the chin.

"Blaine, these men believe you know something. That money can change our family's life forever. If you have something to say, say it. Remember, I have taught you to always speak the truth. Do not be like your bother. Go on now. Be a man. You've nothing to fear."

Blaine swallowed nervously, then finally looked up at Godfrey.

"I was with Clayforth the other night," Blaine said. "A man we had never seen before came up to him. He knew that Clayforth was a runner, for the den, and he asked him if he would put poison in a man's drink. At first my brother said no. But then he showed him gold—more gold than even you have here. He still said no. But he kept showing him more and more gold. And then he gave in."

Blaine took a deep breath.

"You must understand," he added, "my brother had never done anything like that before. But the money—it was too much for him to turn down. He said it would change our lives forever and that we'd never have to come back to this part of town. He wanted to buy mamma and papa a new house somewhere clean and safe."

"Did you see this man's face?" Godfrey asked.

The boy nodded, slowly.

"He was a tall man. Taller than any man I'd ever seen. And he was missing a tooth."

"On the right side?" Godfrey asked.

The boy nodded, his eyes opened wide. "How did you know?"

Godfrey knew, all too well. It was Afget, Gareth's new attack dog. There was no one else who fit that description. And now he had a witness. He had a witness that proved that Gareth's man attempted assassination on him, the King's son. It was grounds to have him deposed. It was the proof they needed.

"I need your son to be a witness," Godfrey said to his father. "What he witnessed is of importance not just to me, but to the kingdom itself, to all of King's court. To the entire Ring. I need him to testify. It will make amends for his brother trying to take my life. None of you will be in danger. You will all be protected, I guarantee it. You can keep all this gold and more."

A thick silence hung over the room, as they all turned to the boy.

"Blaine, it is your choice," the father said.

Blaine looked Godfrey up and down, then looked at his parents.

"Do you promise my parents will be safe?" Blaine asked Godfrey. "And that they can keep all the gold?"

Godfrey smiled.

"All of this and more," he reassured. "And yes, you have my word. You will all be safer than you've ever been."

Finally, Blaine shrugged.

"Then I don't see why not. After all, like you said, papa, it never hurts to tell the truth."

CHAPTER TWENTY EIGHT

Thor galloped back across the desert, getting farther which each step from his hometown, from memories of his encounter with his father—or, rather, the man who had raised him. It had been a life-changing trip, both dreadful and inspiring. The encounter had been painful, yet it had also finally given him the clarity he had always sought. His entire life he had suspected that he was different from his father, from his brothers, from his village; that he didn't belong there; that some great secret about his past was being hidden from him; that he was destined for something, some place, greater.

Now, finally, after hearing everything his father had to say—that he was not really his father, that those were not really his brothers—that his mother was alive—that he was truly different—it all made perfect sense. Despite the troubling confrontation, he finally felt a sense of ease, deeper than he'd ever felt in his life. He was finally beginning to peel back the layers of the mystery of his true identity, to understand more of who he was.

Thor kept turning over in his mind all the things his father said. He was overjoyed to know that his mother was alive, that she cared for him; he could feel her necklace against his bare throat even as he rode, and the feeling comforted him, made him feel as if his mother were right there with him. He could feel an intense energy radiating off of it, and it filled his whole being. She really cared for him. He could sense that. And she wanted to see him. That meant more to him than anything. He was more determined than ever to find her.

But then he couldn't help wonder: if she cared so much for him, why had she given him away to begin with? And why to that man who raised him, and why in that village?

Another question perplexed him even more: who, then, was his real father? The mystery baffled him. Now, not only did he not know who his mother was, but he did not know who his real father was, either. It could be anyone. Was he a Druid, too? Did he live in the Ring? And why had his father abandoned him, too?

Thor felt the ring his mother had given him sitting snug in his inner shirt pocket, and his mind turned to thoughts of Gwendolyn. More than ever, he knew she was the one. He sensed that this ring had come into his life now for a reason, that he was meant to give it to her. He couldn't wait to return and ask her to be his—and if she said yes, to place it on her finger. It was the most beautiful ring he had ever seen, and the idea of her accepting it thrilled him.

Thor kicked his horse, eager to return to his Legion brothers as the second sun fell in the sky. He wanted to finish the rebuilding and get back to King's Court and see Gwen, see Krohn again. He wanted to return to the House of Scholars, to study the map more deeply, and to figure out how he might journey to the Land of the Druids. He had to see his mother. And he had to know who his father was.

Thor felt a sense of sadness as he thought of the man who had raised him. Growing up he had thought the world of him—but the man was nothing to him now. It took so many years for Thor to reach this day, to finally get clarity. He was also, at the same time, beginning to feel a new sense of self-worth. Since this man was not his father, what he thought or how he felt about Thor didn't really matter. He was just a stranger. Thor now felt free to come to his own conclusions about how he felt about himself. At the same time, he could seek out his true father—and that man, Thor hoped, might be a great man, which would make Thor feel an even greater sense of pride in himself. And that man might actually love him for who he is, might be proud of all he had accomplished.

As Thor raced across the wasteland, nearing the village, his horse suddenly pulled hard to the left, surprising him. Thor tried to pull him back on course, but he refused to listen. He brought Thor off course, and as they rounded a small hill, Thor discovered a gurgling stream, cutting through the wasteland, its glowing blue waters contrasting with the yellow desert floor. The horse ran right up to the stream and Thor had no choice but to dismount as it lowered its head to drink.

He must have been thirsty, Thor realized. Yet still, it was strange behavior—his horse was usually obedient. Thor was beginning to wonder if the horse led him to this spot for a reason, when suddenly he heard a voice:

"Sometimes the truth is a heavy thing to bear."

Thor knew the voice, and he turned slowly, overcome with relief to see Argon standing there, in his robes, holding his staff, his eyes shining right at him. He almost looked like an apparition against the desolate wasteland.

"That man was not my father," Thor said. "You knew all this time. Why didn't you tell me?"

Argon shook his head.

"It was not for me to tell."

"And who then is my father?"

Argon shook his head again. He remained silent.

"Can you tell me, at least, anything about him?" Thor pressed.

"He is a very great and very powerful man," Argon said. "One worthy of you. When the time is right, you will know him."

Thor welled with excitement to hear this. His father was a great man. That meant the world to him.

"I feel different now," Thor said, "since discovering the news, since receiving my mother's message. I don't feel like the same boy I was."

"Because you are not," Argon said. "That boy is far behind. You are a man now. There is no turning back. Training can transform you—but so can knowledge. You're not the Thor you used to be. Now you're ready."

Thor looked at him, puzzled.

"Ready for what?"

"Ready to begin your real training," Argon said. "Not your play with swords and sticks and shields—but the training that matters most. Your inner training.

"Close your eyes," Argon said, raising a palm and his staff, "and tell me what you see."

Thor realized now why his horse had led him here. It was not to drink. It was to bring him to Argon, to this unlikely training ground, in the middle of nowhere. Thor would never understand Argon's ways. He seemed to appear at the most unlikely times, and in the most unlikely places.

Thor closed his eyes and breathed deep, trying to center himself, to prepare himself for whatever Argon would throw at him.

"Look into the core of the Ring," Argon commanded. "See all times—past, present and future. What do you see?"

Thor closed his eyes, struggling. Slowly, something was coming to him.

"I see that they are one," Thor said. "I see no division between the past or the future. Time—it is like a flowing river."

"Good," Argon said. "Very good. You are correct. There is no division in time, except for within ourselves. Like a river, it never ends. Follow this river. What do you see?"

Thor struggled to see, feeling a new sense of peace overcome him. This place he stood in felt charged, sacred, and wearing his mother's necklace, he began to feel a stronger energy within him than ever before. Images flashed within him. He began to see visions of the Ring, with more clarity than he'd ever had. It was like it was real. It was no longer fuzzy, as it used to be.

Thor focused and saw a great tide of humanity, an endless number of cities; he looked down on them, as if flying overhead. He watched seasons change beneath him, saw time pass, from decade to decade, century to century. He saw all the people divided. Then he saw all the people as one.

"Good," Argon said. "I sense that you can feel it. The force stream. Now, control the river. Look to the future. Tell me what you see."

Thor closed his eyes, struggling—but nothing came to him. Then he recalled Argon's past lessons, and forced himself to stop struggling. He breathed deep, and tried to allow it to come to him instead.

Thor began to see crystal-clear visions of the future. He flinched inside, was horrified as he watched King's Court overrun. He watched invaders destroy it, raze it, burn it down to the ground. In place of the great city, there was just a mound of ashes.

Thor heard the screams, watched thousands of people fleeing; he saw thousands butchered, thousands more imprisoned, taken as slaves. He watched as a wasteland spread and engulfed the once-bucolic hills of the Ring. He watched fruit fall from trees, saw women taken away. He saw great armies invading, covering every corner of the Ring. And he watched the sky blacken.

"I see a time of great darkness," Thor said.

"Yes," Argon said.

As Thor closed his eyes, he watched a blood-red moon rise over a desolate wasteland. It was night, and he saw a single fire burning in the blackness of the Ring.

"I see a fire," Thor said. "Burning in the wasteland."

"That fire is the source of hope," Argon said. "It is what will rise from the ashes."

Thor squinted and saw more.

"I see a sword," Thor said. "A gleaming sword. It shines in the sun. I see a hundred men being killed one swipe."

"The Destiny Sword," Argon said.

Thor flinched as he watched dragons fly down from the sky, breathing flames onto what was left of the Ring.

"I see a host of dragons," Thor said, voice shaking. "They attack as one."

Thor had to open his eyes—he could stand it no more. The visions were too horrific.

He saw Argon staring back.

"You are powerful," Argon said. "You have seen much. The power within you is strong. Stronger than I thought."

"But tell me what it all means," Thor pleaded, upset. "Is it all true? Will the Ring be destroyed? What will become of King's Court? Of the Legion? Of Gwendolyn?"

Argon shook his head sadly.

"You can't control the future," Argon said. "But you can prepare. You *must* prepare."

"How?"

"You must become stronger. The Ring needs you. You must develop the powers within yourself. You must claim for yourself the power source of your mother, a great Druid, of your father, a great warrior. It all lies within you. Only you are stopping it from shining through. You must accept it. Unleash it. Claim it as your own."

"But how?" Thor pleaded.

"Stop resisting it. Stop fearing who you are."

Argon turned.

"That stream," he said. "Close your eyes. Hear its gurgling. *Really* hear it."

Thor closed his eyes and tried to focus. He heard the delicate sound of water running over rocks.

"Can you feel it?" Argon asked. "Can you feel its current?"

Thor listened to the tranquil sound of the stream, and he felt it moving, felt its current.

"Good," Argon said. "You and the water are one. Now stop the water. Change its course. Turn it upstream."

Thor focused on the current of the water, which he felt flowing as if it were flowing through his own body.

Then, slowly, Thor reached out a palm and directed it towards the water. He could feel the stream's energy source, tickling the center of his palm. Slowly, he willed the current to change directions.

Thor felt a great strength within him, felt the resistance of the water, weighing on his palm, felt himself struggling, as if lifting a physical object. He opened his eyes and was amazed to see that he was stopping the flow of the stream. He was creating a small wall of water, like a dam, freestanding in the midst of the stream, revealing the dry bed underneath it.

"Good," Argon said. "Very good. Now let it go."

Thor pulled back his palm, and the water crashed back down and continued its flow.

"You have mastered a small slice of nature," Argon said. "But nature is not confined to the ground. Nature is all around us. Water flows in a stream—but it also flows in the sky. Feel the clouds above you. Feel how thick they are, how wet with moisture. Can you feel it?"

Thor looked up and was baffled. The sky was clear.

"But it is cloudless," Thor protested.

"Look again," Argon said and raised his staff.

As Thor watched, suddenly the sky above his head darkened with dark clouds, gathering from all corners of the sky. Thor was in awe of Argon's power.

"Now close your eyes," Argon said, "and feel the clouds."

Thor closed his eyes and was amazed to realize that he could feel this cloud, hanging above him like a physical thing. It felt heavy, thick, wet.

"Open it," Argon said. "Open this cloud and let it release its pressure. Let it rain moisture on us. It wants to rain. Allow it to."

Thor found himself raising both palms to the sky, leaning back, and as he did, he felt a great burst of energy rush through him.

Thunder suddenly clapped, and a great wall of water fell down on him. Thor heard a rumbling noise, and an instant later he felt himself drenched, water raining down all around him, landing on the dusty sand, on his head, drenching him.

"Good!" Argon screamed, over the sound of the rain, also drenched. "Now stop it!"

Thor closed his eyes, felt the wall of water, and raised one palm overhead, directing it at the cloud. Moments later, the water stopped.

Thor opened his eyes and was amazed to see the water raining from the sky, but stopping just feet above his head. He was holding it there—and it was sapping his energy. He felt his legs begin to shake from the effort.

"You are tired because you trying too hard," Argon yelled. "Make the cloud disappear!" Argon commanded.

"I can't!" Thor yelled back, shaking from the effort of holding up the rain.

"That is because you think it is hard. It is not!" Argon said.

Impatient, Argon raised his staff and waved it overhead; suddenly, the cloud disappeared. The day was clear and cloudless once again.

Thor looked all around, and there was no evidence that the cloud had ever been there—except for the fact that his clothes were dripping wet. He looked over at Argon in awe. His power was inspiring.

"I can feel my power," Thor said. "But it feels uneven, unsteady."

"That is the human part of you," Argon explained. "You are part human. That is an asset and a weakness. You must learn to master your imperfections. You might never be as strong as your mother; or, you might be stronger. The key lies in your mind, in your resolve, in your developing your skills."

Thor was struggling to comprehend all of this.

"But all of this—moving water, creating rain—I still don't understand how this shall help me in battle," Thor said.

"Don't you?" Argon asked.

Argon suddenly turned, held out a palm, aimed at a boulder and then lifted his hand.

Fifty feet away, an immense boulder, ten times the size of Thor, suddenly shot up high in the air, then, as Argon moved his wrist, it came slamming down with a great crash, a few feet before Thor.

Thor stumbled at the impact as the ground shook, leaving a crater in the earth, insects scurrying in every direction.

Thor looked at Argon with wonder—and fear. He had underestimated him, once again.

"All nature is connected," Argon said. "The water, the rocks, the sky. If you can direct the flow of water, you can direct anything. Even the animals."

Argon looked up at the sky.

"Do you see that bird?" Argon asked.

Thor looked up, and saw an eagle circling high overhead.

"Summon it down to us. Have it land on your shoulder."

Thor closed his eyes, reached up, and tried with all he had to direct the bird's energy. He felt the bird getting closer—but then suddenly flying away. He tried as hard as he could, but he could not control it. He opened his eyes to see the bird disappearing. He lowered his palm, mentally and physically exhausted.

"I'm sorry," Thor said. "I could not control it. It was too hard."

"It was only too hard because you tried too hard," Argon said. "You did not allow it to come to you. You still rely on your human sense of will."

"But I don't see how we can control all animals," Thor said.

Argon raised his staff, and suddenly Thor heard a roar.

He turned and saw a lion walking towards them, quickly, and as Argon moved his hand, the lion followed the direction of Argon's palm. It came up to Argon, sat beside him, and stared out at Thor. Tranquil. Obedient.

Thor was speechless.

"I can't believe it," Thor said.

"That is precisely your problem," Argon said. "If you cannot believe, you cannot create. Because you don't see it, you don't manifest it. You must learn to trust yourself. You know more than you think possible."

Suddenly, a great flash came and Argon disappeared—and the lion with him.

Thor looked about, in every direction, but they were gone.

Thor felt exhausted, but also stronger. He felt as if he had trained all day. He had taken an important step, and he felt his skills developing. But he still knew there was much left to learn, and he wondered if he would ever be able to master it all.

How vast were his powers? What was his destiny? How was he supposed to help the Ring?

Until he met his parents, somehow, he felt, he would never solve the mystery.

CHAPTER TWENTY NINE

Gwendolyn stood amidst the rolling hills on the beautiful Fall day, Krohn playing beside her, flowers in bloom as far as the eye could see, the landscape a tapestry of purples and yellows and whites. She took a deep breath, took aim with her bow, and let the arrow fly.

It whizzed through the air, and barely grazed the target on the distant oak tree. She frowned. It was her tenth attempt at this target, and each time she missed. When she had been younger, she had spent years training with the royal archer, and her aim had been true. She hadn't picked up the bow in years, and she had just expected her aim to be accurate. But it wasn't. Perhaps it was because she was older, or perhaps whatever skill she'd once had just wasn't with her anymore.

Gwen set the bow down and breathed the air in deeply, enjoying her surroundings. She had come out here to clear her mind, to try to get her mind off of Thor. Krohn yelped and pounced in the fields, chasing a rabbit, and she smiled at the sight. He been a true companion since Thor had left, and seeing him made her constantly think of him, and gave her a sense of assurance. She loved Krohn as if he were her own, she could feel his protectiveness, and was so grateful for it. He was growing every day, before her eyes, and was well on his way to becoming a full grown leopard. Sometimes she would look at him and be afraid, until he looked back at her and she saw the love in his eyes.

Gwen looked out at the beautiful fall day, saw the light shifting in the clouds, the distant swaying of the trees, and the field of flowers seemed alive as the wind pushed the colors one way, then the next. As she watched the horizon, she thought of Thor. He was somewhere out there, in that village, rebuilding. She wondered what he was doing right now. She had put on a strong face when she had said goodbye, but inside, her heart had been breaking. She ached to see him again, missed him beyond what she could describe, and she wished more than anything that he was here with her, right now.

Gwen also felt a craving to leave this place. She did not feel safe here anymore, since the attempt on her life, since the Nevaruns had showed up to take her way. She felt some measure of safety living here in her mother's keep, far from the castle, and spending her time secluded from the others, in these hills. She also felt a measure of safety with Krohn here, and in knowing that Thor return soon. She couldn't wait until he returned and the two of them could leave this place for good. In the meantime, she prayed that Godfrey could find the evidence they all needed to bring down Gareth once and for all. If he could, she would not even need to flee; but Gareth seemed indomitable, and she had her doubts whether they would ever be able to bring him down.

Gwen saw Thor's face in her mind, and she remembered back to that moment when he looked as if he were about to ask her something. And then something like fear had crossed his face. She wondered what it was. Was he going to ask her to marry him? Her heart swelled at the thought. There was nothing she wanted more. But she did not understand why he had not asked her yet. Were his feelings not as strong as hers?

She prayed that was not the case. She reached down and grabbed her stomach, remembered Argon's words, and could not help feeling just a little bit stronger each day, feeling with every ounce of her body that she was carrying Thor's child. A mystical, powerful child.

Gwendolyn heard a noise and turned, and in the distance she saw a single man hurrying through the fields, trotting her way. She looked closely, at his short stature, his hunched back, his pronounced limp, and she remembered: Steffen. She had sent one of her attendants to summon him, not knowing if he would come. She was thrilled that he had.

Gwen never forgot those who were kind to her—especially those who saved her life—and she wanted to repay Steffen for his kindness. She hated the idea of him slaving away in the servants' quarters, especially after what he had done for her. It just wasn't fair. He was a good man, who was misjudged by his appearance. She had to admit, even she had misjudged him at first.

Steffen approached, removing his hat and bowing low before her, his forehead drenched in sweat.

"My lady," he said. "I came as soon as you called for me."

Krohn came running over, stood protectively beside Gwen, and growled at Steffen.

"Krohn, it's okay," Gwen said. "He's one of us."

Krohn instantly relaxed, the hairs dropping on his back, his ears lowering, as if he understood. He stepped forward and as Steffen held out a hand, Krohn licked it. He then jumped up and licked Steffen's face.

Steffen laughed.

"He is the most affectionate leopard cub I've ever met," Steffen said.

"If you're on his good side," Gwen replied. "Thank you for coming. I didn't know if you would."

"And why wouldn't I?"

"With Gareth ruling, it seems dangerous to be anywhere near me. After all, look at what happened to Firth. I thought perhaps you might be afraid to be involved anymore."

Steffen shrugged.

"There's little left that frightens me, my lady. After thirty years of sleeping in a basement, I honestly haven't much to lose. I'm not afraid of kings. It's injustice that I fear."

She surveyed Steffen and could see that he was telling the truth. The more time she spent with him, the more respect she had for this man, a funny, quirky man, who saw the world his way. He was much wiser and more intelligent than she had given him credit for, and she felt so indebted to him for what he had done for her. She felt that he was a close friend, one of few people in this court she could really trust.

"I've called you here because I never had a chance to properly thank you," she said.

"You have nothing to thank me for, my lady."

"But I do. And I always repay my debts. I do not hold it fair in my eyes that you continue to be a servant when you have saved the life of a royal. I owe you a great debt, and I wish to repay you. Please tell me how. Would you like wealth? A new position?"

Steffen shook his head.

"My lady, I have no need for wealth. Perhaps in my youth, but not now. I have no place I call home. I sleep in a small room adjacent to the servants' quarters. I have no family—at least none that will acknowledge me. I have no one and nothing in the world. So I have no need for things. That is how it has always been with me."

Gwendolyn felt her heart breaking.

"But that is unfair," she said.

He shrugged.

"That is the way of the world. Some people are born with much, and others with less."

"But it is never too late," she said. "I want to at least elevate your position. I want to give you a job elsewhere, with more dignity."

"As long as your brother is king, I wish to be nowhere near him. The basements suits me just fine."

"And what if there should be a new ruler one day?" she asked.

He looked right through her, understanding her instantly. He was more perceptive than she thought.

"My lady, if *you* are that ruler, and I pray to the gods that you will be one day, then I would be honored to fill any position you would give me. But until that day comes, I am content."

She nodded, suddenly realizing what she would do.

"If that day should come," she said, "I will need many advisors. There will be few that I would trust as well as you. Not to mention, I like your company."

Steffen smiled; it was the first time she had ever seen him smile. It made her sad; she could see the little boy behind his eyes, the one who had once wanted to be loved, but had been nothing but rejected. This might be, she realized, the first time in his life he had ever been accepted, the first time he had ever been picked for anything.

"My lady," he said humbly, a tear in his eyes, "nothing would do me so great an honor."

He suddenly stepped forward, reached down and picked up her bow.

"If I am to be your advisor," he said, "if I may be so bold, perhaps I could start now, with a lesson on the bow and arrow."

He smiled, pointing at her distant target.

"Forgive me, my lady, but I cannot help but notice your aim could use some correcting, if you don't mind my saying."

Gwen smiled back, happily surprised; she was wary that someone in his shape could teach her, but she decided to go along with it and humor him. He was a quirky man.

"I'm glad that you did notice," she said. "Because it needs much correcting. Is archery a skill of yours?"

He grinned as he lifted an arrow, and weighed it in his palm. She had never seen anyone handle an arrow like that before.

"I have few skills in this world, my lady," he said, "but archery is one of them. You would think that I would not—yet something about the hunch of my back has actually made it easy for me to shoot. It always has. My few friends used to joke that I was born in the shape of the bow. But sometimes I think, it is a good thing."

Steffen suddenly placed the arrow in the bow, pulled the back string, then let it go, all while looking at Gwen and smiling.

A second later, there was the sound of the arrow hitting the target, and Gwen looked over, breathless, to see that he had hit a perfect bull's-eye.

She gasped. She could not understand how he had done it: he had been looking at her while he fired. She had never seen anything like that in her life—not even from the royal archer.

"Can you teach me to do that?" she asked, in awe.

"Aye," he said, reaching out and handing her the bow.

She took it and placed an arrow in it, excited for the first time.

"Draw it, let me see your form," he said.

She pulled back the string, her hand shaking.

"Your elbow must be higher. And you must pull your fingers closer to your chin. Your chin should be lowered, your eyes are wavering. Choose one eye. Don't overthink it. And don't hold it so long—your hands will shake."

Gwen let the arrow fly, and again the arrow grazed the target, although this time a bit closer to the center.

"There's a strong wind today," he said. "You must take that into account. Also, the ground you stand on is sloped. Both of those must be adjusted for. Finally, this bow you hoist is too heavy for you. That must be taken into account, too. To adjust, aim a little higher, and more to your right. And bend your knees just a little: they are locked. That will allow you to breathe. Breathe deep, and let it go as you reach the peak of your breath."

Gwen did everything he instructed, and as she let this arrow fly, it felt different this time. She felt more in control.

There was the sound of the arrow striking the target, and she cried out in delight to see that she had hit a near perfect bull's-eye.

Steffen smiled wide, too, and clapped his hands.

"My, you are a fast learner!" he said.

"You are a good teacher," she answered, beaming, proud of herself.

Suddenly, beside them, Krohn started snarling. The hair stood up on his entire body, and he turned, watching the empty horizon, snarling.

"Krohn, what is it?" she asked.

Krohn continued to snarl and Steffen and Gwen exchanged a glance, wondering. Gwen started to become anxious about Krohn's behavior. She had never seen him like this. Was he seeing something?

Suddenly there came a great rumbling, like thunder, and on the horizon, there appeared about a dozen horses, ridden by men in yellow and green armor. Her heart stopped, as she recognized it immediately: Nevaruns. She had assumed they were gone for good, after being chased away at the Hall of Arms. But apparently, they were sneaky. They had been waiting for their chance, waiting for a moment when she was not expecting it.

Now, they charged right for her.

Gwen was kicking herself; she had been so stupid. She should not have left herself vulnerable, alone in the hills like this, especially without her horse, a means of escape. Steffen had no horse either, and they were stuck, helpless, nothing for them to do but wait for their approach. She suddenly wished that Thor was there, by her side, as her heart flooded with panic.

But her heart also flooded with strength, and she felt an indignity rise in her veins. After all, she was MacGil's daughter, a King's daughter, and she bore the pride of a King. Her father ran from no one, and neither would she.

Gwen heard a screech, and high up she spotted Estopheles, screeching, swooping down, circling; she felt her father with her.

"My lady, run!" Steffen screamed.

He stepped forward, snatched the bow from her hands, and faster than any archer she had seen in her life, he reached down and fired three quick shots as the group neared, now maybe thirty yards away.

Steffen's aim was unbelievable. He hit three warriors, each with perfect precision, in their throats, at the base of their collarbones, the arrows going through one end and out the other. Each fell sideways off their horse, dead.

"Never!" Gwen screamed back.

At the same time, Gwen grabbed her bow and fired at the men, too. She missed her first shot. Then she remembered everything that Steffen had taught her. She tried to breathe, to relax. And as she took aim again and let the arrow fly, she was amazed to watch it sail and pierce a warrior in the throat. He reached up, screaming, then fell down, too.

They were so close now that there was no time for Steffen or Gwen to fire. The horses bore down on them and at the last second they both jumped out of the way so as not to be trampled.

The soldiers each jumped from their horses, one tackling Gwen, and the other Steffen, knocking them down and landing on top of them, in their armor. Gwen's ribs were bruised as she hit the ground.

Gwen's attacker reached back with his gauntlet, preparing to backhand her, and she braced herself for the impact, one she knew would shatter her jaw.

But then a great snarling filled her ears, and before her eyes Krohn leapt forward and sank his fangs into the soldier's throat. He shrieked, as Krohn found the soft spot between his plates of armor, and dug in, pinning him to the ground, refusing to let go.

Gwen rolled out from under him and in the same motion, she grabbed his dagger from his belt, and spun around just in time to plunge it into the other soldier diving for her. She stabbed him low in the belly and he shrieked, dropping his club, before he brought it down for her head.

He landed on top of her, limp, and the impact hurt. But she held on and drove the dagger deeper into him, and soon he stopped squirming, dead.

She pushed him off of her.

Another soldier came at her with a whip, about to lash her face, but Krohn turned and leapt, pouncing in the air and sinking his fangs into the soldier's wrist, tearing off his hand in mid-air, the whip with it. The soldier shrieked, sinking to his knees and clutching his bloody stump.

Steffen finally managed to free himself from beneath the other knight, and as he did, he drew his sword and chopped off the handless knight's head.

A soldier attacked Gwen from behind, grabbing her and yanking her to his feet, and holding a dagger to her throat.

"I hope that you always remember that I gave you this scar, princess," he said, his hot breath in her ear. Then he reached up and brought the dagger to her cheek.

Gwen braced herself for the cut, feeling the metal touch her skin—when suddenly she heard a screech, and looked up to see Estopheles, diving down, claws out, right for her. She dodged her head, and the bird swooped straight down and clawed her attacker's face.

He screamed, clutching his eyes and dropping the blade.

Steffen charged forward and stabbed the man in the chest. He then wheeled around and in the same motion, slashed a soldier in the stomach, right before he came down at Steffen with a war hammer.

Gwen, bruised, shaking, covered in blood, looked around at all the corpses and was amazed at the damage they'd done. It was like a mini battlefield, and she and Steffen and Krohn had somehow survived.

But she relaxed too soon: Krohn started snarling again, and Gwen turned and heard another great rumbling.

The horizon became filled with soldiers, hundreds of them, all wearing the yellow and green armor of the Nevaruns.

Gwen's her heart stopped, as she realized that those few knights they had killed had just been an expeditionary party, a small taste of what was to come. Now there bore down on them an entire army, in full force. There was no way they could defend themselves—and nowhere to run.

Steffen stepped forward, fearlessly raised the bow, and prepared to fire. She was in awe at his chivalry, his fearlessness, but she knew it was a losing battle.

"Steffen!" she cried out.

He turned and looked at her, as she laid a hand on his wrist.

"Don't," she said. "We cannot win. I need you elsewhere. Leave this place. Run and get word to Thor, to the Legion. Tell them to find me, wherever I am. That is what I need."

"My lady, I cannot leave you," he protested, wide-eyed, the army getting closer, raising his voice to be heard.

"You must!" she insisted. "I demand that you do. If you care for me, you will. You are needed elsewhere. Without you, I cannot get a message to Thor. You're my last hope. Go. GO!" she screamed, fierce.

Steffen turned and raced off across the fields, sprinting.

Gwen stood there, facing the oncoming army alone, only Krohn by her side, and she trembled inside, but refused to show it. She held her chest out, her chin up, and she stood there proudly, refusing to run. Krohn snarled at these men, not showing an ounce of fear, and she was determined to match his bravery. Whatever would come, would come. At least she would go down proudly.

In moments they reached her. First came the thumping of horses, swirling all around her; then came the scowls of hundreds of angry men, charging for her, holding thick ropes of twine, preparing to bind her. Krohn, undeterred, bravely pounced and tore off the hand of the first man who reached for Gwen.

But another soldier raised a club and brought it down on Krohn's back, and Gwen heard an awful crack. It sounded as if Krohn's ribs were broken—yet somehow, Krohn managed to spin around and bite off his attacker's hand, too.

Krohn leapt for another soldier, sinking his fangs into his throat and clasping onto them while the soldier shrieked. Another soldier smashed him with a mace, yet still Krohn would not let go—until finally another soldier cast a net on him, binding him.

Simultaneously, the soldiers brought their horses to a stop before Gwen, and a group of them dismounted and strutted towards her. One of them stepped out in front, and as he came close, he lifted his visor. She recognized him, from the confrontation outside the Hall of Arms. It was the man to whom she had been sold, the man arranged by Gareth to be her husband.

"I told you I'd return," he said, his face humorless. "You had your chance to come peacefully. Now, you shall learn the hard way of the might of the Nevaruns."

Gwendolyn only dimly saw the gauntlet, behind her, coming down for her face, as she heard the awful crash of metal against her skull, felt the ringing in her ears, and felt herself sink down, unconscious, into the field of flowers.

CHAPTER THIRTY

Luanda snuck through the back streets of the McCloud city, sticking close to the walls, doing her best not to be detected. She had only traveled the city briefly and did her best to retrace her steps, to try to find her way back to where she knew they were keeping Bronson. She passed a horse, tied to a post, and for a moment she turned and glanced out at the horizon, at the sunset, at the open fields, and she wanted more than anything to take the dagger in her hand and cut that horse's rope, mount it, and charge away from here—far, far away, back over the Highlands and to the safety of home.

But she knew that she could not; she had a job to do. However despicable his family was, she still loved Bronson, and she had to save him. She could not live with herself if she did not.

Luanda bit her lip and moved on. She worked her way through the mob, down winding, narrow back streets, through squares, past taverns, whorehouses, streets filled with mud and waste, dogs running everywhere. A rat scurried over her bare foot, and she kicked it off and stopped herself from crying out at the last second. She had to be strong. She only prayed her husband was still alive, and that she could find a way to get them out of here for good.

Before she'd been dragged off to the dungeon, Luanda had watched Bronson get tied up in the town square, made a public example by his father, a laughingstock; she assumed that's where he still stood. She hurried down street after street, trying to remember the way, hoping she was going in the right direction as she followed the thickening crowd. She figured that crowds always flocked towards misery and torture and spectacle.

There came a distant cheer and she assumed she was nearing the city center. Soon it grew more distinct, raucous, and she knew she was getting close.

She walked quickly, trying to keep her head down, hoping no one would notice her. She passed an old woman's stand, draped with various clothing, and as the woman turned away to tend to her dog, Luanda swooped in and snatched a long brown cloak.

She turned the corner and quickly put it on, covering her cold body, and covering her face. She looked every which way, and saw that no one had witnessed her take it, and already she felt better. She tucked the dagger she had stolen into her waist and moved on, slinking through the crowd, and feeling as if she were racing the clock. It was only a matter of time until they discovered she had escaped—and when they did, all of McCloud's men would be on the lookout for her.

Luanda turned down yet another street, the shouts growing louder, and as she did, to her relief, she spotted it: the city square. A huge mob pressed in, swarming around its center; they all looked up and she followed their gaze and was horrified to see, up on a scaffold, her husband bound, his legs and arms each tied in four directions, on a huge cross. He was missing one of his hands, where his father had cut it off, now just a charred stump, and Bronson stood there, head hanging low, body limp. The crowd threw vegetables at him, and he could do nothing but suffer the indignity, as they all heckled him every which way.

Luanda flushed with rage at his treatment and she hurried forward, frantic to get closer, to see if he was alive. From this distance, she couldn't tell.

As Luanda got closer, she noticed him momentarily lift his head, just a tiny bit, as if in her direction, as if maybe a part of him knew. Her heart soared with relief to know that he was still alive. There was hope. That was all she needed.

Luanda realized she would probably get caught trying to free him, and die in the process. But she didn't care. She had to try. If she went down dying, so be it. After all, she was the firstborn child of King MacGil, of a long line of MacGil kings, and it was not in her nature to leave someone behind. Especially her husband, and especially after he had been injured trying to save her life.

Luanda took in her surroundings, desperate to formulate a plan. She didn't know what she would do once she actually saw him, and now that she did, and knew he was alive, her mind raced.

She realized she needed to wait until all these people disappeared, and she needed to wait for the anonymity of night. She didn't know if he would make it until then, but she had no choice. There was no way she could even attempt to get him out in front of this mob of people.

She wormed her way into the town square, walking alongside a stone wall, and searched all the nooks and crannies in the wall until she found one she liked, deep and low to the ground, embedded into one of the ancient stone walls. She tucked herself in it. It was several feet deep, and she sat down, slumping on the ground, and wrapped the cloak tight around her. She disappeared completely inside the small nook, and no one could see her. Her only company down here was the passing rats.

She sat there, and waited. Twilight was already coming, and soon, night would fall. Eventually, all of these disgusting McClouds would disperse back to their homes. Eventually, she would be alone here. And then she would make her move.

*

Luanda opened her eyes with a jolt and looked around, wondering where she was. She had fallen asleep, had wakened in the midst of fast, troubled dreams, and she chided herself, breathing hard. She had resolved to stay vigilant, to stay awake, but her wariness must have gotten the best of her. She looked out at the dark, at the absolute stillness of the town square, and wondered what time it was. At least the sun had not broken yet. And now the square, as she'd hoped, was completely empty.

Save for one person—the one who mattered most: her husband. He still stood up the scaffold, bound to the cross, hanging limply. She did not know if he was dead or alive. But at least he was alone.

Now was her chance.

Slowly, Luanda crawled her way out of the crevice, her legs and arms stiff from being curled up so long. She stood, stretching them, and surveyed her surroundings. Bronson was so high on the cross, she needed a way to get him down—and once she got him down, she needed a way to get them out of there.

But she saw no horse anywhere, no means of escape, and there was no time to search for one. It was now or never, she knew. She would just have to get him down, then figure out what to do with him then.

Luanda made her way stealthily across the square, ducking low; she reached the scaffold and climbing her way up the back steps. As she approached, she heard Bronson moaning, and was glad to hear sounds coming from him. He was alive.

Luanda came up behind him, climbing all the way to the top of the scaffold, a good ten feet off the ground, and stood beside him.

"Bronson," she whispered in his ear, as he stood there, delirious. "It's me, Luanda. I'm here."

Bronson raised his chin and looked over at her with one eye open; she could see a small smile at the corner of his lips. But his lips were chapped, and he was too delirious to open his mouth to speak.

"I'm going to get you out of here, do you understand me?" she said.

Slowly, he nodded back.

Luanda removed the dagger from her belt, reached behind him, and cut the thick twine binding his arms to the cross. As she did, he suddenly slumped and fell over, collapsing onto her. The weight of him was unexpected, and sent her crashing down onto the podium with a loud noise, the hollow wood reverberating in the town square.

"Halt! Who goes there!" called out a stern voice.

Suddenly there was a torch in the blackness, and a horse came charging towards them. Luanda looked up, terrified, to see one of McCloud's men, a royal guard, racing right for them.

She had to think quick.

Luanda jumped to her feet, pulled the dagger from her waist, and as the man charged for her, she reached back and threw it.

She prayed to God that her aim was true. It was a reflex, throwing knives, something she had done since she was a child. It was the one skill she had. And now, she prayed those years had paid off.

There was a noise of blade entering flesh as the guard screamed; she watched as the blade pierced his throat and sent him flying backwards, over and off his horse. The horse kept charging, though, right for her, and Luanda reached over and grabbed its reins, before it could take off again. She then grabbed Bronson, dragged him to his feet with all her might, and draped his body across the horse. She jumped on the horse, kicked it, and the two of them took off.

She heard a chorus of voices in the distance, behind her, but she did not stop or turn to see who was chasing her. She took off down the winding streets of this town, hoping and praying she could get out of here soon.

Her prayers came true. After several more turns, she found herself out under open sky, in the open fields, charging, heading West, into the setting of the second sun and the rising of the first moon. In the distance, as a silhouette, she could see the Highlands, and her heart soared. Just over those mountains, there was safety. If she made it, she vowed she would never cross to the McCloud side again.

She could hardly believe it.

They were free.

CHAPTER THIRTY ONE

Reece woke to the breaking dawn of another day, the first to rouse. He looked around the dying embers of the bonfire and saw all of his Legion brothers still sleeping around it under the open sky. He had been thrilled when Thor returned the night before, and the two of them had stayed up half the night talking. At some point they had drifted off, and Reece had been plagued by troubled dreams. He kept seeing Selese's face. In one dream, he saw her in a rowboat, adrift at sea, drifting away from him on strong tides; in another he saw her dangling over the edge of a cliff, holding his wrist. In all these dreams she was slipping away from him, and he kept trying to save her, but it was always too late.

Reece had awakened sweating, looking frantically for her. Of course, she was not here. He had not spoken to her since she'd rejected him the day before; he'd tried to forget about her, spending the rest of the day throwing himself into his work, helping the villagers rebuild, trying to push her from his mind.

Yet with every stone he'd laid, with every bit of labor, he thought only of her. For some reason, he just could not shake her from his mind. Despite himself, he had grown fond of this little village, of this simple place beneath the wide open sky, its simple people, its calming ways. It was such a refreshing change from King's Court. And yet he knew that his time here was almost done, and that he would likely never see Selese again.

Reece paced in the early morning light, tormented over it. She had left things off in an ambiguous way, and he could not be entirely certain if she did not like him. He knew that if he did not try to speak with her now, one last time, then he would never come back here, never take that chance again. He knew that if he returned to King's Court without taking that chance, without closure, it would haunt him.

Reece felt stuck between two worlds, desperately needing to talk to her again, yet afraid, unsure if she wanted to see him. Her words had been confusing. On the one hand, it had felt like a rejection; but on the other, she had not entirely closed the door, and had made that cryptic reference to admiring persistence. She was a mystery—and that was partly why he liked her. He had never encountered anyone like her, who kept him on his toes as she did. He'd finally met someone who didn't care about riches or titles or status, who could care less about who he was, or where he was from. She was as pure and genuine a person as he'd ever met—and that just made him love her all the more.

He did not know why he was so obsessed with her. Was it because she had brought him back from the dead? Or was there something else? He felt an intense connection to her, one he could not shake, and he had never felt anything like it before. He could not ignore it, no matter how much he tried. He was burning up inside.

Reece could stand it no longer. He had made up his mind.

He finally turned and hurried off, turning down the streets of the small village, marching with determination to Selese's cottage. He was overflowing with things to say to her; he needed to know why she had spurned him, and how she really felt about him. He was carrying on a whole conversation with her inside his head, and by the time he reached her door and grabbed her knocker, he was already worked up.

He slammed her knocker several times, the only sound in the sleepy village, reverberating throughout its empty streets. It sounded way too loud, and as a dog began barking in the distance, he felt conspicuous, as if he might wake this whole town up.

He slammed the knocker again and again, until finally he heard a voice.

"All right all right!" came a sleepy voice behind the door.

Reece stood back, suddenly realizing what he had done, suddenly realizing that he was slamming on her door at the crack of dawn—and he felt embarrassed. Now he wanted to turn and run—but it was too late.

Selese yanked open the door and stood there, staring back at him in the early morning sun, wrapping a shawl tight around her shoulders, looking sleepy and very annoyed.

"What has gotten into you?" she asked. "It is not yet sunrise, and yet you slam my door as if an army is advancing."

Reece stared back, tongue-tied.

"So?" she prodded, annoyed.

Reece stood there, forgetting everything he'd wanted to say.

"I um…" he started, then stopped.

Why did she have this affect upon him?

"I came to say good morning," he said.

Her eyes opened wide.

"Good morning?" she repeated, incredulous.

180

Then she burst out laughing, right in his face.

"Have you lost your mind?" she added.

Now it was Reece's turn to get mad.

"Listen," he began, no longer able to contain himself. "It's not right what you're doing here. Playing games like this. I need you to be honest with me. No more of this."

She looked at him, baffled.

"No more of what?" she asked. "Are you dreaming?"

"No more of this game we're playing. I need you to tell me the truth."

"I'm not playing any games with you," she said. "I don't even know you."

He examined her, frustrated.

"So are you telling me you're not feeling what I'm feeling?" Reece asked, wanting to get to the point. He needed to know, for his own clarity of mind.

She blinked, taken aback.

"And what is it that you are feeling?" she asked.

"Enough of the questions!" Reece demanded, at the end of his rope. "I came here because I love you. Do you understand? I *love* you. I'm not sick. I'm not delirious. I'm awake. I'm in my right mind. And that's how I feel. And that's the end of it!" he yelled, angry, his voice rising,.

She looked at him, surprised, as if looking at a crazy person; then, slowly, a smile formed at the corner of her mouth.

"But you don't even know me," she replied. "How can I believe it's true? How is such a thing possible?"

Reece's heart fell.

"So are you saying you don't love me then?" he insisted.

"I don't even know you," she responded. "I'm not saying that I don't love you. I'm not saying that I do. It is not a word I would use lightly. And not with a stranger."

"Well, how are you supposed to know me, if you won't give me a chance?" Reece pressed.

Now it was her turn to blush.

"You are royalty," she said. "I am a village girl. It would not work out between us."

"And how can you be so sure?" Reece demanded. "Because I think it could."

She looked him, her eyes growing serious for the first time, as if finally truly hearing him.

"What are you asking?" she asked.

Reece took a deep breath.

"I'm asking you to come with me. I'm saying that I want to take you away from here. I'm saying that I want you to give us a chance. I mean what I say. I'm not a passerby. I take love very seriously. And I know how I feel about you. I've been up all night long—and I can think of nothing else."

Selese's cheeks reddened, and she shifted, flustered.

"Tell me," Reece asked, calming. "Do you not think of me at all?"

Selese looked down to the ground, reddening herself.

"I've thought of nothing else since you left yesterday," she said softly, looking down, as if afraid to admit it.

Reece's heart swelled. He felt like shouting from the rooftops. He could hardly conceive that she felt the same.

"Then why do you resist me?" he pleaded.

She looked up, her eyes wet.

"You would tire of me in a day," she said. "I would just be an oddity, the village girl brought to King's Court. Everyone would gawk at me. You would move on to someone else. I won't put myself through that."

"Nobody will gawk at you," Reece insisted. "Least of all me. I could care less what others think. I want you there. I want you with me."

She looked into his eyes, and for the first time, he could really feel her feelings for him. He could not wait for an answer any longer: he leaned in, placed a hand behind her head, pulled her close, and he kissed her.

She did not resist. She did not kiss him back, but she did not pull away, either. The feel of her lips on his was exhilarating, and he kissed her as long as he could, not wanting to let go. As he did, he felt transported to another place. He felt that this was the woman he was meant to be with.

Suddenly, a horn sounded, cutting through the morning sky, and Reece turned as the whole village began to run, heading in one direction. He spotted a single man galloping towards the village center, in a hurry, coming from King's Court. A messenger. He knew instantly that, whatever it was, it could not be good.

*

Thor stood in the early morning light of Sulpa, and turned with the rest of the village as he saw a lone messenger galloping towards him, riding across the wasteland from the road to King's Court. Thor squinted into the light, wondering if it were an apparition, but the horns sounded all around him, and he knew it was real. At first he felt on guard for battle, but then he realized it was just a messenger, and his heart beat faster. Whatever it was, it could not be good. Not by the way this man was riding.

As the messenger neared, Thor ran out to meet him, and his heart dropped further as he realized who it was. Steffen, the hunch back, the one who had saved Gwen's life. He was charging hard, and his face was bloodied and covered in sweat, and clearly he had been riding all night. Thor could feel the urgency coming off of him, even from here, and every fiber in his being told him that something was wrong.

Thor ran out to greet him, beyond all the other villagers, at the village gate, and Steffen dismounted, breathing hard, and hurried up to Thor.

He half bowed.

"My liege," he began, gasping for air.

"Bring him water!" Thor ordered, and a village boy ran up with a bucket of water. Steffen took it, leaned back and drank, gulping it down quickly, then dumping the rest of it over his head.

He wiped his face with the back of his hand, took several deep breaths, and looked up at Thor.

"My liege, something terrible has happened," he began. "It is Gwendolyn."

Thor's heart pounded.

"We were ambushed by Nevaruns," he continued. "At first, just a handful, and we managed to kill them. But then, a greater army came. They overwhelmed us. It was just Gwen and I and Krohn, alone on the hilltop. No one came to our defense."

Steffen broke into tears.

Thor stepped forward, flooded with panic, grabbed the small man by his shoulders and shook him.

"Tell me what happened!" he demanded. "Is she okay!?"

Steffen shook his head.

"She told me to come find you. I wanted to stay and fight to the end. But she insisted I come and get you. When I left, they were closing in on her. There was nothing else I could do. I don't know if she's even alive."

Steffen wept, and Thor stood there, overwhelmed with guilt. He hated himself for leaving Gwen alone, for not returning sooner. He couldn't stand the thought of her being taken away, unprotected, all by herself. He felt torn to pieces.

And then he felt a new feeling rising up in his veins: a desire for vengeance, and a desire to save her, if she was alive.

There was no time to waste.

"TO THE HORSES!" Thor screamed out to his Legion brothers, who were already gathered around him, listening to every word.

Within moments Thor was on his horse, as were his brothers, and he kicked it harder than he'd ever had in his life. He rode from this place, riding with everything he had into the wasteland, towards King's court.

He only prayed that Gwendolyn was still alive.

CHAPTER THIRTY TWO

Thor galloped at the head of the small group of Legion members racing for King's Court, all of them exhausted, riding all day, without a break, pushing their horses too hard. The second sun was now long in the sky as Thor charged across the drawbridge, through King's Gate, and past the Royal Guard, not even slowing. His friends kept up with him as they charged beneath the tunnel and out the other side, creating a storm of dust as they entered into King's Court.

They kept charging, cutting across the court and out a gate on the far side, Steffen leading them to the field where Gwen had been surrounded. Thor's heart was thumping in his chest as he prayed beyond hope that maybe, just maybe he would find her here alive. And Krohn, too.

But the way Steffen described it, he knew the chances were slim. She could be dead. They both could be.

Thor had to see for himself. He felt so grateful that all of his friends backed him up and rode with him on this journey, refusing to go elsewhere. Not one of them hesitated, even for a moment. He truly felt as if these were his brothers now.

They rode and rode, across fields, up and down hills, and through an immense field of flowers. As they climbed a bend, Thor spotted Estopheles, circling high up, and he felt that they were close. They rounded another hill, and Thor's heart stopped as he saw the carnage before him. He continued to charge, heading forward, as if into a nightmare.

There, on the hilltop, were what appeared to be several bodies, Nevarun corpses, wearing their distinctive green and yellow armor. He could see the bloodshed even from here, and even more so, he could sense it, in the very fabric of the soil. A great calamity had happened here. And he hated himself for not being here to protect Gwen.

Thor and his men charged to the hilltop, and as they reached the group of bodies, they all dismounted, Thor's horse barely stopping as he jumped down and ran, searching all the bodies on the ground, desperate, tears flooding his eyes, hoping and praying one of them might be Gwen. He saw the frozen corpses of the Nevaruns, arrows piercing their throats, blood staining the field, and he could see what a vicious battle had happened. He could see at a glance that everything

Steffen had told him was true, and he was more grateful than ever to Steffen for doing his best to defend Gwen.

He scanned the faces desperately, as did his Legion brothers, running from one body to the next; but his heart already told him what he knew to be true: Gwendolyn was not here. She had been taken away.

The realization hit him like a hammer. On the one hand he was relieved that he did not find her corpse. That meant there was at least some hope that she was alive. Yet on the other hand, he imagined her kidnapped, stolen from this place, and all the terrible things that might have happened to her since, and his body burned with a sudden desire to save her—and a desire for vengeance.

As Thor continued to scan the bloody grass, he spotted something that made his heart sink: Krohn lay there, motionless, on his side, blood pouring from his head. Thor hurried over to him, dropped to his knees, and ran a hand along Krohn's hide. He could see him breathing, shallow, and was greatly relieved. He saw the blood on his fangs, and glancing at the corpses, he could tell the damage that Krohn had done, and he felt overwhelmed with gratitude towards him for protecting Gwen—yet also overwhelmed with guilt.

"Krohn," Thor said softly, nudging him. His body was still warm, but Krohn did not respond.

"Krohn," Thor urged, shaking him. "Wake up! Please!"

Thor shook Krohn harder and harder, until finally Krohn opened one eye, just a crack. Then the eye closed again. Thor could see that he was suffering, that he was badly injured. He sensed that if he did not get help soon, he would die.

Thor wasted no time. He picked up Krohn him, surprised at how heavy he had become, slung him over his shoulder, and carried him over to Steffen's horse, draping him along the back of it. Krohn lay there, limp, like a saddlebag.

Thor turned to Steffen.

"Bring him to the healer. Right away. Waste no time! Tell her to use everything in her power to save him. GO!"

Without wasting a moment, Steffen remounted his horse, Krohn draped across the back of it, and galloped off down the hill.

Thor turned and faced the Legion members.

"I have to find Gwen," he said grimly. "Her blood is on my head. I cannot wait another minute. If there's any chance she's alive, every moment counts. I don't expect any of you to come with me. I will be up against the entire Nevarun army, and will be vastly outnumbered."

Reece stepped forward, and clutched the hilt of his sword.

"Just the kind of odds I like," he said.

"And I," Elden added.

"And I," O'Connor chimed in.

"And we," chimed in the twins.

"We would never leave you to face an army alone," Reece said. "Not after all we've been through. After all, Gwen is my sister too. And one day she will be your wife."

"Your blood is our blood," Elden added.

Thor nodded back, understanding and overwhelmed with gratitude. He would have done the same for any of them.

"Are you sure this is a chance you wish to take?" Thor asked. "This is my battle. I do not want to drag you into it."

"If you ever think we would let you go alone," Reece said, "you're crazy. So let's stop wasting time and bring back my sister."

Thor looked at the faces of his Legion brothers, saw the determination. In his time of great despair, he had never been so appreciative.

As one, they all mounted the horses; Thor kicked his into a gallop, racing through the field of flowers, down towards the distant road that led farther and farther away from King's Court. As he went, Thor unconsciously checked all of his weapons at his waist, the ones strapped to his back, on his saddle, all along his horse. He was fully armed. That was good. Where he was going, he would need every single one of them. It was a suicide mission.

And if he had to die this way, trying to save Gwen's life, then so be it.

*

Thor rode harder than he ever had, his Legion brothers at his side, charging farther and farther south, heading towards the distant province of the Nevaruns. He had followed the tracks left by the hordes of warriors who had trampled the fields of flowers, leading them back onto the main road leaving King's Court. It appeared from the markings that they had come for Gwen with a band of at least a hundred warriors, by the width and breadth of the crushed grass, the broken branches, the horse prints left in the dirt. It was clear the direction they were heading, and the markings still looked fresh, giving Thor hope. Maybe he could catch her in time.

As Thor continued to ride, kicking his horse yet again, he prayed he could catch them before they entered their fortified city. They had to overcome them on the road if there was to be any hope. He hoped that the group of invaders would slow at some point, giving Thor a chance to catch up. He assumed that they must; after all, once they were far from King's Court, what could this army of a hundred Nevaruns, fierce, savage warriors, have to fear from anyone? They would probably slow to a trot, or even a walk, and take their time heading back to their province with impunity. The thought of Gwen being among them burned Thor alive; it was too much to bear. He hated Gareth with a passion unlike he'd ever felt, and vowed to take revenge.

Thor knew that Gwendolyn was strong, fierce and proud. He saw the damage she had done back in the battlefield, with Steffen, and he had been impressed, though not surprised. He prayed that somehow she could draw on that strength to stay calm as they took her away, to have faith that Thor would come get her. He assumed they wanted her alive, as a trophy wife, to rub it into the face of the MacGils for all time.

Thor was determined to change that.

They charged and charged, the second sun nearly setting, Thor and his men out of breath, their horses out of breath, charging harder and longer than he ever had in his life—and finally, they reached a plateau, high up on a hill, from which they were afforded a commanding view of the countryside. Thor saw spread out beneath them the vast array of the southern provinces of the Ring, rolling hills and valleys against an awesome fall sky, clouds streaking every color, trees of every color swaying. And there, on the horizon, he spotted the huge entourage of Nevaruns, riding south, cutting through the fields. Thor was encouraged to see that they had slowed their pace, and were now moving along at a trot.

For the first time, he knew they could catch them.

Thor kicked and screamed at his horse, and the others did too, and as one, they all charged down the hill, keeping the Nevaruns in sight as they followed their trail. Thor rode faster than he ever had, down rolling hills, over dirt roads, across meadows, and through a winding forest. They got closer and closer, the Nevaruns just a few hundred yards away.

As they got within bow and arrow range, Thor caught his first sight of Gwendolyn, just for a brief moment and was immensely relieved to see she was alive. She rode on the back of their leader's horse, her wrists bound, her head down in shame, as he rode triumphantly in front of her, an arrogant smile on his face. They rode at the head of the contingent, several feet in front of everyone else, as the man led his victorious army home.

Thor could not help but notice that this army had left a trail of devastation in its path, pillaging small villages, from which smoke rose up on the horizon. Technically, these Nevaruns owed allegiance to the MacGils, as they were on the MacGil side of the Highlands; Thor felt certain that they would have never acted with such impunity under her father's reign. But they were separatists, always hard to control, and now that Gareth was king—and had invited them to take away his sister— clearly, they did as they wished. They were never really loyal to the MacGils or the McClouds. They appeared to be loyal to anyone they did not feel like killing at the moment.

As they neared, still undetected, Thor realized that they needed to formulate a plan. After all, there were only nine Legion members, while there looked to be at least a hundred Nevaruns. Not only that, but the Nevaruns were huge, fierce warriors, half breeds, who lived for war, and lived for killing. Thor recalled Kolk's stories of gaining his scars by their hand.

They could not face them head-on. Despite whatever erratic powers Thor might have, it would still be a losing battle. Thor knew it. His powers were not developed enough, and he could not rely on them. And if they gave way, it would be a slaughter. He had to come up with a strategy.

As they rode and rode, he wracked his brain, thinking of the best way to attack these men.

Thor surveyed the surrounding landscape, and he had an idea. He could see that around the bend, if they followed this road, the army would pass through a narrow strip, between two cliffs. The strip was a good hundred feet long, and for those hundred feet, the army would be vulnerable.

Thor looked up, to the top of the cliffs, and saw boulders perched at its edge. He had an idea.

"Conval, Conven!" he yelled out.

They rode up beside him.

"Do you see the top of those cliffs? I need you each to ride up to either side of them, and when I give a sign, release those boulders. It will crush the men below. Meanwhile, the rest of us will charge down below and attack whoever survives of the group. GO!" he commanded.

Conval and Conven split off from the group, and they charged up the grassy slopes leading to the top of the cliffs. Thor led the remaining men around the other side, taking the long way around so as not to be detected, and hoping to surprise the Nevaruns when they came out the other side. They took a path through the woods, circling all the way around, and he stopped at the edge of the tree line, all his men stopping with him, and waited.

Thor watched Conval and Conven take position at the cliff top, hundreds of feet above the Nevaruns, who suspected nothing. Thor sat there on his horse, waiting, watching, trying to be patient. He needed the boulders to do as much damage as possible, and needed to wait until the Nevaruns entered deeper into the chasm. He had to get as many of them as he could in one shot. And he also had to make sure that Gwen was first safe out the other side.

His horse prancing, Thor watched the opposite end of the chasm carefully, waiting for the first sign of Gwen's exit, his heart pounding. He had to see Gwen's face before he gave the signal.

Finally, after what felt like forever, the leader walked out on his horse, slowly, Gwen on it behind them—and Thor gave the signal.

Thor charged out of the woods, charging right for them, raising up a great battle cry, all his brothers charging with him. At the same time, Conval and Conven began to furiously push the boulders over the edge.

A great rumbling followed, as boulder after boulder went tumbling down, hundreds of feet, landing with a mighty crash into the chasm. There arose the cries and screams of dozens of men, as the boulders came raining down like hail, causing one great boom after the next, and the ground shook with the impact.

The Nevaruns broke out into chaos. Those that survived, narrowly dodging the boulders, burst out of the chasm, racing forward, close behind their leader and Gwen. Thor was hoping only a few would survive—but more of them escaped than he would have liked. There seem to be about thirty still alive, charging towards them, like ants, out of the chasm, and rushing to meet Thor's group of seven. He was badly outnumbered. But he had no choice now but for a head-on confrontation. At least he had killed dozens of them; he would rather face thirty of them than a hundred.

A battle horn erupted from the Nevaruns and these fierce warriors barreled down on Thor.

Thor heard the whizzing of an arrow, and glanced over to see O'Connor firing three arrows as he rode. Thor watched them sail and was impressed by his friend's aim, the three arrows finding their targets with deadly precision, three Nevaruns falling from their horses. Inspired, Thor raised his sling and hurled it, careful not to hit Gwen or their leader, and with his perfect aim, took out two soldiers himself, hitting each in the side of the head and knocking them off their horses.

Elden followed suit and threw his throwing hammer, and Reece threw his throwing axe, and they took out two more soldiers. The numbers of Nevaruns quickly shrank as they all braced for impact, Thor and his men now outnumbered only three to one.

Those were still tough odds, especially with warriors like the Nevaruns, who had devoted their entire lives to combat. None of them seemed afraid, and none of them even had a moment's hesitation as they charged for Thor and his men, wielding tridents and axes and halberds as if they had been wielding them since birth. They let out a fierce battle cry themselves, and moments later, the two groups met in the middle in an ear-shattering clash of arms.

The fighting was fierce. Their leader singled out Thor and charged him directly, wielding a two-handed battle axe with a single hand and bringing it down right for Thor's head. Thor had to be careful in how he defended himself, given that Gwen rode on the same horse. The leader, of course, knew that, and he smiled, reveling in it. Thor was compromised.

Thor raised the sword Kolk had given him, and blocked the blow at the last moment. It was one of the fiercest blows Thor had ever received, and he could feel the warrior's strength reverberating through the handle. There was a great clang of metal, Thor's arms shook, and he closed his eyes as he held his new sword, made of a material he did not know, praying that it did not split in two.

He was relieved that it did: it stopped the axe but inches from his head.

Normally Thor would have swung around and slashed back—but with Gwen on the back of his horse, he could not risk it. He was forced to just keep riding, past him, and as he did he caught a quick glimpse of Gwen's eyes, wide with fear, as she sat there with her hands bound behind her.

"THOR!" she screamed out, frantic.

But there was no time for Thor to look back. As he charged into the group, two more warriors came at him, one swinging a war hammer sideways, right for his ribs. Thor leaned back at the last second, and the hammer just missed, saving him from crushed ribs; he then raised his sword and brought it down on the man's extended arm, chopping it off, the arm and hammer falling down to the ground as the man shrieked.

The other soldier swung his axe sideways for Thor's head, and Thor ducked at the last moment as it went whizzing by. He then swung around with his sword and chopped off the soldier's head; it bounced off and rolled to the ground, as the man's body continued to ride, headless, for several more feet, until it finally slumped over and fell to the ground.

Thor had no time to rest on his heels: he was attacked in quick succession by Nevaruns on all sides, and with all manner of weaponry. He felt a hard blow on his shoulder, resonating against his armor, and he realized he had been hit by a mace, the clang ringing in his ears; luckily his armor had blocked it from piercing his skin, but the pain from the deep bruise shot up and down his arm.

Another soldier charged Thor from the side, raised his shield, and used it as a battering ram, something Thor did not expect; he smashed Thor hard in the side of the head, and sent him tumbling end over end off his horse, landing hard on the ground with a clang of metal.

Thor tumbled on the ground, winded, as horses stampeded all around him, battle cries rising up in all directions. As he rolled, he looked over and saw Reece, slashing and parrying with two soldiers, holding his own, but badly outnumbered; he saw O'Connor reach up with his bow to take a shot, but watched as a Nevarun knocked the bow from his hand with a trident before he could release. He saw Elden wield his war hammer with two hands and knock a Nevarun off his horse—only to see another Nevarun jab Elden from behind with a javelin, knocking him off his horse and down to the ground face first.

Thor saw the three other Legion members they had ridden with, boys he did not know well, and watched them fight gloriously. One of them managed to stab a Nevarun in the throat, killing him—but in the same moment, he was pierced through the chest with a spear. He cried out, and Thor felt his pain as he slumped off his horse, heading to the ground, dead.

The other legion member stabbed a Nevarun with his spear in the stomach, injuring him—but he was attacked from behind by two others, one of whom cut off the legs of his horse, while the other smashed his head with a hammer, killing him instantly.

The final Legion member leapt off his horse in a brave show of glory and landed mid-air on two Nevaruns, tackling them down to the ground before they could swing at him. He drew his dagger and stabbed one in the throat, then slashed the other. But at the same moment, he himself was pierced through the back with a trident, and he let out a great cry, as he collapsed to the ground, dead.

That left just Thor, Reece, O'Connor and Elden, the four of them against the two dozen or so Nevaruns who still remained. They had done much damage, had dwindled the Nevaruns numbers greatly, but they were still badly outnumbered, and at this pace, their chances did not look good.

Thor, on his knees, reached up to block a great sword blow from a Nevarun, coming down for his head, and as he did, he looked up into the sunset sky and saw, in the distance, Conven and Conval, charging down the mountain, coming to reinforce them. The Nevaruns didn't expect them, and as they charged for the battle, Conven and Conval each raised a spear and hurled it, killing two more men from behind. They continued to charge, raising two more spears and hurling them, killing two more Nevaruns from behind, before the group caught wind of their advance.

Now the odds had changed. Now it was six of the Legion against twenty Nevaruns, and Thor felt a renewed sense of hope.

Thor finally managed to roll out of the way of the attacker bearing down on him, then swung around and killed him. He rolled again, took out a short spear, and hurled it at another attacker who galloped towards him, piercing his throat before the attacker could unleash his trident. The man, wounded, threw his trident at Thor, but off-balance, and the weapon sailed through the air and missed him by an inch, plunging into the ground beside him.

Another Nevarun came for Thor, this one wielding a three-headed flail with a long chain. Thor ducked, and the three spiked, iron balls whizzed by his ear, grazing his helmet and just missing him. As the man past, Thor loaded his sling and hurled a rock, hitting the attacker on the back of his head and sending him from his horse, dropping the flail.

Thor dove to the ground as a horse rode by, just missing being trampled, and grabbed the flail lying on the ground, with its long chain, then rolled around, got to his feet, and swung it at his two oncoming attackers. He connected with them both, knocking them both off the horses, landing on the ground with a clang of metal. He swung it again, raising it high above his head, and before each could get up, knocked them back down to the ground.

Thor heard a screech overhead and looked up to see his old friend, Estopheles; as a soldier charged Thor from behind, javelin raised high, Estopheles dove down and bit the man's wrist right before he released it. The soldier screamed out, dropping his javelin and falling from his horse with a clang of metal; Thor grabbed the javelin, spun around, and plunged it into the man's chest.

But Thor suddenly felt the wind knocked out of him as he was tackled hard from behind, driven down, face-first, into the ground. A warrior landed on top of him, with a full plate of armor, crushing him; Thor spun, wrestling with the man and reaching up and grabbing his wrist, right before he sliced Thor's throat with a dagger. Thor held his wrist at bay, arm shaking, then finally lifted his head and head-butted the man, breaking his nose.

The soldier cried out, and Thor threw him off of him. As he threw him, the man landed in the path of another horse, and was trampled instantly to death.

Thor was beyond exhausted, struggling to catch his breath, while all around him his six brothers were fighting for the lives; he could see they were all starting to lose the battle. O'Connor cried out as a Nevarun managed to slice the side of his bicep, blood squirting out; Elden received a mighty mace blow on his shoulder, sending him stumbling back onto the ground; Reece ducked the blow of a sword, but Thor could see his reflexes were not as quick as they should have been, and he almost lost his life. Thor knew he had to do something quickly, or else his brothers would all die.

Thor felt a heat, a power rising up within him, and he prayed to God that this time he could control it. Just enough to get them all out of this, to get Gwen to safety.

Please God, help me through this. Help me win this battle.

Two more soldiers charged for Thor, and one of them reached back and threw a throwing knife right at him. Thor saw it tumbling end over end through the air, saw it coming, too-fast, right for him. He had no time to react. He stood there, defenseless, and raised his palm, trying to summon his power to stop it.

The blade froze in the air a second before it reached him, and then dropped harmlessly to the ground.

Thor raised his other palm, feeling a power surge through him greater than he had ever felt, and knew that this time something was different. Something was shifting within him, and he felt more powerful than ever.

Thor summoned the earth to obey him. He felt the cracks on the ground, felt the contour of the boulders, and then moved his hands in both directions, trying to command the earth to open up.

There came a great rumbling noise and the ground began to tremble, then to shake, and a chasm began to open up in the earth. The earth began to split in two, separating, opening several feet, the gap becoming wider and wider. Several soldiers, charging for him, dropped into the chasm, shrieking as they and their horses plunged down to the depths. Another Nevarun, fighting with Elden, stumbled backwards, falling into the chasm right before he dealt Elden a fatal blow.

Thor looked over to see a Nevarun raise a double-handed axe high overhead and bring it down for O'Connor, who lay there, prone. He was about to kill him. Thor swung his palm in his direction, and directed a ball of energy at him. The soldier went flying, backwards, off his feet, dropping his axe and falling into the chasm, sparing O'Connor. Thor spun and directed his palm towards another soldier who was lunging his sword for Reece's back, and he managed to stop the man's arm in mid-air, allowing Reece enough time to spin and strike the man with his sword.

Thor spun again and again, stopping all the Nevaruns from attacking his friends, sparing each of their lives and allowing each of them to prevail, and kill their attackers. The battlefield began to quickly shift, with only a handful of Nevaruns remaining.

Thor was beginning to feel optimistic when suddenly he felt a great blow on his back, like that of a hammer, smashing into his armor, and knocking him down to the ground.

He hit the ground hard and rolled to his feet to see their leader, facing him, wielding a two-handed war hammer in just one hand. In his other he held a long chain, dangling from his palm, which he swung overhead. He wore a malicious smile. Behind him, Thor could see Gwen, tied to his horse, forced to watch, helpless, eyes opened wide in panic and desperation.

"You thought you could steal my girl from me," the man growled down to Thor. He swung the chain around his head, and Thor raised a palm to use his energy to stop it.

But for some reason, his magic would not work against this man. As Thor jumped to his feet, the chain continued to swing through the air, wrapping around Thor's ankles again and again; the warrior yanked it, and Thor fell flat his back, his feet tied together, helpless on the ground. Thor did not know what power this man wielded, but it was intense, unlike any warrior he had ever fought.

While Thor lay there, helpless on his back, the warrior stepped forward, raised his hammer high, and brought it down right for Thor's face.

Thor rolled out of the way at the last second, and the hammer sank deep into the earth.

Thor sat up, feet still bound, and reached over to draw the sword on his belt.

But the warrior backhanded him before he could draw, knocking him back down to the ground.

Thor lay there, his head ringing, defenseless on the ground as the man stood over him, extracting his hammer from the earth, and raising it high again. He was prepared to bring it down right on Thor's face. Thor lay there helpless, and there was nothing he could do.

"Say good night, young one," the warrior said, smiling wide.

Suddenly the hammer froze in mid-air, as the man's eyes open widened.

Thor at first was confused; then he saw an arrow pierce the man's throat, protruding out the front.

The warrior stood in place, frozen, holding the hammer high as blood gurgled from his mouth, dripping down his chest.

Then he dropped the hammer, landing on his own head, and collapsed onto the earth, right beside Thor, dead.

Thor looked up to see Gwendolyn. She sat there on the horse, holding a bow and arrow, having just shot the man. She had somehow managed to sever the cords that bound her wrists, and her hands trembled as she looked down at Thor.

Thor loved her more in that moment than he could ever say. He sat up, unwrapped the chains at his feet, and ran over to Gwen, jumping up, mounting the horse, feeling her arms wrap around him, her head lean into his back, and feeling overwhelmed with relief. She was safe. And they were together again.

Thor surveyed the battlefield and saw three Nevaruns left. One was being finished off by Elden, the other by O'Connor, and the final one fought hand-to-hand with Reece. As he watched, Reece suddenly slipped and the warrior prepared to bring his sword down.

Thor galloped over to him, and before the soldier could chop off Reece's his head, Thor pulled a short spear from the horse's saddle and hurled it. It pierced the man's back, came out the other side, and he collapsed to his knees, dead.

Thor sat there on the horse, with Gwen, and looked around. It was a field of carnage, filled with the corpses of thirty Nevaruns, demarcated by the chasm of the open earth. Pools of blood were everywhere. Three were only five Legion members left alive, in addition to Thor: Reece, O'Connor, Elden and the twins. They were all wounded, exhausted, breathing hard. But they were all victorious.

Thor raised a single sword high in the air, and the thrill of victory rushed through his veins.

"LEGION FOREVER!" he yelled out.

The others turned and raised their swords in response.

"LEGION   FOREVER!"

CHAPTER THIRTY THREE

Andronicus rode his horse in a rage, leading his vast army along the edge of the Canyon, heading north, marching for the Eastern Crossing of the Ring. As he marched, more and more Empire troops filled in behind him, arriving in droves from his fleets of boats landing on the shores. Andronicus had been deeply embarrassed by that McCloud prisoner who had duped him, who had led him to believe that he knew the way to breach the Canyon. It had been years since Andronicus had been duped by anyone, and he realized that his overzealousness to cross had allowed him to be weak, to be fooled. His body still shook with rage at the slight, even though he had already killed the man. He wished he could find a way to track down the man's family, and kill them, too.

As Andronicus rode, he was more determined than ever to breach the Canyon somehow, to wreak havoc on the Ring, to make all these humans suffer. Yet without being able to cross, there was little he could do. He knew that it was a futile mission at this point, that all of this mobilization had been for nothing. Yet still, he hated the idea of just turning back and leaving this place, of going back home in disgrace. Especially now that all of his men were here, and more and more were arriving with each moment.

He figured he could at least work his way up to the main McCloud crossing, the bridge guarded by all those McCloud soldiers, and see if perhaps he could goad any of them to walk out from the safety of the Canyon, if any of them were that stupid. Maybe he could torture one or two of them. Maybe even kill some more. That might at least appease his mood.

Andronicus could also use the opportunity to test the Canyon again, just in case there was a breach somewhere. He could throw some of his own soldiers over the edge, and see if they died. Who knows? Maybe, just maybe, he could find a chink in the armor somewhere.

Andronicus rode slowly, the sound of thousands of boots marching behind him in unison, as he proceeded along the edge of the Canyon. Finally, they turned a bend, and he saw his objective before him: there was the Eastern Crossing of the Canyon, hundreds of McCloud soldiers lined up alongside the bridge, all the way into the

McCloud side. What Andronicus would give to be on that side of the Ring. He could taste it from here.

Andronicus saw the McCloud troops tense up as his army approached the main entry to the bridge. He led the way, all the way up to the very edge of the Canyon, standing but feet away.

A tense silence hung over the two armies. The McCloud soldiers, wisely, stayed on the bridge, on their side of the energy force, not daring to leave the protection of the Canyon.

Andronicus nodded towards one of his commanders, and the commander shoved forward several soldiers, who charged for the McCloud men, swords drawn. The ten unlucky soldiers charged right for the bridge—but the second they crossed the line, onto the bridge, entering the mystical air of the Canyon, all ten of them were eviscerated, burned alive, and fell, nothing but ashes, down at the feet of the McCloud soldiers.

Andronicus frowned. Nothing had changed. There was still no way in.

"Come out here, to this side of the Canyon, and face us in battle like real men!" Andronicus boomed, his voice echoing throughout the Canyon, as the hundreds of McCloud men stood at attention on the bridge, all in perfect discipline, none of them daring to move. They were too smart for that.

The two armies stood in a silent standoff. Andronicus was feeling desperate.

"Let me across this bridge," Andronicus boomed out, trying another tactic, "and I will give you all riches beyond what you could ever dream. You will become Empire soldiers. You will have ten times the gold. Each one of you will become generals in my army. Anything you wish for will be yours."

Once again his proclamation was met with nothing but tense silence, as the soldiers all stood in perfect attention, none of them moving. There was nothing but eerie silence, and the howling of the wind. The mist of the Canyon blew over them in waves, enveloping them, coming and going as they stared out.

Andronicus was stumped. He suddenly snatched a bow and arrow from one of his soldier's hands, pulled back and fired it at the closest McCloud soldier.

But the second the arrow hit the invisible shield of the Canyon, it disintegrated.

Andronicus grabbed a dagger from his belt, and threw it.

That disintegrated, too.

He leaned back and roared, in a rage, not knowing how to cross. It was the one spot left in the world that stumped him, the one thing left he could not have.

Andronicus had no choice. He had to turn back home. He had been duped, and he had to admit it. He would have to find another way, another time, to cross the Canyon, to subdue the Ring. The longer he waited here, the more time he wasted.

But before he left, Andronicus had to let his bad mood out on someone. So before he turned to leave, he grabbed one of his common soldiers, raised him up high above his head with two hands, then ran for the Canyon, and threw him over the edge. As his body crossed the edge of the Canyon, Andronicus expected the man to disintegrate, to crumble into ashes, as the others.

But Andronicus was shocked as he watched this man's body fly through the air, over the rim of the Canyon, perfectly intact, then plunge down below, screaming and flailing all the way down to the bottom, to his death.

Andronicus stood there, blinking several times, not understanding what had happened. It was as if the shield had suddenly been turned off.

Andronicus grabbed another soldier and shoved him, this time right down the center, towards the bridge. The man was terrified, seeing what had happened to his peers, but Andronicus jabbed him in the back of his neck with a spear, and the man ran obediently, bracing himself with his hands before his face as he ran towards the bridge, expecting to die.

But this time, something different happened: the soldier kept running, right onto the bridge, not disintegrating as the others had. He stood there, in the midst of the McCloud soldiers, alive.

The McCloud soldiers all seemed shocked, too. They jumped into action and attacked the lone soldier, killing him on the spot.

They then turned and looked at the Empire army with a whole new respect—and fear. No longer was there a barrier between them. Something had happened.

The hundreds of McCloud soldiers slowly stepped backwards, began to retreat, looking nervous, not understanding what was happening.

Andronicus could not understand it either. The shield was down. It was really down. What had happened?

He would not wait to find out.

"CHARGE!" he screamed.

Thousands of his men rushed forward, onto the bridge, stampeding it, slaughtering the McCloud men as they went. The remaining McCloud soldiers turned and ran.

Andronicus watched, waiting to see what would happen, if the shield would somehow come back up.

But to his amazement, his men were fine. They kept charging, all the way across the bridge, and onto the McCloud side of the Ring. They continued charging, standing firmly on McCloud soil.

Safe.

The shield was down.

Andronicus smiled, happier than he'd ever been in his life. He drew his sword, and charged with them. He blended with the stampede, and he killed some of his own men on the way across the bridge, just for fun. He felt like a little boy again.

In moments he landed himself on the McCloud side of the Ring, feeling the soil of the Ring beneath him for the very first time. It was a moment he had dreamed of his entire life. He could not believe it.

He was *here*.

Andronicus knelt down and felt the soil with his palms, as all his men rushed past him, then leaned over and kissed the earth.

He looked up and saw, on the horizon, the McCloud city.

He grinned, wider than he ever had in his life.

It was time to pay McCloud a visit.

CHAPTER THIRTY FOUR

As Thor rode back for King's Court, Gwen on the horse behind him, Reece, O'Connor, Elden and the twins riding alongside them, he felt weary but overflowing with gratitude. The second sun was setting and they all rode at a comfortable trot into the magnificent sky. Thor felt beyond weary, every muscle in his body hurting, as if he had just been through a war.

But having Gwen with him, feeling her hands clutch his chest, her cheek resting against his back, took all of his weariness away. Having her with him made him feel that all was right in the world. He was beyond grateful that she was alive, that she had not been injured, that the Nevaruns had never had a chance to have his way with her. He was grateful that they had survived the encounter, and that he had been able to save her—and that she had saved his life. He felt as if all of his prayers had been answered.

As they rode back towards King's court, Thor felt triumphant, but also the sting of tragedy, as he thought of their three Legion brothers who had died in battle, whose corpses they carried home now, slung over the back of their horses. And while on the one hand he felt like a returning hero, he also felt a sense of apprehension, as he did not know what they were returning to. After all, it was Gareth, the still lawful king, who had arranged for Gwen to be taken away—and it was to Gareth's court that they were returning. Gareth was increasingly unhinged, that much was clear, and now that there was a full-fledged rift between The Silver and these new men Gareth had brought in, the tension had never run so high. It felt as if King's Court was on the verge of a civil war, and that all that was needed was a spark. And as Thor charged back towards the place with Gwendolyn, in defiance of Gareth's orders, he could not help but feel as if maybe he carried that spark.

Thor braced himself. He was too weary for another battle now. But that might be just what he was walking into.

Thor knew that Gwendolyn and the others had to either find a way to depose Gareth, or that they all had to flee King's Court for good and find a new home, setup a new court elsewhere. It was not safe here anymore.

As they neared King's Court, Thor knew that the first place they had to go was the Hall of Arms, to meet up with the Legion and see whichever soldiers were currently here. He knew that many of them, like Kendrick, were still stationed in the field, rebuilding and refortifying the Ring. But several fine warriors, including Kolk and Brom, were still stationed here—and Godfrey was here, too, their best hope at finding the proof they needed to indict Gareth.

As Thor and his men trotted through the open plaza of King's Court, crowds of onlookers gathered, watching the ragtag group in wonder, and Thor could feel the stares, feel word already beginning to spread. He knew it was only a matter of time until word of their arrival reached Gareth and his men, and he turned sharply towards the hall and doubled his pace. He needed to rendezvous with them before anything happened.

Thor and the others entered the plaza before the Hall of Arms, and several members of the Legion and The Silver were milling around outside of it and looked up at them in surprise as the group rode in on their horses, covered in blood, wounded from the battle. One of the Legion members called out, and soon many more came rushing over, as Thor and the others dismounted.

Thor heard a whining, and his heart leapt as he looked down and saw Krohn, being led towards him by Steffen. He knelt down, elated to see him well, and hugged Krohn as he leapt into his arms, limping, looking weak, but very much alive. Gwen knelt down and hugged Krohn, too.

"Illepra took good care of him," Steffen said, smiling.

Krohn licked Thor and Gwen all over, and they kissed him back.

The doors flew open and several members of The Silver came pouring outside, milling excitedly around Thor, Gwen and the others; they were swept up in the crowd and ushered inside the hall, the doors closed quickly behind them.

As Thor entered the Hall he could feel hundreds of eyes on him. The Hall was packed, overflowing with Silver and Legion members, all of whom came hurrying over to the group. At their head was Kolk and Brom, along with Atme and several other famed warriors whom Thor recognized.

Kolk, then Brom, embraced Thor, then the others, and Thor could see the relief in their faces.

"You have returned," Kolk said. "We heard, too late, of Gwen's capture, of your expedition. You should have come to us first. We would have joined you."

"There hadn't been time," Thor said.

"Gwendolyn!" came a voice.

Godfrey rushed over and embraced her, relief on his face.

"You're alive," he said, shocked.

All the soldiers looked at Thor and the surviving Legion members with a new respect, with a look of awe. Thor felt proud. Surrounded by these men, he felt as if he could finally take a deep breath and let down his guard.

"Not all of us made it back," Thor said, his voice growing deeper, more authoritative. "Three of our Legion members died, I'm sorry to say. There were nine of us."

"Against a hundred Nevaruns," Reece added.

"And where are these hundred warriors now?" Brom asked, stepping forward, putting a hand on his sword's hilt. "Are they pursuing you?"

Thor shook his head gravely.

"They are all dead, my lord," he said gravely.

Brom's eyes opened wide with a new look of respect, looking them all up and down.

"Are you saying that the six of you killed a hundred of the Ring's fiercest warriors?" Brom asked.

"There had been nine of us, my lord," Thor corrected. "Three have died. But yes."

Kolk stepped forward and laid an approving hand on Thor's shoulder.

"You have done the Legion proud," he said.

Thor cleared his throat.

"I feared you would be upset," Thor said. "We have rescued the King's daughter, but we have broken the King's Law to do so, as she was given legally. We may have also sparked a war with Gareth. I'm sure he will not let this lie."

"Then let him try!" Brom yelled. "We fear no one. And no, we are not upset. We are proud of your actions. Anyone coming here to take away the King's daughter against her will deserves death."

"AYE!" screamed the room.

"Even if it was a lawful edict of the King?" Reece asked.

"What King?" Kolk called out.

"AYE!" echoed the room.

"And I have proof of Gareth's treachery!" Godfrey called out excitedly.

The room turned to him, riveted.

"There is a boy who is willing to be witness to the crime. He has agreed to testify against Gareth, for his attempted assassination of me."

The room gasped, breaking out into an excited murmur.

"The boy is being kept safely in the castle. I was awaiting the return of the warriors—and now that you are all here, and we are ready, we can all go to the Council together, and bring the boy and present the evidence. With a witness, the Council will have no choice but to legally depose Gareth."

"And if they do not?" Kolk asked.

"If the council will not take action," Brom said, "then it is clear that we, The Silver, The Legion, the King's men, no longer have a place here at King's Court. If so then we shall all leave this place and set up a new court elsewhere!"

"AYE!" echoed the room.

"My lady," Brom said, turning to Gwen, "we are prepared to fight to the death for you, just as we had for your father, to instill you as ruler. When the Council sees our proof, we will lawfully depose Gareth. And then we shall instate you as Queen. I ask you again: is this an honor which you will accept?"

Gwen looked to the floor, then looked up.

"It is time to end my brother Gareth's rule," she said. "And if my being queen is what it takes, then so be it."

The room erupted into a cheer.

"And if we are forced to leave this place," Kolk said, "then Gwendolyn, you shall be our ruler, in absentia. We will set up our own King's Court elsewhere."

"AYE!" echoed the room.

"We can venture to Silesia!" boomed a voice. They all turned to see Srog standing there, in the distinctive red armor of the West. "You can all come to my city. It is fortified with a thousand men, and we can set up a new King's Court there! Gwen can rule there, until Gareth falls and we return!"

"AYE!" echoed the room.

"Let us hope that this boy is a faithful witness," Kolk said, turning to Godfrey, "and that we need not go anywhere. Godfrey, are you sure he is true?"

Godfrey nodded back.

"He awaits us even now. Time is precious. Let us go and end Gareth's reign once and for all!"

"AYE!" screamed the room of men.

As one they all turned, headed out the hall, and marched for Gareth's castle. Thor felt the excitement and anticipation in the air like a palpable thing, and he knew that in just moments things would never be the same at King's Court again.

CHAPTER THIRTY FIVE

Thor marched with the large group of soldiers, Gwendolyn at his side, Godfrey leading the way with the young boy in tow, as the huge group of men wound their way through King's Castle, down corridor after corridor, their footsteps echoing as they marched towards the Council room. Thor could feel the momentousness of the day, the great anticipation that hung in the air as they neared the Council room. Finally, they had what they needed: Godfrey had a witness, the Council was in session, and with a witness, lawfully, the Council had to depose Gareth. Once they did, his reign would be over once and for all, Gwendolyn could be installed as ruler, and life could go back to how it had been at King's Court.

But then again, knowing Gareth, Thor also felt a sense of dread, a pit in his stomach, knowing he seemed to have a way out of almost everything, how he was always one step ahead of everybody. Thor looked around, at all the formidable warriors around him, and wondered what would be if somehow Gareth found a way out of this. Would there be a full-fledged civil war? Would they all leave King's Court, never to return again?

Thor tried not to think of these things as they turned down the final corridor and marched, dozens of them, all armed, for the huge doors of the council hall. The royal guards outside the door stiffened, eyes opening wide in fear at the site of the small army.

"Open these doors at once!" Brom commanded.

The guards glanced at each other, hesitating for just a moment, then must have realized they had no choice. They reached over, yanked open the huge doors, and stepped aside.

Thor marched with the others into the huge council hall, their boot steps echoing off the vaulted ceilings. They all filled the room. Heads turned, and the council stopped.

Before them were dozens of council members, seated at the wide, semicircular table, all facing Gareth, who sat up on his platform, on his throne, clutching its arms and looking down on the whole room. There was a frenzied look in his eyes, and he seemed more desperate than ever.

Behind Gareth stood dozens of armed soldiers, Kultin's men, his private fighting force, all with hands on their swords, as if waiting for any calamity that might happen. Brutes, all of them.

The councilmembers stood and turned as the group entered, fear on their faces.

"What is the meaning of this?" Aberthol asked, standing, looking over the faces. "Gwendolyn," he added, "you of all people know it is against the law to interrupt a Council meeting."

"Forgive me," she replied. "But we bring news worthy of interrupting these proceedings. In fact, we bring news that will change the fate of the Ring forever."

Gwendolyn stared coldly up at her brother, and he looked down at her with a cool hatred. He seemed startled to see her alive; he had probably assumed she would be far from here by now, in the hands of the Nevaruns. Gareth's face had sunk deep into his cheekbones these last days, and he seemed more insane than ever.

Godfrey stepped forward.

"I have with me here a young boy," Godfrey called out, "who will stand as witness to my brother Gareth's treachery. Gareth hired a man to assassinate me—I, a member of the royal family!"

The room broke out into an outraged murmur.

"This boy here was witness. He will proclaim once and for all what Gareth has done, and you, the Council, will have to take lawful action, and depose our King!"

The murmur in the room continued, as numerous councilmen and lords looked at each other. Gareth just continued to stare down coldly at it all, expressionless.

Aberthol turned and looked towards Gareth.

"Are these charges true, my Lord?" he asked slowly.

Gareth smiled down at the room.

"Of course they are not," he said. "Godfrey is a scheming son who has always wanted his father's throne. He would make up any charges against me he could to depose me."

"I do not seek the throne," Godfrey countered. "I have no wish to rule. Gwendolyn will be the next ruler."

Gareth snorted down.

"No she will not," he said "I am ruler. By law. And no words from a boy will change anything."

"My Lord," Aberthol interjected, "if this boy is a true witness to an assassination attempt, the law mandates us to hear his testimony and to rule as a Council."

A thick silence hung in the air, as Gareth scowled back, then finally, shrugged.

"If you want to hear the boy, then hear him," he said nonchalantly. "Send him forward."

The boy looked up at Godfrey, and Godfrey nodded back down to him, then gently nudged him. The boy tentatively stepped forward, towards the center of the room, into a shaft of light that shone down from the ceiling. He seemed scared, as he looked up, looking from Aberthol to Gareth.

"Tell us truly boy," Aberthol said. "What did you witness?"

The boy stood there, hesitating to speak. Then finally, after several long seconds, he called out.

"I saw nothing!"

The room erupted into a shocked gasp.

"What do you mean, boy?" Godfrey yelled down, shocked, outraged. "Tell them what you told me! Tell them what you saw! Do not be afraid. Be honest now!"

The boy looked again at Gareth, who seemed to nod back to him.

"I saw nothing!" the boy yelled out again. "I have nothing to say!"

Godfrey examined the boy with a confused expression, while Gareth smiled, satisfied.

"As you were saying, my beloved brother?" Gareth asked.

Godfrey frowned back at Gareth

"You've gotten to the boy somehow!" Godfrey yelled.

Gareth leaned back and laughed.

"You have a useless witness," Gareth said. "Your pathetic plan to oust me failed. I still sit as true and rightful and lawful King. And there is not a thing you can do about it."

"Aberthol, you must do something!" Godfrey pleaded. "It is obvious he has gotten to the witness. This boy saw what he saw. My brother tried to kill me!"

Aberthol shook his head sadly.

"I'm afraid that without evidence, the law is the law. Whatever may have happened, Gareth must remain as King without proof to the contrary."

"You are a liar!" Godfrey screamed out across the hall to Gareth, red-faced, drawing his sword as he bore down on him.

The sound of the sword being drawn echoed throughout the chamber, and as soon as it did, suddenly there came the sound of dozens of swords being drawn, as all of the fierce warriors behind Gareth jumped into action.

The Silver and Legion responded, drawing their swords, too.

There came a tense standoff in the room, rows of soldiers on both sides standing with swords drawn, facing each other. The room was thick with tension.

"The law is on my side," Gareth said slowly, deliberately. "I can have all of you imprisoned here today, every single one of you."

"You can only imprison us by the law of King's Court," Gwendolyn called out, stepping forward. "But as of today, we are no longer members of King's Court. None of us. I and this force will leave this place for good. You can sit there and rule unlawfully in our father's throne, and we will rule in own court, in absentia. And if you try to send men to take me away again, we will consider it an act of war, and I assure you, we will fight back. You have lords loyal to you. We have lords loyal to us, too. As of this day, we no longer serve you. If the Council will not depose you by rightful law, then we shall leave this place and form our own council."

"You can leave King's court if you wish," Gareth said, "but you shall now be known as heretics and traitors. You are breaking the King's law. If I ever encounter you in the field, I will kill you all. And if you ever come to King's Court again, you will all be killed."

Gwendolyn shook her head.

"You are a pathetic human being," she said. "I curse the day you became my brother. Father looks down at you in disgrace."

Gareth threw his head back and screamed with laughter.

"Father looks down at no one. He is dead, my dear. Don't you remember? Someone killed him."

Gareth screamed and screamed with laughter.

They had all had enough. They turned as one and stormed out the hall, the dozens of them marching away, down the corridor, out of this place. As they prepared to walk out the doors and never see King's Court again, they were accompanied all the way by the sound of Gareth's laugher, echoing off the ancient walls.

CHAPTER THIRTY SIX

Erec rode on the forest path, heading north, finally, after all these months, heading back to his home, back to King's Court, this time, with his new bride-to-be, Alistair. She rode on Warkfin behind him, clutching onto him, as she had been for hours as they entered the thick wood. Erec had not stopped galloping since he'd rescued her from that lord's castle, wanting to gain as much distance from the place as possible.

Erec recognized this wood: he was now on the outskirts of Savaria, hardly a day's ride away, and as he rode between the thick trees, he turned and checked back over his shoulder one more time, wanting to make sure they were not being followed. They were not. The horizon sat empty, as it had every time he'd checked that day, and for the first time, as they entered the tree cover, he felt they could relax.

He slowed the horse. Poor Alistair had been gripping his chest for so many hours, he was sure that she could use some rest. And so could he. He was beyond exhausted from the intense battle, and from the non-stop riding. He hadn't slept in days, and this seemed like a good place to rest.

Erec found a secluded spot, well-sheltered, beside a lake, protected by tall, swaying trees, and he stopped before it and dismounted and held out a hand to help Alistair down. The feel of her hand, of her soft skin, electrified him as he helped her down off the horse; she looked exhausted, but as beautiful and noble as ever. He was thrilled to be by her side after all those days of fighting for her, after all the days of being apart—and after almost losing her. It had been too close of a call. He was ecstatic that he had saved her from an awful fate, and determined that the two of them should never be apart again.

As the two of them stood there, she turned and looked up at him, the waters of the lake reflected in her soulful eyes. She looked back at him with such love and devotion, he felt his heart melt. He knew deep in his bones that he had made the right choice. There was no finer woman he could hope to be with.

"My Lord," she said, looking down to the ground softly, "I don't know how to thank you. You saved my life."

He reached down, placed a finger under her chin, leaned in, and kissed her. They kissed for a long time, and her lips were the smoothest thing he'd ever felt. She leaned in, kissing him firmly, running a hand along his cheek, as he ran a hand along hers. He reached up and brushed back her hair gently, outlining the curve of her beautiful face. He had never seen anyone so beautiful, from any corner of the kingdom, and he could hardly believe his luck to be with her.

"You have nothing to thank me for," he replied. "It is you who has saved me. You saved me from an empty life, from searching for my love."

She took his hand and led him to the mossy ground beside the lake. They sat down beside the crystal clear waters, and as the second sun began to set, she leaned into him, resting her head on his shoulder, and he reached over and draped a hand around her shoulder, holding her tight.

"I waited for you every day with bated breath," she said, "as you competed in your tournaments. When they sold me into slavery, I fought with everything I had. But they were too powerful for me. I cried and cried for days, thinking only of you."

The thought tore Erec up inside.

"I'm sorry, my lady," he said. "I should have known the innkeeper would deal with you in that way. I should have been there sooner to protect you."

She smiled up at him.

"You protect me now," she said. "That is all that matters."

"I shall protect you with everything I have, for the rest of my days," he said.

She leaned in and they kissed again, holding it for a long time.

She pulled back, and he looked into her eyes, and was entranced.

"My lady," he said, "I can see in your eyes that you are of special birth. Can't you tell me your secret?"

She turned and looked away, a sadness overcoming her face.

"I don't want to withhold anything from you, my Lord," she said. "But I made a vow, never to reveal were I am from."

"But why such a vow?" he asked. "Could the place be so terrible?"

"The place was beautiful, my Lord," she said. "More beautiful than anything I have ever seen. That is not why I left."

"Then tell me," he said, intrigued. "Tell me at least one thing about your past. Am I correct? Do you hail from royalty?"

She looked to the lake, sighed, waited a long time, then looked back at him.

"If I tell you one thing," she said, "will you vow not to ask again?"

Erec nodded back.

"I vow," he said solemnly.

She looked into his eyes, then finally, said:

"I am daughter to a king."

Erec, despite himself, was amazed at the news. He had sensed it, but to hear her say the words surprised him. Now he was infused with a burning desire to know which king she hailed from; why she had left; why she had chosen to become a maidservant; what had happened in her past; why the secrecy. He was dying to know more.

But he had vowed, and as a man of honor, he would not break his vow.

"Very well, my lady," he said. "I shall not ask you again. But know this: whatever it is that happened in your past, I am here to protect you now, and I love you more than my heart can say. You and I shall start a new life together. One that you shall be proud to speak of for the rest of your days."

She broke into a wide smile.

"I would like that," she said. "I would like to start life over again."

Alistair leaned in and kissed him, and they held it for a long time, as a light breeze caressed them.

"Every night," she said, "in my servitude, I prayed for a man like you. Someone to appear and rescue me from all of this. But I never dreamed someone as great as you would arrive. Every prayer I have ever had has been answered in you, and I shall spend the rest of my life in your devotion."

They kissed again, and as twilight rose, they lay down on the grass, kissing in each other's arms. And for the first time in as long as he could remember, Erec felt as if everything were right in the world.

*

Erec woke at the crack of dawn, sensing something was off. He looked all around, alert. He still held Alistair in his arms, as he had all night long, and could see the content smile on her face. He felt deeply relaxed having her with him. The trees were still, the lake gentle, and all he could hear was the sound of the first birds beginning to wake.

Yet still, the warrior instinct within Erec told him that something was wrong.

He jumped to his feet, threw on his chainmail, and walked over to Warkfin, who he could see was prancing just the slightest bit, his ears moving back. Warkfin sensed it, too: something was off.

As Erec stood there, he began to feel the slightest tremor in the earth, and he knew something was happening. He quickly hurried over and roused Alistair.

"What is it, my Lord?" she asked, waking with concern in her eyes.

"I do not know," he responded. "But we must move quickly."

He picked her up and mounted her on the back of the horse, then jumped up himself, mounted on the front, and kicked it.

They rode down the forest trail, to the top of a small hill, where he had an advantageous lookout over the hills below. As they reached the top he stopped, and was shocked by what he saw.

Hundreds of men in armor rode in his direction, wearing the distinctive shiny green armor of that Lord from Baluster. They had followed his trail. They were not letting it go: they wanted vengeance. This Lord was even more powerful than Erec had thought: even in death, his men would not let it go.

Erec realized in an instant that he had a war on his hands.

He dismounted, turned and looked up at Alistair.

"Listen to me carefully," he instructed, intense. "You must ride far away from here, before this army arrives. Take the path through the forest, and stay north. It will bring you to Savaria. Seek out the Duke and my old friend Brandy. They will take care of you. You will be safe there."

She sat there on the prancing horse and looked down at him with terror.

"But what of you, my Lord?" she asked.

"I must stay here and confront this army," he said.

Her eyes opened wide in panic, as she looked from Erec to the horizon and back again.

"But my Lord, you are terribly outnumbered," she said. "You cannot survive!"

He shook his head grimly.

"Whether I survive or not makes little difference," he said. "What matters is that you survive. If they kill me here, today, they may be satisfied and turn back; and if you are safe within the gates of Savaria, they will not pursue you. But if you stay here with me, you will die—or worse, be captured. If I die, I will die content knowing that you are safe."

She looked down at him, tears rolling down her cheeks.

"My Lord, please don't do this!" she pleaded. "Why can we not flee together?"

Erec shook his head.

"I swore an oath of honor," he said. "As a member of The Silver, honor is my badge. I can never run, from any foe, for any reason. I am sorry, but my honor obligates me."

He came close to her, his heart breaking to see her distress.

"Know how much I love you," he urged. "Now go!" he called out, and slapped Warkfine hard, startling him and forcing him to take off, Alistair hanging onto the reins, but looking back over her shoulder, weeping.

"MY LORD!" she screamed.

Warkfin was well-trained, and he knew what Erec wanted, and he knew he would not stop until he took her far from here, to the Duke's Palace. Erec felt a sense of ease watching her ride off, knowing she would be far from the battle.

Erec turned, looked back out over the hill, and surveyed the army, getting closer and closer. The rumble could be heard even from here, and he steeled himself for battle.

He drew his sword, the clang reverberating in the hills. High up he heard the screech of a bird. It was days like this that he had been born for. He might die on this day, he knew. But he would at least die facing the enemy, fearlessly, in one great clash of honor.

CHAPTER THIRTY SEVEN

Thor stood with the huge entourage of Legion and Silver as they all finished gathering their weapons from the Hall of Arms, gathering their belongings from the barracks, and preparing to leave King's Court for good. It was a huge and growing force, and Reece, O'Connor, Elden and the twins joined Thor, Gwendolyn and Godfrey as they all spent their final moments gathering whatever they could carry. Together, they all walked from the hall, out the great doors for the last time, Krohn whining at their side.

The huge, armed group wound its way into the plaza of King's Court, towards King's Gate, beyond which was the drawbridge and the road that would lead them away from King's Court forever. As they went, a small army in and of themselves, the very face of what would be the new MacGil court, people gathered all around and watched them go, eyes opened with wonder and fear. Word had spread of the rift, and as they went, some people watched in wonder, while others joined their group, deciding to abandon Gareth's court and go with them. It was heart-wrenching. Thor felt as if the kingdom were being split in two with each passing step.

As they neared the stone gate, the final exit, Thor took one last look back over his shoulder at King's Court, at this place he had grown to love, to call home. He hated that Gareth was ruling, that he had ruined this place for all of them, had usurped it as his own, this place that had been ruled by MacGils for seven hundred years. There was nothing that they could do about it.

Gwen squeezed his hand, and Thor looked into her eyes and could see her relief to be leaving, and to be with him. He felt the same. At least she was safe. They walked together, hand in hand, proudly, walking through the archway.

"Do you think we shall ever return?" he asked Gwendolyn.

She looked out sadly.

"I don't know," she answered.

"Not with this King," Reece chimed in. "If we ever return, it will be on our terms."

Suddenly a horn sounded, and pandemonium broke out all around them.

Thor spun with the others, and saw people swarming about in every direction, as an agitated buzz spread through the streets. Several messengers, out of breath, came running towards Thor and the others.

"The Sword!" one of them screamed, frantic. "It's been stolen!"

An outraged gasp spread through the crowd, followed by a long murmur.

"Speak clearly man," Kolk yelled at the man. "What do you mean?"

"The Destiny Sword! It's gone! And the Canyon—the Shield is down!"

An outraged cry rose up through the streets, a cry of panic, as all the soldiers turned and looked at each other. Thor looked at the others, could see the fear in their faces, and he felt it too.

The shield was down. They were all vulnerable, defenseless, the entire Ring. There was no longer anything standing between the Empire and them. The Empire's million man army could enter, could attack at any moment.

"But how is it possible?" Reece asked.

"The Destiny Sword has remained at King's Castle for seven generations!" Godfrey called out.

"It would take ten men to even hoist it!" Brom yelled. "Where could it have gone? Who could have taken it?"

"They have caught the thieves!" a messenger yelled back. "They are in the town square even now, about to be hung!"

As one, Thor and the others all ran across the plaza, turning down a street that led to the large, open square in the center of King's Court.

A huge mob swarmed around the scaffold, on which four men stood bound, nooses about their necks. The men looked panicked, desperate, as they looked out at hundreds of people.

On the far side of the square stood Gareth, with Kultin and his fighting force, looking down at the criminals. Thor and the men entered on the other side of the court, and it was utter pandemonium. Finally, a horn blew, and a silence fell over the group.

"Admit what you have done!" yelled out an executioner.

"We are part of a group that stole the Destiny Sword!" one of them screamed.

The crowd broke out into an outraged murmur, and finally fell silent.

"And tell us where the sword is!" the executioner cried out.

"The rest of our group has taken it far from here. They have been carrying it all night. They are already across the Western Crossing of the Canyon, and have already boarded a ship. They are taking it into the Empire. As we speak, it is already across the sea, in a foreign and hostile land. You will never get it back!"

The crowd cried out again, in an outraged murmur.

"Silence!" Gareth screamed.

Slowly, the crowd quieted.

"And what was your reason for stealing the sword?" Gareth called out. "What is its destination?"

The criminals stayed silent this time, refusing to speak.

Finally, one of them lifted his head.

"We have vowed to never tell!"

The crowd broke out in another murmur, until finally Gareth stepped forward, with his entourage of men, and faced the executioners.

The crowd fell silent.

"Kill these men!" he commanded the executioner.

The crowd broke out into a cheer.

"But my Liege, you promised—" one of the criminals began to cry.

Gareth nodded, and before the man could finish speaking, the floor dropped out and they all hanged.

The crowd cheered in satisfaction, as the corpses dangled in the air.

The crowd began to disperse, in an agitated stir.

"The Destiny Sword stolen," O'Connor whispered.

"It is unthinkable," Elden said.

"The shield is down," Conval said.

"We are defenseless," Conven added.

Kolk, Brom and the men huddled close around Thor, Gwendolyn, Godfrey and all of the others.

"We must hurry from this place," Kolk said. "We must get as far from King's Court as possible and fortify our new home."

"That is pointless now," Brom said. "If the shield is down, we are not safe anywhere. If the Empire invades, the Ring will be overrun by a million men. Nothing will stop them."

"What we need is to get the shield back up again," Kolk said. "And for that, we need the Sword."

"But you heard the thieves," Reece said. "It is already far from here. Deep inside the Empire."

"Then we must go and get it back," Brom said.

With his words the huge group of knights fell silent, looking at each other grimly. For the first time, Thor could see fear in their faces.

"Is there anyone among you men that will volunteer to venture into the Empire and search for the sword?" Brom called out, facing the Silver.

The group of knights, all Silver, the finest warriors Thor had ever known, all stood there, silent. None of them stepped forward.

"My lord, it would be futile," one of them said. "You know that. A small band of warriors would never survive such a deep foray into the Empire. It has never been done before in the history of the Ring."

"And we don't even know where the Sword is!" another said. "The Wilds stretch millions of miles. It could be anywhere!"

"It would be a suicide mission," said another. "There is nothing we can do but brace ourselves for an attack."

"I will go," Thor said, stepping forward into the huge circle of men.

They all fell silent, so silent, one could hear a pin drop.

Thor could feel all the stares, and he felt himself racing with energy, felt more alive than he ever had. He knew it was crazy, reckless, that the chances were impossible. But he also felt that this was what he was born for, felt proud of himself for not giving into his fear. It wasn't about surviving. It was about honor.

"You have a big heart, Thorgrinson," Kolk said. "And you do the Legion proud. But you would not survive. Not even you."

"It is not about surviving," Thor said. "It's about doing what is right. For our kingdom. For all of us."

The men remained silent.

"But no one else volunteers to go with you," Brom said. "Even among these brave and fine warriors. And I cannot blame them."

"Then I will go alone," Thor said, resolving himself. He was determined.

"I will join him!" came a voice.

Thor turned to see Reece step forward, beside him.

"And I!" said O'Connor.

"And I!" said Elden.

"And we!" said the twins.

Thor felt emboldened as all of his friends stepped forward, the group of six standing as one, ready to face death together.

Kolk shook his head.

"You are crazy, all of you," Kolk said, "and the bravest men I've ever seen."

Brom stepped forward, placed a hand on Thor's shoulder, and looked him in the eye.

"Whoever you are, boy," he said, "you do your ancestors proud."

He examined Thor deeply, as if deciding.

"Go then," Brom finally said. "Find the sword. Bring it home. The fate of our kingdom rests on you."

"We shall leave King's Court and journey to Silesia and form a new court in your absence," Godfrey said. "We will await your return. Be quick about it. And don't die."

The men dispersed, and Thor stood there, feeling his world changing, reeling all around him. Then he felt a hand on his wrist.

Thor looked over to see Gwendolyn standing beside him, tears in her eyes. His heart broke at the sight of her.

"Before you leave, talk with me a minute," she said.

Thor walked with her, stepping away from the crowd, and they took privacy behind a stone wall. She looked up at him, and a tear rolled down her cheek.

"I don't want you to go," she said. "Please. Not after all we've been through."

"But if I don't, the shield will stay down," Thor said. "The Empire will attack. We will all be finished."

She shook her head.

"We are all finished anyway," she said. "The Sword is gone. The shield will never go up again. You will never find it. You will just die alone out there. If we are to die, I would rather that we die together."

Thor shook his head.

"Then your death, all of our deaths, would be on my head, because I had not tried to find the Sword. I must do this Gwendolyn. You, of all people, must understand. Please. I do not want to leave you. Know how much I love you. I wish for nothing more than to stay by your side. But I must do this. For our kingdom. For the Ring. For honor. Don't you understand?"

She nodded slowly, looking down at the ground, wiping her tears.

Thor felt the ring his mother had given him, burning inside his shirt, and at that moment, he wanted more than anything to get down on one knee and to propose to Gwendolyn, to ask her to be his wife. A part of him felt that this was the moment.

But another part of him felt it would not be fair to her to propose. He was about to leave, to head off into what was a likely death. If she were to be married to him, that would leave her a widow, forever. It would not be fair to her.

Thor decided to keep the ring where it was, and as soon as he returned—*if* he returned—he would propose to her then. Then, they could live together forever.

He reached down, raised her chin and looked into her eyes. He smiled down at her, wiping away her tears, and leaned in and kissed her.

"I love you, Gwendolyn," he said. "More than I could ever say."

She choked up in tears, crying, and threw her arms around him and hugged him tight.

"I hate you for going," she said.

"You will be safe this time," Thor said, his heart breaking. "You will be with all these men. You will run your own court. An entire army will be protecting you. No one can hurt you now."

"It is not for myself that I fear," she said. "It is for you."

Thor finally pulled her back, and looked deeply into her eyes.

"I will return to you, my love," he said "Not the moon and the stars and the heavens in the sky can keep me from you."

She smiled up weakly, a tear running down her cheek.

"I wish I could believe that," she answered.

CHAPTER THIRTY EIGHT

King McCloud burst from his castle as the second sun was setting in the sky and ran across the plaza of his royal court, filled with rage. He leapt onto his horse, followed by dozens of his loyal men, and kicked, taking off at a gallop through his small city, through one of the arched gates, and onto the dusty road leading up the mountain. He kicked the beast harder and harder, outrage burning through his veins. He had just received the news that his son had escaped, his bride with him, had broken free from his grasp before he'd had a chance to torture and kill them both and make a public display of them.

McCloud burned with the indignity of it all. He could not believe that little witch had outsmarted him. He had been in a foul mood since returning home, and now he was in an outright fury. If it was the last thing he did, he would hunt them both down, find them before they could reach the safety of the MacGil side, and torture and kill them both himself.

McCloud galloped, dozens of men following, desperate to reach the hilltop outside his court where he could have a good vantage point, see exactly where they were, and decide how best to hunt them down.

Ungrateful little boy, he thought. He realized now that he had made a mistake to let Bronson live all these years. He knew from the time he was born that he should have had him killed—should have had all of his sons killed—so that no one could ever threaten to depose him. He had been too soft. Now he had paid the price.

He had also been foolish to keep that MacGil girl alive as long as he had. He knew from past experience that it was always a good idea to kill women as soon as possible, and not take any chances with them. He again had become too soft in his old age, and he resolved to be crueler and more vicious than ever before.

McCloud screamed and whipped his horse again and again, until it bled, the horse screaming, as they all charged and finally crested the top of the hill.

From this vantage point, the setting sun flooding the sky in scarlet, matching his mood, McCloud could see on the horizon his son, Bronson, with Luanda, riding for the Highlands. His anger burned anew. It looked like they had a good day's ride on him, and catching them would not be easy. No matter. He would hunt them down, make a sport of it. He would ride all night if he had to, and would not rest until he pounced on them and crushed them to death with his bare hands.

McCloud sat there on his horse, watching, breathing hard, and was about to whip his horse again, to charge off after them, when suddenly, something came into view which confused him. He blinked several times, unsure what he was seeing.

Before him there came into view an army of horses. It was the biggest army he had ever seen, unlike anything he had ever laid eyes upon. It appeared to be a million men, covering the entire countryside, swarming his way, like a swarm of ants.

He turned, and in every direction they were there, millions of men, turning his land black with their bodies, their horses, closing in on him from every direction. He could not understand what was happening. From their dress, they appeared to be Empire men. But it was not possible: they were inside the Ring. Across the Canyon.

Did the shield fail? he suddenly wondered, his heart skipping a beat.

Before McCloud could process it all, suddenly there crested above the hill, right in front of him, a thousand men, just a few feet away—and at their head rode Andronicus, on a single horse, twice the size of his.

Andronicus sat there, on his horse, a few feet before McCloud, grinning down at him, an evil grin, his fangs protruding, his sharp teeth glistening in the sunset. His demonic yellow eyes told McCloud all he needed to know: he had been beaten.

McCloud was suddenly overwhelmed with panic, and he turned and looked behind him, as if to flee—but an instant later thousands more Empire men closed in from behind.

He was completely surrounded. There was nowhere to run.

McCloud swallowed hard. For the first time in his life, he felt what it was like to feel real fear. He felt what it was like to be utterly defeated.

McCloud licked his dry lips as he looked up at Andronicus, wondering if there was any way out of this.

"My Lord," he said to Andronicus, his voice shaky, all of his confidence gone.

"You had your chance to strike a deal with me," Andronicus snarled, an ancient deep voice, rumbling forth from his chest. "And you refused."

"I am sorry, my Lord," McCloud said, his voice catching in his throat. "I was just about to send men to you, to send you a message, that I wanted to let you in."

"Were you?" Andronicus said.

He leaned back and roared with laughter.

"Somehow, I doubt that very much," Andronicus answered. "You are a poor liar. But it wouldn't have mattered anyway. In my world, there are no second chances."

He leaned back and smiled wide.

"Now you will learn what it means to defy the great Andronicus."

CHAPTER THIRTY NINE

Thor sat on his horse and they rode at a walk, leading the small contingent of his six friends as they broke away from the huge fighting force of Silver and Legion who had come to see them off. The six of them stopped before the main bridge for the Western Crossing of the Ring, Krohn at their side, and before stepping foot onto the bridge, Thor and his brothers turned and saw the hundreds of Legion, of Silver, standing there, seeing them off. They all stared back with solemn faces, faces filled with awe and respect. Whatever happened, whatever lay before them, he felt as if he had found a home. A family. A *real* family. And he knew that was a very rare thing. For that, he would be eternally grateful.

Kolk raised a single fist high in the air, then turned it upside down, a salute of the highest honor and respect. All the other men followed, saluting Thor and his friends—and they returned the salute. Thor felt the sacredness of the quest before him, and he resolved to do whatever it took to save his kingdom.

Thor looked over and saw Gwendolyn's face, standing amongst them, crying, and he met her eyes. He could see the love in her eyes, and he sent the love back. He cared for her safety more than for his own, and he prayed with all that he was that she would be safe amidst these great warriors. As he looked at her, he could already see MacGil in her, could already see the great leader that she would become. He was filled with pride for her.

Thor knew that if he did not leave now, he never would. He had to steel himself.

He turned, his friends with him, and as one, they rode their horses slowly onto the bridge.

Lined up alongside the bridge were hundreds of MacGil soldiers, and they all stood at attention as they went. As Thor and his friends passed, the soldiers all raised their fists in salute. Hundreds of men on both sides saluted them as they went.

As they proceeded further over the bridge, beginning to cross over the Canyon, Krohn at their side, further and further from the safety of the Ring, the eerie mist of the place began to rise up and envelop them. Thor did not know what lay ahead. He knew it would be dangerous. He knew it could take months, years. He could not imagine the lands they would see, the monsters they would meet, the battles they would face. He knew their chances were slim. And he knew they might not ever find the Sword. It was not a quest for the light of heart. It was a quest of heroes.

As Thor walked, he was beginning to realize that it was not the objective that made one a hero—it was the journey, the quest itself. The willingness to accept it. Life was short. He realized that now. It was not about how he ended it. It was about how he lived it.

And as he looked up, at the great expanse of wilderness before him, he knew that, for the first time in his life, he was about to truly live.

NOW AVAILABLE!

A VOW OF GLORY
Book #5 in the Sorcerer's Ring

"A breathtaking new epic fantasy series. Morgan Rice does it again!
This magical sorcery saga reminds me of the best of J.K. Rowling,
George R.R. Martin, Rick Riordan, Christopher Paolini and J.R.R.
Tolkien. I couldn't put it down!"
--Allegra Skye, Bestselling author of SAVED

In A VOW OF GLORY (Book #5 in the Sorcerer's Ring), Thor
embarks with his Legion friends on an epic quest into the vast wilds of
the Empire to try to find the ancient Destiny Sword and save the
Ring. Thor's friendships deepen, as they journey to new places, face
unexpected monsters and fight side by side in unimaginable battle.
They encounter exotic lands, creatures and peoples beyond which they
could have ever imagined, each step of their journey fraught with
increasing danger. They will have to summon all their skills if they are
to survive as they follow the trail of the thieves, deeper and deeper
into the Empire. Their quest will bring them all the way into the heart
of the Underworld, one of the seven realms of hell, where the undead
rule and fields are lined with bones. As Thor must summon his
powers, more than ever, he struggles to understand the nature of who
he is.

Back in the Ring, Gwendolyn must lead half of King's Court to the
Western stronghold of Silesia, an ancient city perched on the edge of
the Canyon that has stood for one thousand years. Silesia's
fortifications have allowed it to survive every attack throughout every
century—but it has never been faced with an assault by a leader like
Andronicus, by an army like his million men. Gwendolyn learns what
it means to be queen as she takes on a leadership role, Srog, Kolk,
Brom, Steffen, Kendrick and Godfrey by her side, preparing to defend
the city for the massive war to come.

Meanwhile, Gareth is descending deeper into madness, trying to fend
off a coup that would have him assassinated in King's Court, while
Erec fights for his life to save his love, Alistair and the Duke's city of
Savaria as the downed shield enables the wild creatures to invade. And
Godfrey, wallowing in drink, will have to decide if he is ready to cast
off his past and become the man his family expects him to be.

As they all fight for their lives and as things seem as if they can't get any worse, the story ends with two shocking twists.

Will Gwendolyn survive the assault? Will Thor survive the Empire? Will the Destiny Sword be found?

With its sophisticated world-building and characterization, A VOW OF GLORY is an epic tale of friends and lovers, of rivals and suitors, of knights and dragons, of intrigues and political machinations, of coming of age, of broken hearts, of deception, ambition and betrayal. It is a tale of honor and courage, of fate and destiny, of sorcery. It is a fantasy that brings us into a world we will never forget, and which will appeal to all ages and genders.

About Morgan Rice

Morgan is author of the #1 Bestselling THE SORCERER'S RING, a new epic fantasy series, currently comprising eleven books and counting, which has been translated into five languages. The newest title, A REIGN OF STEEL (#11) is now available! Morgan Rice is also author of the #1 Bestselling series THE VAMPIRE JOURNALS, comprising ten books (and counting), which has been translated into six languages. Book #1 in the series, TURNED, is now available as a FREE download! organ is also author of the #1 Bestselling ARENA ONE and ARENA TWO, the first two books in THE SURVIVAL TRILOGY, a post-apocalyptic action thriller set in the future.

Among Morgan's many influences are Suzanne Collins, Anne Rice and Stephenie Meyer, along with classics like Shakespeare and the Bible. Morgan lives in New York City.

Please visit www.morganricebooks.com to get exclusive news, get a free book, contact Morgan, and find links to stay in touch with Morgan via Facebook, Twitter, Goodreads, the blog, and a whole bunch of other places. Morgan loves to hear from you, so don't be shy and check back often!

Books by Morgan Rice

THE SORCERER'S RING
A QUEST OF HEROES (BOOK #1)
A MARCH OF KINGS (BOOK #2)
A FEAST OF DRAGONS (BOOK #3)
A CLASH OF HONOR (BOOK #4)
A VOW OF GLORY (BOOK #5)
A CHARGE OF VALOR (BOOK #6)
A RITE OF SWORDS (BOOK #7)
A GRANT OF ARMS (BOOK #8)
A SKY OF SPELLS (BOOK #9)
A SEA OF SHIELDS (BOOK #10)
A REIGN OF STEEL (BOOK #11)

THE SURVIVAL TRILOGY
ARENA ONE (Book #1)
ARENA TWO (Book #2)

the Vampire Journals
turned (book #1)
loved (book #2)
betrayed (book #3)
destined (book #4)
desired (book #5)
betrothed (book #6)
vowed (book #7)
found (book #8)
resurrected (book #9)
craved (book #10)